JUST ONE KISS

THE LAST CHANCE ACADEMY

EILEEN DREYER

NEW YORK TIMES BESTSELLING AUTHOR

OHB

For the Divas
I wouldn't be here without you.

PROLOGUE

The shadows were deep, but the shadows were always deep in the old building, especially at this time of night. Their implied menace went a long way toward keeping the younger girls in their beds. Who knew, after all, what could be hiding in dark corners where the cold breezes from the moors crept in through loose windows and swirled around bare ankles?

On the other hand, the shadows that quelled the young were also very handy for hiding all manner of nefarious behavior.

"Hurry! We don't have much time."

"Well, if it hadn't taken you so long to get past the lock…"

"Or if you hadn't stopped to sample the loot."

"If both of you wouldn't waste time arguing about everything."

Their bare feet made little sound on the cold stone floors. They knew exactly how to sneak past enemy doors, even as they clutched unwieldy treasure in their arms. It did make opening those doors an exercise in balance that looked more like dancing lessons than theft. But they'd had enough practice to see it through. Besides, once inside, they were greeted like the heroes they were.

"Our bedtime snack is here!"

Whispered thanks met them as they began to pass out their booty, girl by girl. Even for the excitement that spread down the long room, the noise was minimal. A quiet thank you, a delighted sigh of anticipation. A muffled crunch as a prize was consumed. Reward enough and more for the chances the burglars had taken. Nutrition shared for girls regularly made to go hungry for the lesson of discipline. Or the greed of the administrators, as all the girls knew.

The sneak thieves had just made it to the last bed when the dormitory door slammed open. These new intruders were not nearly as careful nor as quiet. And they held a lantern high enough to light over thirty girls from ages seven to fourteen crouched on spare beds, suddenly frozen in place, half with purloined bread in their mouths, panicked eyes facing their doom, jaws still working to get their treats consumed before they were confiscated.

Standing by the furthest iron beds, the three miscreants stood as straight and tall as they could, considering one was a head shorter than her comrades. They quickly hid the remaining loot behind them rather than lose it.

"You three," Miss Larinda Chase accused in failing tones. "Why does it always have to be you three?"

"Because," a little voice piped up from the middle of the room, "they're our fairy godmothers. They promised they would always grant our wishes."

Not exactly. They had promised they would always respond to appeals for help. It didn't make the next hours of cold isolation crouched in dark and narrow closets any warmer. It did make the headmistress's consternation more satisfying. And it made their sentences at Last Chance Academy less onerous, at least until the next year when Georgie, Charlie, and Eddie Packham helped foment rebellion and overthrew the administration. But that is a story for other times. This is the time to talk of fairy godmothers.

MAY, 1814, MAYFAIR, LONDON

*L*ady Georgianna Packham would have known sooner that her help was needed if she hadn't been busy chasing Napoleon across the plains of France.

"And then General Wellington and Daddy Hill pushed Marshal Soult across the River Nive," she said, bouncing the painted horse and soldier across the bright blue scarf that wound over the rumpled sheet representing the battlefield.

"Daddy Hill?" her brother Geoffrey asked, his seven-year-old rump in the air as he repositioned the French troops farther east, knocking some over as he'd been wanting to do since they started the lesson. "Why would a daddy lead troops? That's silly."

Georgie nodded and shoved a loose curl behind her ear as she pointed to the tiny lead soldier in his distinctive scarlet coat who sat at the front of the British troops. "His real name is General Rowland Hill. But he has taken such good care of his men that they nicknamed him 'Daddy.'"

"My lady."

Georgie looked up from where, also on hands and knees, she

was knocking down some more French cavalry for Geoffrey. "Yes, Minta?"

The tidy redheaded maid perched in the doorway bobbed a bit of a curtsy. "Back door, miss."

Georgie nodded. "Well then, I'm afraid we'll have to wait for the Battle of Paris. Read the rest of those dispatches, Geoffrey. We can set up when I get back."

Geoffrey, busy engaging a blue-clad soldier against one in red, merely nodded. Seated next to him, thumb in mouth, three-year-old Emily nodded right along.

Giving Emily a quick buss on the cheek and Geoffrey a tousle, Georgie climbed to her feet, where she settled her dress and repinned her hair before following Minta out into the nursery hallway.

"Don't know how you can enjoy playin' soldiers an' all, miss," Minta said with a shake of her head. "Bloody business, it were."

"I'm afraid it was, Minta. But this is the best way to lock knowledge into little boys' heads. And if Geoffrey wants to be a soldier, he needs to learn it."

Minta shook her head. "Seems to me he needs to learn that soldierin's a trial and a bloody business."

Since Minta had grown up in the train of the British Army, she should know.

"Which is why you and I will sit down with him right after we get Wellington safely through the battle of Toulouse," Georgie answered, "so he can know the good *and* the bad."

Minta didn't seem enthused. "Won't help, you pardon me sayin'. Bloodthirsty buggers, men, the lot of them."

Georgie smiled as she started down the first flight of narrow servants' stairs toward the kitchen. "Oh, I know. But at least we can say we tried."

Georgie wondered what time it was. She always lost her sense of it while instructing the children. The light had begun to slant, though, so rather a surprising time for a call. Then again, the call had come to the kitchen door, which meant it was completely unofficial.

"Did the person identify themself?" she asked her maid.

"No'm. Just said she needed a fairy godmother."

Georgie fought the urge to scowl. It had been four years since she'd earned that annoying nickname. Anyone would think people would have begun to forget. But no. At least once a month one of her ex-classmates showed up at the back door, bouncing from foot to foot, skirts clutched in her hands, eyes flickering around the kitchen, where by now the staff was so inured to these unorthodox visits that they went about their business as if nothing unusual was happening.

It seemed she was to have another.

"Neither Charlie nor Eddie was available?"

"Lendin' library, what I hear."

Georgie recognized the girl standing in the kitchen the minute she entered. Georgie smiled to herself. She really should not call her a girl. But any of the students younger than she and her cousins would always be thought of as *girls*. And this one looked like it.

Thin, pale, blonde, with her hands predictably tangled in her skirts and her eyes on a swivel, Priscilla Mayhew stood on one small foot and watched the kitchen staff as if expecting them to decamp to peach on her to her parents for being there.

"Hello, Priscilla," Georgie softly greeted her, stepping out onto the kitchen proper.

Priscilla startled like a wild filly. "Oh, Lady Georgiana..." Even her curtsy looked frantic.

Georgie gave her a sincere smile. "You know perfectly well it is Georgie. After all, we both survived Last Chance Academy. Would you care to come with me? Mrs. Barnes, our housekeeper, has a lovely little parlor she is kind enough to lend me on occasion."

Mrs. Barnes, who looked more like a sergeant major than a housekeeper, gave a stiff nod and then, as if she couldn't help it, a wink. "Go on wit' ya now, girl. Minta, let Nanny know them hooligans is up there on their own."

Priscilla blinked like a baby bunny at Mrs. Barnes's broad western accent. "She is not from London, is she?" she whispered as she followed Georgie from the wide, green-walled room and down the narrow servants' corridor.

"No. Mrs. Barnes is from The Castle. She is convinced we would all run mad if she weren't about to manage us."

She was also kind and patient enough to allow strange young women to sneak in the back door for help.

"Here we go," Georgie said, pushing open the door into the housekeeper's sitting room.

Georgie had always loved it here. Rather than solemn and important like the public rooms of the house, Mrs. Barnes lived amid chintz and overstuffed sofas. Smelling of cinnamon and furniture polish and warmed by a constant fire, it reminded Georgie of a room from a fairy tale.

Priscilla blinked again. "Oh, my. This is..."

Georgie nodded. "Lovely, yes. Please. Sit."

Priscilla shook her head in some wonder. "Like a nest."

She sat and looked around, as most visitors did, no matter the room. Her next question was also inevitable.

"You really all live in this one house?"

Georgie smiled. "All thousand or so Packham cousins. With my mother and father so often preoccupied with government affairs, Uncle Samson in default charge of the family, and Aunt Ellen and Uncle William dying so young, it seemed easiest to keep us all in the immediate vicinity to more easily maintain supervision. It has actually worked out quite well.

And I only need run down the corridor to see Charlie and Eddie."

Georgie spent the time until the tea service arrived asking after Priscilla's parents and younger sister, who had been a year behind her in school. They chattered until tea had arrived, been poured, and waifish Priscilla had devoured three seed cakes and a slice of bread and butter. One of the great mysteries of life, Priscilla's frail frame, considering what she put away at a sitting.

"Now then," was all Georgie had to say.

Priscilla sputtered a bit, then set down her cup and clasped her hands like a novice in church. "My life is over," she whispered.

Georgie might have been far more concerned if this statement hadn't been the opening line of almost every visit she'd had.

"How is that?" she asked equably, having long since learned that an air of calm saved much time and drama.

Priscilla let loose a pathetic little sob. Georgie waited patiently. Priscilla wasn't one for show. Her pale little face was pinched and sad. Georgie knew that whatever it was, she would help the girl.

"Timothy," Priscilla whispered, head down.

Now Georgie worried. "*Your* Timothy? The Squire's son? What about him?"

Not dead, Georgie prayed. She'd met Timothy. He was everything Priscilla needed. Calm, certain, loving. And right next door.

Priscilla shook her head, still focused on her twining hands. "He is...*lost* to me."

Georgie took a slow breath to keep from saying what she instinctively wanted to. *Had he no compass? Could he not read the stars? I thought he was smarter than that.*

"Lost how, Prissy?"

Finally, the girl looked up to expose huge, tear-swollen blue eyes. "My father," she gulped. "He won't...he has forbidden..."

Georgie sighed. Oh, dear. Not something as simple as a lost bracelet or ill-timed *billet doux,* then. A real problem.

"He won't allow you to marry Timothy."

This time Priscilla shook her head so hard that two pins flew out of her tightly curled hair. "Oh, Georgie, what shall I do? My father has arranged a marriage for me to the Marquess of Coleford. I can *not* marry him. He's so old! And he's poor." Now came a real sob. "And he...he lives in...*Wales!!*"

Oh, dear. Poor Priscilla. After being raised in London and Oxford, she must think Wales was comparable to the moon. Georgie could have told her that Wales was perfectly lovely. Wild and beautiful with a wonderful store of fairies, gnomes, and pixies to liven any fireside. But considering the woeful look on Priscilla's face, Georgie suspected that pixies would never balance out a loss of home and society.

Georgie suspected that, given the challenge, Priscilla would do perfectly well anywhere she went. But she'd never been made to. Every minute she was not incarcerated in Last Chance Academy, she'd lived no more than two rooms away from her mother and younger sisters. Which meant that not only would she be miserable in a marriage that involved travel to Wales, her husband would be even more miserable.

Timothy, on the other hand, lived down the lane. A perfect distance for a committed homebody.

"I don't suppose you have a lost bracelet you'd rather I find," Georgie tried.

Priscilla hiccupped in surprise. "Pardon?"

Georgie waved her off. "Nothing. Merely thinking out loud. You have spoken to your father? He knows how worthy Timothy is?"

Priscilla also had a nice line of scowls when she wanted to.

"Do you really think that my father would ever consider a squire's son as worthy as a *marquess*?"

Georgie sighed. "Yes. Quite." She thought a moment. "The Marquess of Whom again? I don't recognize the name."

"Well," Priscilla said, finally pulling out a handkerchief to mop her eyes. "He *is* from Wales."

"Yes, I see."

"And he just returned from the army to take up his duties here. The inheritance was evidently a surprise." Shockingly, she grinned. "Not a pleasant one either, from what I heard. He had evidently been perfectly happy on his horse, tromping about all over Spain. Now he must deal with leaky roofs, sick tenants, and mangel-wurzels. Whatever those are."

Georgie actually knew. She sincerely doubted Priscilla cared.

"And all without sufficient funds," Georgie said with a nod.

"Living on River Tick."

Georgie chuckled. "Priscilla. What would Lady Chase say?"

For the first time, Priscilla chuckled right back. "That language is not up to the standards of Lady Chase's Academy for Civilized Ladies," she pronounced in an uncanny replica of the headmistress's nasal voice.

Georgie laughed right along with her. "But his name?"

"The Marquess of Coleford. Peter Prentice...something. Colonel Peter...er..."

"Greyville?!" Georgie retorted, not only surprised but impressed. And oddly disconcerted.

Priscilla immediately brightened. "Then you *do* know him. You could *talk* to him."

Georgie shook her head. "I know *of* him. Quite a renowned hero. Mentioned in almost as many dispatches as the great man himself."

Enough to make an impressionable girl fall madly in love, if she just went by the tales of his heroism and daring-do. She and

Georgie and Eddie had pored over the dispatches as if they were The Monk. Perhaps she should talk Priscilla into meeting the Colonel. From what Georgie had heard, Prissy's heart might be won over with no more than one look at him.

Although Georgie suspected he didn't look quite so majestic in the country tweeds and muddy boots he'd need for dealing with mangel-wurzels as he had in his flashy Dragoon's uniform. At least from the reports she'd had.

How odd, she thought to herself, considering the pale beauty before her. When she realized just who the Marquess of Coleford was, Georgie didn't feel nearly so inclined to push Priscilla into his arms just to get her out of Mrs. Barnes's sitting room.

"Well?" Priscilla asked, leaning forward. "Can you help me? Us?"

Georgie considered. "Does your Timothy know about this tangle?"

Priscilla lost another hairpin. "How can I tell him? It would break him!"

"I suspect he'll find out when he sees you walking out of St. George's on the Marquess's arm."

Blast. It seemed she had run out of patience. And Priscilla was watering up again.

It was all Georgie could do to keep from sighing. "You must speak to him, Priscilla. Is he here or at home?"

"Oh, he never leaves Oxfordshire."

"Then write him a letter."

Priscilla's eyes grew large. "Write an *unmarried* gentleman?"

Georgie got to her feet and stepped to the window to keep from choking the girl. "Priscilla, please do not think I am such a gudgeon I don't know that you write him faithfully while you are in town."

The raging blush was all the answer she needed. Blushes were so convenient for ferreting out the truth.

"Tell him. Make it simple and straightforward. No letters blotched from tears."

"And I shall tell him you will solve the problem?"

Georgie finally allowed herself a sigh and looked out to the back garden. "Tell him I shall try."

"And the other godmothers?"

"If they have time. That is all I can promise."

Priscilla got to her feet. "I knew you'd help me."

Georgie turned, not wanting the girl to be mistaken. "I said I'd *try*. That is all I will promise."

Priscilla ran up and gave her a quick, hard hug. "That is the only promise I need. You can do *anything*."

Georgie opened her mouth to refute such an absurd claim, but she never did. She knew it wouldn't do any good. Priscilla would believe what so many other people did, that Georgie could do *anything*. Well, she was tired of doing everything. One more season, her mother had promised. One more and she could dispense with the expectations of the *ton* and choose her own path. Georgie was counting the days.

Lately she'd been thinking of living in one of the little stone *cloghan* huts out by her cousin's horse farm in Ireland, with only the wind, ocean, and seabirds for company. It had begun to sound so enticing. In the meantime, she had a problem to solve.

After watching Priscilla skip out, repairing her hair with the recovered pins as she went, Georgie retreated to her own sitting room upstairs to think. Maybe she should start an investigation agency instead, she thought with a wry smile. Charge for all those lost bracelets and inconvenient *billets-doux* she was so good at tracking down.

It took only another ten minutes for the inevitable invasion.

She didn't even bother to turn when she heard the steps in the hallway.

"That was Priscilla Mayhew we just saw leaving out the back, wasn't it?" her cousin Charlie said as she walked in.

Georgie nodded.

Her cousin Eddie followed on Charlie's heels. "You are about to do something foolish," she said, her voice nearly as soft as Priscilla's. "Aren't you?"

Georgie sighed and got to her feet to face her cohorts. "I very much fear I am."

Charlie laughed. "Well, good. We got here just in time."

2

————

The planning meeting commenced the next afternoon after the cousins had collected some vital information. Georgie was working on preparing the lesson on the Battle of Toulouse when the door opened.

"Do we have a plan yet?"

She looked up from her mother's Chinoiserie desk to see her cousin Charlie standing in the doorway to the Chinese Salon. Obviously, time to put away the work she'd been doing for the work she needed to do. "Do I have my intelligence yet?"

Charlie strode in. "Eddie said she would meet us here. All I could get from my dance partners last night was that Greyville's men adore him and won't hear a bad word spoken against him."

"Greyville?"

Charlie shrugged and began to stride about the room as if caught in a prison cell rather than one of the most opulent rooms in Clevedon House. "He prefers it to the new title. Says he's not used to it yet. Actually, prefers *Grey*, but I am not that lost to good manners."

Georgie turned back to her work, but she was grinning to herself. Charlie always moved as if she brought a strong wind in with her. Georgie had always thought that this room should have been Charlie's. The décor was exotic, the furniture shining mahogany, a hue that seemed positively tame compared with the red of Charlie's hair, and the brilliant red silk wallpaper writhing with ornate dragons that seemed just about ready to incinerate the furniture, much as Charlie often did.

Perhaps it was the Breslin red hair from her mother's side of the family, or the no-nonsense attitude of a girl brought up amid four brothers and a sportsman father, or the lightning quick mind that flared just as quickly to temper. But Charlie somehow matched the energy in this room.

"Well, think of something," she said now as she plopped onto a scarlet silk settee, her orange muslin gown clashing violently with the scarlet material, which Georgie knew delighted Charlie no end. Georgie wagered that her cousin would stay right there until one of the other adults came in to catch her and all but collapsed in horror. "I'm bored."

"How can you be bored?" Georgie asked absently, collecting the newspapers she had been perusing and putting them into a pile. "You have only this week disgraced yourself in a phaeton race with Cyril Wright, beat my father to flinders in a mad game of chess, and sent Jalbert into spasms insisting that he include curry in the menu so you can practice for when you travel to India."

Picking up a Belle Assemblée, Charlie flipped through it. "Should I go unprepared? Ramdas from the General's house gave me several recipes and promised to secure the curry for me."

"So, it's India now? What happened to the Amazon?"

Charlie waved a small hand. "I stand a better chance of finding someone on their way to India. I shall not give up on the Amazon, however. In the meantime, I. Am. Bored."

Georgie nodded and checked her questions one last time. "Let me get Geoffrey through Toulouse while we wait for Eddie."

Charlie harrumphed. "You do know we have a perfectly good tutor who is supposed to be teaching these lessons."

"He has enough strife just getting the boys through Greek and Latin and Mathematics. Besides, I find this fun."

"You never found it fun before..."

Georgie grinned down at her work. "Before the very Colonel Greyville whom I am about to rescue from an ill-considered marriage, came to our attention?"

Charlie smiled down at the magazine she really wasn't reading. "I assume you shall have to meet him," she mused.

Georgie couldn't deny that her pulse picked up a bit. She found herself wanting to smile. She couldn't deny she'd been thinking a bit too much about her upcoming meeting with the Colonel. "He needs to find an alternate bride. I can help."

"And how do you plan to do that?"

"Well, I don't know yet. That is what the meeting will to be about."

Charlie didn't even look up. "*You* could marry him."

Georgie raised her head and looked out the window. "I doubt it. I suspect that a man who is that used to giving orders would not deal with a woman who is as well. Besides, all we know about him is what the dispatches tell us. He is exceptionally talented at disposing of Frenchmen. Not necessarily a talent conducive to marital harmony."

"Unless you need some Frenchmen killed."

"Rather doubtful. What if he is a tyrant, a sadist, a man with unnatural tastes? What if..."

Charlie grinned. "He doesn't *bathe!*"

Georgie shuddered. She admitted it was her own personal quirk. She was known throughout the *ton* as being very particular about her dance partners. No one else could definitively say why. It had nothing to do with station or elegance. In fact, two of her favorite partners were younger sons just out of university looking for polish.

In the end, the *ton* just labeled her a bit snobbish. Daughter of a powerful earl and all. Only Charlie and Eddie knew the truth. Georgie literally gagged at the smell of an unwashed body. Especially if the person had been lazy enough to believe that a good dousing with cologne would conceal all ills. Georgie had actually kissed Beau Brummel's hand once in gratitude for his bringing cleanliness into fashion.

Not the smell of hard work, she admitted. Prissy's beau Timothy had carried the scent of the stables on him, and an honest hard day. He had also smelled of fresh air, gorse, and rain. The unwashed dandies in town smelled of slovenliness, selfishness, and sloth, even clad in the latest, most precisely tailored fashion, which should have shattered Weston's heart.

And people wondered why she had turned down four offers since she'd come out at seventeen. It would have been more, but she had never let those gentlemen close enough to risk the question.

The real aversion also quite nicely covered her real reason for not marrying, which would have confused even those who loved her.

"I'll try again tonight at the Wilkenson's ball," Charlie offered. "I imagine I could quiz a few of Gabe's chums. Several are home on leave."

Gabriel, Georgie's cousin, and Charlie's older brother. Captain Gabriel Stephen Aloysius Packham, of the Lifeguards.

"Although," Charlie grinned, "I'm not sure they could be a reliable judge of whether Colonel Greyville *smelled*. Men are much less sensitive about that sort of thing."

Georgie smiled right back. "Especially those used to living off the land and sleeping on the ground."

"And consorting with sheep."

"Charlie!"

Charlie opted for wide-eyed innocence. "Pushing them aside so they can sleep on the ground," she clarified, her eyes sparkling just a little too much.

"Who smells now?" they heard from the doorway.

It was Eddie, munching on an apple as she entered. As opposed to her cousins, Eddie bore the classic pale English blonde-haired, blue-eyed beauty, which was almost washed out by the boring pastels she insisted on wearing.

"No one smells," Georgie answered, putting her maps and papers aside.

Charlie grinned. "Yet. What news, Edwina?"

Eddie scowled at Charlie's address, even as she shoved her cousin to the side of the settee and plopped down next to her, her own cream muslin day dress complementing the scarlet cushions perfectly. "It is the concerted opinion that the tack to take with Priscilla's father is to make him see that Prissy would pine for her family in *far off* Wales, where the marquess will need to stay for quite a while to restore his property."

"And we will do that how?"

"I don't know yet. While I have been assured Mr. and Mrs. Mayhew would be very susceptible to the threat of their family being so catastrophically divided, the Mister doesn't attend many social events. I'll work with Prissy to see how to get his attention. Possibly mention that I haven't seen my beloved sister for *so* long because she's in...*sob*...Wales."

Both cousins nodded. It never occurred to them to worry about the fact that Eddie had no sister.

"Well," Charlie said, tossing the magazine back onto the table. "Whatever we do, we should do it soon. Certainly before Prissy's father inserts the notice."

Georgie tucked her stack of papers into the bottom drawer of the desk. "I very much fear the notice has gone astray," she said as she casually stood and straightened out her lemon morning dress.

Both cousins stopped in place. "You didn't!" Charlie crowed. "Of course you did. How?"

"A certain reformed pickpocket who has been helping at the orphanage."

Eddie shook her head. "You, Lady Georgiana, are devious."

Georgie gave her cousins a dignified bow. "We needed time."

"To see to the colonel."

"Yes."

"And nurse his wounded heart."

She sat in the dragon-armed side chair. "I sincerely doubt that will be needed."

"But it might be wanted."

"What might be wanted?"

The cousins turned to see Georgie's mother stroll in, the picture of aristocratic elegance in a robin's-egg blue walking dress that accentuated the kind of blonde elegance Georgie envied. The Countess's hands were full with the morning post, and her sharp brown eyes as calm as a bishop's over prayers.

"What are you girls plotting now?" her mother asked.

"A picnic in Richmond," Georgie said.

"A visit to the Tower," Charlie said at the very same moment, reclaiming her seat in a dignified way that fooled no one.

The duchess nodded absently and walked over to the Chippendale writing desk Georgie had just surrendered. "Well, whatever you are up to, make sure you take John along."

"Of course," the cousins responded, knowing that John the footman would never peach on them.

"And fit in time to see your grandmama. She has complained."

"She always complains," Charlie protested.

The Countess gave Charlie a gimlet stare. "Only when her favorite granddaughters do not visit. And when you do, Charlotte, if you love your grandmother, try to wear something that doesn't clash with her furniture and confuse her bees."

Charlie grinned and spread her skirts a bit. "Yes, Aunt Arabella."

The Countess's sole comment was a muffled "Hmph," as she sat to attack her usual pile of correspondence.

"Mama," Georgie asked of a sudden.

The Countess did not look up. "Yes, dear?"

"Do you know anything about the new Marquess of Coleford?"

Her mother's head snapped up as if she had heard angels sing. "Who, dear?"

Hope lived eternal in her mother's breast. Georgie kept telling her that she had three more daughters who would eventually need her devoted guidance to look for husbands. But her mother said quite clearly that all her varied accomplishments would mean nothing if she could not successfully marry off her favorite oldest daughter.

Considering the fact that in addition to providing an heir and spare to the Earl along with four other hopefuls, the Countess was not only one of the country's leading political and diplomatic hostesses, but chair of several charitable boards that benefited everything from orphans to war widows, Georgie thought it should be enough for one woman. What was a daughter here or there?

Her mother obviously mistook Georgie's interest and glowed.

"As a matter of fact," she said, turning a bit in her seat, which just made her golden chignon glow in the sun that poured in. "I was just hearing about him at the St. Pancras Orphanage meeting. Poor man. Quite a heroic soldier, one of Wellington's favorites. It's not bad enough he was wounded, but he comes home to find that his two cousins have been lost to influenza. Not that they were such a great loss themselves, may God forgive them. The two of them ran the Marquessate right into the ground with sport, liquor, and...well...."

"Women," Georgie and Charlie chimed in.

Eddie blushed.

Georgie's mother blushed right alongside, which was charming at her age. She scowled. "I don't know what I did to deserve you scamps."

Charlie positively grinned. "You married my papa's brother and inherited the whole lot of us. It is quite a good thing that you like us all so much."

"Yes, dear." The Countess was nothing if not diplomatic.

"The Marquess?" Georgie prompted. "What injury? I read nothing about it in the dispatches."

Her mother huffed. "You and your brothers. Poor man was injured on the very last day of fighting. He might have lost his leg, I believe."

Georgie felt as if she'd been punched. No. Not such a magnificent man.

"Well, that should put him in a better mood," Charlie muttered.

Georgie and her mother both glared. Eddie just shook her head.

"The estate is bankrupt," the Countess said, "with only the entail keeping it together. It simply isn't fair that he must come home to that. I hope he can find a way out of it."

All Georgie could offer was a faint, "Indeed."

"Why do you ask?"

Georgie was no fool. She was an expert at diversion. "One of the girls from school mentioned him. Geoffrey followed him quite closely on the Peninsula, so I wondered." She saw her mother's brightening expression and held up a hand. "Casually."

There was nothing for her mother to do but return to her correspondence.

There was more Georgie could do. She did it the next morning.

~

PETER PRENTICE PHILPOTT MARSDEN GREYVILLE, Marquess of Coleford, Earl Whitmore, Baron Llanthony, known to his friends as Grey, had the head from hell. He hadn't meant to overdo it the night before, but his old tentmate Rob Glenn had stopped in London on his way through to the family pile somewhere in the Midlands. Not that Grey knew where that was. His branch of the family had never been invited to their own family pile, much less anyone else's.

He was invited now, by damn. Amazing what a title could do for a chap. Even if it came with no money. He imagined he would be quite the popular guest anywhere in the empire now. But first he had to survive his first foray into epic debauchery since the night he'd bought his colors. Hell, he'd felt better after Badajoz. And he'd been recovering from a bullet to the back. This time it was merely his thigh. And it didn't hurt unless Grey was forced to stand on it more than a few minutes.

"Here, sir," a melodious voice interrupted his misery. "We thought we might need this."

Grey opened one eye where he sat slumped over on the side of his bed to find a white-haired scarecrow clad in a black suit and red eyepatch bent before him, bearing a glass of something noxious on a silver tray. He could have sworn he saw the stuff smoking.

"Braxton," he growled, "Only the King is allowed to use the royal *we*. On an ex-batman from Stepney, it sounds ridiculous."

"Yes, my lord."

Grey winced but grabbed the glass. "I don't suppose we could go back to Colonel."

"We could not, my lord."

Grey squinted up at him. "I believe you have been working toward this position since I met you. You were never in the same place as my cousins, were you?"

"We were with you, my lord," Braxton intoned piously, straightening to valet poise. "All the way across the Peninsula."

Grey might have despaired of the man if he hadn't caught the glint in the old poseur's eye.

"Yes, Braxton," Grey admitted, "you were."

And if Braxton hadn't slogged through every mile of mud alongside Grey the last six years and kept him alive after Badajoz, Grey might have been less genial. And trusting. Taking a deep breath, he downed whatever Braxton had put in that glass. When it didn't take the top of his head off, he did his best to ignore the stench and handed the glass back.

"Major Glenn is a bad influence, Braxton. It is undoubtedly a good thing he is on his way north."

"Perhaps tomorrow, my lord. Today he is collapsed in the Brown Guestroom."

Grey prayed for his stomach to settle. "Serves him right. That wallpaper should give him nightmares. What time is it?"

"Ten. You have a visitor who wishes to speak to you."

"Don't be absurd. It's too early."

"She said she would wait."

That got Grey's eyes wide open. "She? Er, we didn't bring her home last night as well, did we?"

That got an actual grin from his batman. "No, my lord.

Nothing but Dragoons in the house 'til she arrived." He scowled a bit. "Well, and the young people."

That made Grey flinch. Another surprise inheritance he'd discovered upon arriving home. "And the young people are?"

"In the breakfast room trying to see if they can finish the cinnamon buns before you get down there."

Grey bolted to his feet, his distress was so great. "Good God, man. Why didn't you tell me? If I don't save the bakery products, we'll have a disaster all over the dining room table."

"Yes, my lord."

By the time Grey had managed to shave, dress, and brush his hair into some semblance of order, Braxton's magic elixir had begun to work. At least Grey could turn his head without feeling as if it would spin off across the floor, and his stomach mostly stayed in place. His civilian attire still felt odd, especially since he was fifteen pounds shy of that long-ago day when he'd had it tailored. The tobacco brown jacket hung loose, and he thought he'd need to move the buttons on his pantaloons. He supposed that sooner or later he'd have to get into Weston for some new togs. Especially since he would soon have the money to do so.

Ah, and there went his stomach again.

"Braxton," he said, buttoning his coat. "I don't suppose I had a nightmare where I agreed to marry a perfect stranger in order to save other perfect strangers."

"No such luck, my lord. We believe congratulations are in order."

Grey closed his eyes again for a moment. The future suddenly looked far bleaker than the battlefields of Spain. In another week, he would have to face the battlefields of Wales. Wales, by God, which according to his mother's description was more foreign a country than Spain. And including, as Braxton put it, 'the young people.' And all that after he met with the eighteen-year-old virgin he was to take to wife. Why had he ever left the battlefield?

Sighing, he straightened his shoulders, as he did every time he went into battle, and strode from the bedroom that was as new to him as everything else in his life.

At least he hoped his imminent wife might have better taste than his cousins had. The master bedroom he had inherited with its heavy maroon flocked wallpaper, velvet hangings, and elk heads, for the love of all that was holy, was just as liable to give him nightmares as the Brown Guestroom.

"Where is the, uh, visitor?" he asked as he descended the stairs, Braxton following behind.

"The gold parlor, my lord. It seemed the least…"

"Distressing?"

"Indeed. Place to wait."

"Well, I will be with her after I make sure the breakfast room is still in one piece. And Braxton?"

"My lord."

"Please see to it that I do not see another dead animal head in this house. Or on the property, come to think of it. My digestion is perilous enough as it is."

His first indication that more disasters lay in wait for him came as he stepped off the staircase.

"I cannot get down!" He heard a piping young voice protest, as if it were a grave injustice to her. Which, having gotten to know Sophie over the last few days, he was certain she felt it was.

"That," a strange woman's voice answered quite calmly, "is a problem."

Grey stopped on the spot. Why was a strange woman in his breakfast room sounding very much like a governess? He turned to Braxton, who simply shrugged.

"You have to get me *down*!" Sophie insisted.

"As a matter of fact," the voice responded. "No, I do not."

There was a pause. "Then what shall I *do?!*"

He knew he should be in there. It occurred to him that Sophie's voice was not only beginning to sound frantic, it was coming from well above the floor. Even above the table. Oh, lord. The shelves.

He resumed limping at a faster pace. Then he heard the quiet voice again and slowed just outside the door.

"Well, I am not quite sure what you shall do," the calm female voice answered. "It might be something you consider before you climb shelves the next time. There might not be anyone around to get you down. Which means you could easily fall trying it yourself. Or you might simply be stuck up there all day long. And then you would miss out on this cinnamon bun. Would you like another piece, Amelia?"

"Yes, please," came the shy response.

"And your...puppy?" the female asked.

That earned the kind of delighted giggle he had only rarely heard since the girls had joined him. If this strange woman was looking for a position, he might well give her one. Especially if she was truly as complacent around that dog as she sounded. Along with the girls, Grey had inherited a wolfhound the size of his charger who disliked everyone but the girls.

"He doesn't eat cin'mon buns," Amelia confided. "He eats roast."

In fact, he'd eaten the roast from last night's dinner.

"*I* want a cinnamon bun!" Sophie insisted, her voice sounding thin and fractious.

Grey knew he should get in there before she began to throw one of the ugly bric-a-bracs on the shelves at whoever was in the room.

"I'm certain you do," the woman answered. "What do you think we should do about it?"

"You should get me *down!*"

"And why should I do that?"

"Because you're a grown-up. That's what grown-ups *do!*"

Grey caught himself just shy of laughing. There was nothing like the logic of a child.

"Is that what you were taught?" the female asked. "Oh, my. I'm afraid it doesn't work that way in my house. Children who disobey and put others in danger because of it must decide for themselves how to go on. Don't you think? I might add that if you need help from someone, you might think of how best to acquire it."

"In your house?" Amelia asked. "Are you a mama?"

Her chuckle set off odd shivers in his chest. "Oh my, no. But there are quite a few children in my house. At last count, I think it was about ten."

Good God, Grey thought. Was an orphanage mistress here to beg money? It would certainly explain her patience.

There was another long pause. Grey looked up to see that his nursery maid was standing stock still just on the other side of the open door, her eyes wide and her hands full of small sweaters. He put his finger to his lips. He had to see how this was settled. Not one person in the house had had any luck getting Sophie to behave since he'd arrived.

"Miss Georgie?" Sophie's voice suddenly sounded small and uncertain.

"Yes, Sophie?"

"C-could you...help me?"

Silence.

Even smaller. "Please?"

A chair scraped across the floor. "Of course I will, sweetheart. Come here."

Grey would have moved, but suddenly there was the sound of a little girl crying. "I...I was scared."

"Of course you were, baby. It is awfully high up there. Did the room look any different?"

"Scary. I thought it would be fun."

"I know. Exploring *is* fun. I love to explore. But I try very hard to prepare first so that I don't put myself or anyone else in danger. What if there had been no grown-up to get you down? If you'd fallen, you might have squashed your puppy." She waited for a watery giggle. "Or worse, Amelia. She would be a little blonde splat on the floor."

Now there were two childish giggles. Grey waited no longer. Straightening his coat, he continued into the room. And stopped. There, standing with Sophie curled into her arms as if she'd always belonged there, was a perfect stranger. A perfect... Grey felt the oddest lurch in his chest. She was not beautiful. Not in the way Iberian women were, flashy and sultry. Not in the way of aristocratic Englishwomen, sleek and prim and superior. Although he could see that she was one by her boarding-school posture and perfect grooming. But her eyes were just a bit tilted, her hair a lush mahogany, her figure much too curvy for fashion. She was a square jaw and broad forehead away from traditional prettiness, but there was a life in those strange green eyes that was compelling. He suspected she would be like the night sky. Familiar feeling until you looked at it long enough and discovered untold treasures.

There was something else familiar as well. Something he couldn't put his finger on.

Even with Sophie in her arms as if she'd held her forever, she dipped a perfect curtsy. "Good morning, my lord. I apologize for bothering you."

"By saving this little monster from breaking my floor?" he asked, with a grin for Sophie.

"I climbed to the top," Sophie announced proudly. Then

suddenly, her face crumpled a bit. "But I forgot to prepare for 'sploring."

"I suspect you won't again, poppet," he said, stepping all the way into the breakfast room. "Did I hear there were cinnamon rolls?"

"Here, Uncle Grey!" Amelia piped up. She tried to lift the plate with her chubby little four-year-old fingers but only ended up sliding the remaining rolls off onto the table. One hurtled over the side to be devoured in one gulp by the mass of grey fur and sharp teeth crouched below the table.

"Oh, no," Amelia groaned, squeezing her eyes shut and scrunching down in her seat so that her fine blonde hair covered her face, an instinctive move of protection Grey had seen too often from both girls.

For a moment he froze. He didn't know what to do with little girls, especially little girls who betrayed a past he didn't even want to consider. He was the only one here who should instinctively anticipate violence.

There was nothing for it. With a quick look up at the stranger whose expression betrayed her own cautious dismay, he stepped up to crouch beside Amelia's chair.

"I believe," he said, knowing his voice was too gruff, "that your...*puppy*," he said with another quick look at their guest, "is happier than I have seen him. I also believe I can spare a roll for him. As long as he has the manners not to deposit it back upon my carpet."

She was still curled in a defensive position. "I should have 'pared," she whispered, sounding anguished.

"Oh, dear," the strange woman murmured, sitting Sophie back in her seat. "I didn't mean to..."

Grey smiled quickly up at her. "Amelia was trying to help. Helping is a wonderful thing."

"It is indeed," the woman said. "Both girls offered to help me finish a cinnamon bun. They were gracious enough to take two pieces, so I didn't have to eat the whole thing by myself."

Finally, she got giggles from both little girls, even though a bit weak.

Grey regained his feet. "Can I assume you are the lady who wishes to see me?"

Her smile was less assured. "I am. If I could have a few minutes of your time?"

"Did you 'pare for the consequences?" he asked.

Her smile grew a bit. "I certainly hope so."

"Then, ladies," he said, with a bow to the girls. "If you will excuse us for a minute."

"Talk here," Sophie commanded. "We like her."

"Sophie," the woman said. That was all. Sophie.

And Sophie ducked her head. "Please."

"We cannot," she said. "But I will stop back in to say good-bye. Would that suffice?"

Amelia scrunched up her face. "Suff...."

The lady smiled. "My apologies. I got ahead of myself. Would that be all right? Please?"

Both little girls grinned and nodded before returning their attention to breakfast.

"There had better be at least one of those left when I get back," Grey warned. "You know I have a great appetite."

"Pro-*dijus*." Sophie nodded, proud of the word she'd picked up from him.

"Pro-digious," he agreed.

Quickly bending, he dropped a kiss on one white-blonde little head and another caramel-colored. The dog momentarily looked up as if expecting his own tribute, sighed, and dropped his chin back to the floor.

The nursery maid finally made it into the room as Grey escorted his guest out.

"I don't suppose you've come to apply for a position as governess."

Her smile was breathtaking. Madonnas bore smiles like that. He'd seen them in churches all over Spain.

"I fear not. I have quite enough challenges at home." She gave him a quick look from those pale green eyes that he felt straight down to his groin. "I must beg your attention on another matter."

"So I hear. It must be urgent if you came so early in the day."

"I do apologize for the time," she said. "But I needed to see you before you did something foolish."

And that was when Grey's day got even worse.

3

___

"I believe introductions are in order," Greyville said as Georgie followed him into the grimmest room she had seen since boarding school. Good heavens, she thought, looking around at pea-green wallpaper and heavy gold furniture left over from the previous century. Or possibly the one before that. The room could give one indigestion.

The marquess gave his own look. "Appalling, isn't it?"

She shook her head in wonder. "Nauseating."

For a moment she was plagued by guilt. She suspected this was their best parlor. And she was taking the funds away to improve it. But then she thought of Prissy trying to live up to the power and strength that emanated from this man like the heat of the sun, and even with only a moment's acquaintance knew that poor Prissy would never survive him. For the first time in her life, Georgie questioned whether she'd make it out of this room unscathed. And oddly, all that did was inspire the most delicious shivers.

"You seem to know who I am," the marquess said, closing the door enough for privacy without sacrificing propriety. "I hope you aren't here to raise money."

Georgie blinked away the distraction. "I beg your pardon?"

He stopped. "For the orphanage?"

She was probably staring. "What orphanage?"

He offered a slight, wry smile. "You mean there can be another reason for a young woman to be in charge of ten children in one house?"

It took a second for her to connect the question to previous statements, leaving her with her own rueful smile. "You have obviously never met my family. We are known for being...prolific."

For a minute he just stared. She could watch him do that all day. He was even more than the dispatches had intimated. Lean, hard, tall, with the unmistakable posture of an officer in an elite corps and the lithe grace of a natural horseman. His face was all angles, weathered by a Spanish sun so that his water-blue eyes looked ghostly against the tan and the unusual salt-and-pepper of his thick umber hair. Even the scar that marred his left temple intercepted his eyebrow at a perfect angle. He was compelling, enticing. He was, unfortunately, unforgettable.

And he smelled...delicious. Cinnamon and sandalwood and cedar. She might be in trouble here. And she hadn't even checked to see if he had two legs.

"Oh, my God," he suddenly said, eyes widening a bit. "I knew I recognized those eyes. You're one of the Mad Packhams!"

Well, that brought Georgie caroming back to reality. "You must know one of the boys."

"I know all three of them. Mad as snakes, the lot. The most misnamed miscreants I've ever met."

She could afford a smile. "The Archangels, you mean? Yes. I am inclined to agree, but then I grew up with the monsters. And really, if your parents conspired to name you after angels but your sisters after British kings, how would you react?"

His scowl lightened. "I'd run off to war to prove I was more than feathers and haloes."

She nodded. "Exactly. Evidently it is an age-old Packham proclivity."

"And do you kings attempt to prove yourselves as more than scepters and bad habits?"

Georgie still smiled, but only out of habit. "Females do not get that chance, my lord. Even Packhams."

"And yet, here you are, breaching my castle for some reason. I'd have to assume that means you are Michael's sister."

She frowned. "I am."

"I might have known. His etiquette is just as dismal."

A bit of his glow dimmed for Georgie. "I would assume etiquette would not be as vital on a battlefield as, say, courage," she said, leveling a glare on him. "Or adaptability. Or brains."

It seemed she had surprised him. His sudden grin set her skin humming. Oh, dear.

"Well, there you have me," he admitted. "He is all of that." His shrug was a work of art. "As, I am forced to admit, are his cousins. Always up for an adventure."

Georgie nodded. "You do indeed know them, then."

For a second, he looked conflicted. Not certain, she knew, how to go on.

"The introductions," she said, dipping a belated curtsy. "Since we have no mutual acquaintance to pretend we haven't been speaking to each other for the last twenty minutes, allow me to introduce myself. Lady Georgiana Packham."

"Also known as The Termagant," he offered, eyes lighting.

She all but reared back. "I beg—"

He shook his head. "You do know that that is what your brother calls you. You were evidently a trial to him growing up, your ladyship."

Finally, Georgie could really smile. "As a matter of fact, I was. I hope I still am. It is, after all, the sworn duty of every sister."

His smile softened, and Georgie wanted to just bathe in it. "And now you have come to be a trial to me, I presume?"

"I fear that I am. I have come on behalf of a schoolmate. If you would hear me out."

He finally motioned her to one of the garish gold satin settees that were even more uncomfortable than they looked. Georgie thought they might have been stuffed with horsehair. Or nails. And amazingly enough, even her perfectly mild forest-green lustring walking dress clashed with the color. She would have loved to have seen what Charlie would have braved against it.

"You really do need that cash," she mourned.

"What?"

She looked up to see that he had perched on another of the torturous structures. He sat just as uncomfortably as she. But she didn't want to insult him by jumping straight into his lack.

The good news was that he seemed to be in possession of both feet.

Well, that was rude, Georgie thought. *Good thing he wasn't a mind reader.* She did wonder how to find out about his injury, though.

A topic for another visit. She had to find a way to broach her mission.

"Should I ring for tea?" he asked.

"Thank you, no. I shared some with the girls."

He frowned, vaguely waving a hand toward the dining room. "How did you...er..."

"Recognize the sounds of imminent disaster from down the hall?" She gave a small smile. "The surfeit of siblings and cousins in my own home. One learns to be ever on the alert for trouble."

He nodded, still looking uncomfortable. "Then you all really do live together? I thought Rafe was exaggerating."

It seemed she was always explaining their living situation.

"Since my father is away so much, it seemed more convenient to put my uncle in charge of the estates, and more convenient yet to collect all the children into one place. Add to that the children of my other uncle, whom we sadly lost some time ago, and it is an edifying and lively arrangement."`

"And beneficial for the familiarization of the logic of small girls," he agreed. "Thank you. I suppose I will pick up the knack eventually."

She smiled, suddenly beset by the urge to reach out to this quite human man. She had spent so much time reading about his heroic feats she wasn't prepared for the flash of helpless emotion on his face at mention of the little girls in the breakfast room.

"They are very dear," she began.

His sigh was heartfelt. "They are also a trial. Soldiers are not trained in the gentler arts of miniature tea services and conversations with dollies. They also follow direction with more alacrity."

"They are not...?"

"Mine? They are now. They were my cousin Peter's girls. Both he and their mother were lost to the influenza."

"Poor babes." Poor Lord Coleford, obviously caught in a dilemma. "They have no other recourse?"

He betrayed himself with a quick flash of anger in those sea-bright eyes. It was the frown that followed that pulled at Georgie even more strongly, since she suspected it was weighted with the burden of fragile little girls.

"A grandmother," he said with another shake of his head. "If you are here long enough, you might well meet her. She frequently descends, hoping to catch me in the act of locking them in the attic and making them live on water and mouse droppings."

"She must love them quite a bit."

His glare was brief but furious. "Their money, rather. Their grandfather was wise enough to protect their dowries from his son. But that is a topic for another time. Thank you for saving Sophie from herself."

Now her smile was genuine. "You have your hands full with that one. She's bright as a penny."

"She is five and wishes to adopt the lion at the Tower."

"Perhaps a kitten instead."

His scowl was belied by a certain twinkle in his eyes. "Brutus would have the thing for breakfast."

"I assume that is the horse under the table who was doing away with the dropped bun bits."

"It's what I call him. Irish wolfhound."

"Yours?"

"Good Lord no. Theirs. I'm actually quite surprised he let you near the girls. He is quite protective."

Georgie nodded. "A good thing, with Sophie's independent streak."

"It's just too bad we can't train him to catch Sophie when she climbs."

"So, the shelves aren't the first ascent?"

"Just the latest."

Georgie kept wanting to reach out to him, just to make physical contact. "That must be a lot to come home to, along with everything else."

That quickly, his mood cooled. He raised one eyebrow. "How is it I can help you?" he asked in a manner of officers everywhere reclaiming the conversation. After all they had discussed, this had evidently been the step too far.

Georgie drew in a breath. Now that she was for it, she had no idea how to broach the subject. "My lord…"

She got yet another scowl, this one of impatience. "I would prefer Grey, if you don't mind," he said. "Or Greyville. I have yet to accommodate myself to a title that was never meant to be mine."

Georgie nodded in commiseration. "I am sorry."

He scowled. "Not nearly as sorry as I. If I may say so, I make an exemplary soldier. I suspect my skills will not be quite what is needed for a marquessate."

"Don't be silly," she retorted. "You have been notorious for your quick thinking, your courage, your determination, your adaptability. I suspect all will be needed."

His expression of horror was comical. "Good God. You don't read dispatches, do you? Didn't your brother tell you that most of what is written is to encourage the public to pay more taxes?"

Georgie kept finding herself smiling, this time to acknowledge the truth. "My youngest brother is looking to a life in the army. I have been trying to instruct him so he can make an educated decision. Dispatches are his preferred primer."

For a moment the marquess—*Greyville*—sat in silence. Georgie suspected he was wanting to tell her some truth, something never included in dispatches, which she had long since suspected had been purposely kept out of Michael's letters as well. She held her breath, waiting.

In the end, he just shook his head. "You were about to tell me why you came."

Ah, so they were back to that. Every time he revealed a bit more of himself Georgie found it harder to break the news.

She picked a bit at the embroidered Grecian key design on her dress. "Er, well, the truth of the matter is, your…er, Greyville, I had a visit the other day from, well, from Priscilla Mayhew."

That got his attention. He went very still, a hunter catching a scent. "And?"

Georgie wanted very badly to get up and move. But if she did, so would he. They could very well end up dancing around the room and getting nothing done. And the less she had to do with this room—and her task—the more comfortable she'd be.

So, she forced herself to face him. "How did her father broach the marriage to you, my lord?"

She had heard the description that a person's face set like granite. Suddenly she understood it. This was not going to be easy. She was sorely tempted to bring up his little cousins again, just to see him smile.

"I do not believe that can be of any concern to you, my lady." His voice was as stiff as his features.

She sighed. "Prissy made it my concern, my lord. She begged me to intercede."

"Intercede? What in blazes for?"

Georgie fought the urge to twist her hands like a supplicant. She was so glad she wasn't facing this man across pistols. He would have dropped her without firing a shot.

So she drew another breath and dove in. "She asks to be freed of the engagement."

It seemed she'd managed to surprise him. "I beg your pardon?"

She straightened, as if that would bolster her courage. If only Priscilla had asked her to find a lost bracelet.

"Priscilla was never apprised of the engagement until her father had signed the papers. She is...er, afraid that her affections have already been given."

He blinked at her as if she'd just spoken Chinese. "What does that have to do with anything?"

"What does it...." Before she knew it, Georgie was on her feet after all. "Tell me you are joking, my lord."

He rose right in front of her. He topped her by a good six inches, and right now every inch of him pulsated with fury. "I was about to say the same thing to you, madam. I believe this interview is over."

She scowled right back at him. "That would be *my lady*, Greyville. I am not married."

"For which I'm sure some poor sod is eternally grateful."

It took most of Georgie's social discipline to keep from gasping. "Why, you bully. You would really tie a woman to you who would resent you every day of her life for taking her away from the boy she loves, just to make your life a bit more comfortable."

His sneer was as impressive as his smile. "Try not to be so melodramatic, *my lady*. The girl is eighteen. She doesn't know what she wants. But I guarantee she will be happy with being a marchioness."

Now Georgie's gorge was really rising. "If you believe that, sir, then it is obvious you never met her. I'm sure she was an easy solution to your problem. But as I was trying to teach Sophie just now, impulse is not always a good predictor of outcome."

"You think my decision was impulsive."

She shrugged. "You came home to a disaster. Everyone knows of your financial difficulties. Add to that the girls? You saw a way out. You jumped at the chance."

He leaned closer, which should have intimidated her. She wondered why it excited her instead, straight down to her toes. "I wonder that you considered me worth consulting, ma'am, if that is what you thought of me."

"Actually," she retorted, determined not to retreat an inch, "I think Priscilla is worth saving from an ill-advised match. And the more time I spend with you, the more convinced of it I am."

Why did his eyes have to be so compelling? Why did she want to ease that deep crease between them? Why did she want to *touch* him? It would do her no good. It would certainly do Prissy no good.

"And if I graciously step away," he retorted, "who will take her place? You?"

He took her breath away. "And make us both miserable? No thank you. After meeting the girls, however, I will submit to helping you find someone else."

"I don't want someone else!" he bellowed.

Georgie shook her head. "Is this your normal method of solving a problem, my lord? Shouting it down?"

He glared. "It has certainly worked the last ten years!"

She did her best to smile. "Yes, but I am not bound by any oath to listen to it."

He leaned in a bit. "Nor am I bound by any social convention to stay around and listen to *you.*"

She couldn't help herself. "Is it that you are afraid you'll lose the money," she demanded, "Or the argument?"

She actually silenced him for a moment. She knew it wasn't going to last long, and when it was past the windows would rattle. "My lord...Grey..."

He slashed a hand through the air. "Enough!"

"Stop it!" a voice piped up from the doorway. "Stop yelling at her!"

Georgie whipped around to see they had company. She thought she had never seen anything so brave. Two little girls, who she suspected had long suffered from someone's temper, stood foursquare in the doorway, clutching each other's hands like a lifeline, their features sickly pale and their eyes full of tears. Facing the man who now had the power over their lives in order to protect her.

She would have run to hold them if Greyville hadn't got there first. Suddenly he was on his knees, his arms around them both, holding them close. Georgie thought her own heart would explode.

"What is this?" he asked, letting an arm loose to wipe at small tears. "Lady Georgiana's personal army?"

Sophie sucked in a shaky breath. "You...you...."

"I was yelling," he said, his voice unspeakably gentle. "I know. I am too used to yelling. The army is a noisy place, and that is how we get each other's attention. It doesn't mean anything. Does it, Lady Georgiana?"

He didn't even look her way. He didn't need to. "Remember I said that there were ten children in my house?" she asked the girls. "Well, the truth is that with everybody else who lives there, eighteen people wander in and out of my house all the time. And that's without the servants. So, you can imagine how noisy it gets there. Yelling does not frighten me."

Sophie straightened, her head back. "It doesn't frighten me either. But sometimes it scares Amelia. 'Cause she's little."

Georgie stepped closer and crouched alongside Greyville. "Then his lordship and I will practice our quiet voices until Amelia is more comfortable."

Greyville got to his feet. "Oh, I'm not sure I can do soft, Sophie. I sound like I'm growling."

Amelia giggled, the sound like sparkles on the sea. "Just like Bark."

"Bark?" Georgie asked, accepting Greyville's hand to stand beside him.

Sophie put two fingers to her lips and whistled. The wolfhound skidded into the room, nearly toppling both girls and Georgie, who thanked heavens she was used to large animals.

"Sit, you silly," Sophie told him.

He sat right next to her, his tongue lolling, his shaggy head above Amelia's. Georgie noticed that he didn't look to the girls. His focus was entirely on Greyville.

"I'm glad you have Bark," Georgie told the girls. "That way yelling won't scare Amelia so much. Because Bark would never let anyone hurt you, would he?"

"Not anymore."

Oh, God. Much more time with these two would shatter Georgie.

"Then make sure you keep him with you," she said. "Isn't that right, Lord Greyville?"

"Indeed." Even his voice sounded a little thin. She suspected he had caught the girls' body language long before she had.

"Now, girls...and Bark," he said, giving them each a formal little bow. "May Lady Georgiana and I have a few more moments to talk? I promise we will not yell."

Georgie wasn't sure he should make promises that would be so hard to keep, especially considering what she still needed to say.

Sophie considered both adults with her brittle, wise eyes, and finally nodded. "We still have one cinnamon roll. But prob'ly not for long."

And with an impish grin, she tugged her sister out the door. Bark waited a few moments more, his attention focused solely on Greyville. Then he simply stood and turned to follow the girls down the hall.

"You could almost swear he spoke to you," Georgie marveled.

"The doggie translation of 'don't hurt my girls?'" Greyville nodded. "It is the sole reason I let that hairy horse in the house. They need some security."

She looked after them, thinking of what Greyville faced. "How long have they been here?"

"Ten days. Until I got home, they were with my cousin's solicitor. He had no idea how to deal with little girls." Sighing, he scraped his hands through his hair. "No more than do I."

Again, Georgie was beset by the urge to reach out. To ease the tight set of those shoulders. To comfort a man who resembled stone. "The situation is more complicated than that. Isn't it?"

He nodded. "You saw their reactions. The defensive postures. I'm very afraid my cousins didn't know how to raise children either."

"You really are quite good with them," she said and smiled. "Take it from someone with experience."

He rubbed at his temple. "Thank you again for your help."

Again, Georgie had to dive into deep water. "Does Prissy know you've inherited them?"

For the longest moment he just looked out the door, as if seeing the sisters holding onto each other as they retreated to the breakfast room. Then he shook his head.

It was Georgie's turn to sigh, and it was heartfelt. "You do remember that Prissy is only eighteen."

"Women have been mothers by that age."

"You know perfectly well this is not the same. Prissy is a sweet girl. But she isn't..."

He turned to her. "What? She isn't what?"

Georgie faced him, even as her knees shook. "Up to this."

He glared at her again, his hand fisted at his side. "Why are you even getting involved?" he demanded.

Georgie offered a rueful smile. "Because Prissy asked me. She's too afraid to ask her father and more afraid to ask you. It is pointless to ask her mother. Mrs. Mayhew would marry you herself to connect such a title to their name."

"But you wouldn't?"

She shrugged. "I already have an illustrious title attached to my name. It is not quite as delightful as it sounds."

"So says a woman who has everything."

She laughed. "Anyone who can say that has never been a woman."

"A fact patently obvious to all." He looked down at her. "What, then, do you want that you don't have?"

But that list was too long, and too much of it unrecognizable to men. So, she settled for, "The freedom to make my own choices."

It took him a second, but he finally shook his head. "Obviously a subject too complex to be solved over a morning visit."

She ducked her head, conceding. "And without even the benefit of tea."

"Or brandy."

She was tempted to sit back down but realized that would put her in even more danger of attraction. She needed to get out before she began to see his side of the question. And before she actually did touch him. She was very much afraid that would change everything.

"Do me a favor," she said, then shook her head. "No. Do *yourself* a favor. You haven't met Prissy yet, have you?"

"I have not."

"Do so. As soon as possible. Then come see me, and we can begin looking for a wife who would be strong enough to support you and those little girls."

He still frowned. "Is this a service you perform for everyone?"

"For no one, actually. You may consider yourself special. And now, I have two little girls I must bid farewell to. Thank you for your time."

And before she could change her mind, she curtsied one more time and headed out the door.

❧

GREY STOOD there for the longest moment listening to the faint murmurs of that woman bidding the girls goodbye before Chalmers, the butler he had inherited with everything else, showed her out the door.

He was just about to head into his office to pen a note to his fiancée when Braxton stepped into the room.

"Eavesdropping again, Braxton?"

"Only in the most respectful way, my lord. We believe it was needed."

"Oh, do we?"

"Indeed. A certain gentleman is waiting in your office to discuss your travel schedule. And there are rumors from the kitchen, where the cook's assistant is walking out with a certain groom, that the young persons' grandmother is planning a surprise visit to them today."

Grey scrubbed at his face, suddenly beset by a new headache. "And I have a fiancée who doesn't seem to want my poor self."

"And, if you'll pardon our saying, milord, a grandmother who will use the opportunity of your trip to take advantage."

"A grandmother who makes Brutus growl and bare his teeth."

"A grandmother who might well be able to convince the Chancery that a single man is no guardian for little girls."

Hearing the bright chatter of those two little girls, Grey fought a fresh wave of fear that he would ultimately fail them. "And damn it all if I don't know that. It seems my clever plan to acquire a wife has suffered a set-back."

"A thought which has occurred to us as well. Whatever you do choose to do, Colonel, you're running out of time to do it."

"And damn it if I don't know that as well."

4

———

*A*ll Grey could think as he sat on yet another painfully uncomfortable settee in the fussily overdecorated gold drawing room at the Mayhew house, a cup of tea balanced on one knee and a piece of dry seed cake on the other, was that he should have met his fiancée before he signed for her. He should have at least met her mother.

"We are *so* honored to have you here, your lordship," Mrs. Mayhew trilled, fluttering the lace square in her plump little hand like a flag of surrender. "Are we not, Priss-Priss?"

The only thing keeping him from wincing was the too-obvious strain on his fiancée's features, tightening even further at her mother's obsequiousness. He might have better withstood the assault to his senses if his head wasn't once again caught in a vise of late-night drinking. Rob Glenn had not moved on. And after a few hours of refighting battles over Rob's excellent whisky, Grey had somehow let loose the information that he was being forced into marriage. So, Rob had decided to stay, to "help a comrade," he'd said with a lopsided grin and a slap to the back.

Grey just wished his friend were here now to take some of the attention from the mother. Rob was at least an earl.

"It was nice of you to visit, my lord," his fiancée said in a near-whisper.

He hated to agree with The Termagant, but she was all too correct. This was a girl. Unformed, unsophisticated, unhappy in the extreme. Possibly even more unhappy than he was. And yet, looking at the predatory gleam in her mother's eye, Grey suspected that he would have had an easier time getting out of the Tower than this marriage.

"Will you be at the Conynghams' tonight, my lord?" the mama asked now, patting at overcurled hair that was a yellow color he suspected wasn't found in nature. "I am certain you will be delighted to hear that our Priss-Priss will be performing. She plays the harp like the veriest angel."

Something else he should have learned from the Termagant, he supposed. Whether he would be able to withstand fifty years of a frightened, rabbity wife and rapacious in-laws. He suspected he would end up at the gallows for throttling his solicitor, who had set up this unholy alliance. Right after he throttled the mother.

"I wish I could be there, ma'am. But I fear I have duties that will keep me away."

Thank a merciful God.

Should he bring up the girls? He suspected he already knew how the news would be received by both mother and daughter. The mother would gush about ready-formed families and how her darling was a natural-born mother, and the daughter would lose the rest of her color and faint right off her chair. He was ashamed at how tempting the idea sounded. At least it would break up this stultifying conversation. No, not conversation. Monologue.

"...and, of course, like any well-bred girl, our Priss paints the most delightful watercolors. Why, her painting of Mayview—that is our estate in Oxfordshire, of course—is worth hanging at the Academy, I vow. But it is in her sweetness with her younger sisters that I am most proud of her. So patient. So loving."

Grey all but stopped breathing. So. She knew. The woman's eyes were sharp as sheared glass. He felt a noose tighten around his throat. The question was, did the girl know? If her blank expression was any indication, he suspected not. Which meant the real question was, should he bring it up now? Get it right out in the open to see her reaction.

He simply wasn't sure he had the courage. He was beginning to respect the Termagant for trying to help this poor, wan girl. Priscilla Mayhew would be indescribably beautiful for the right man, all innocent, golden English beauty. But he knew without a doubt she would never bloom for him.

And yet, he couldn't imagine a way to give her the freedom to marry that boy she loved.

"How delightful," he responded when the mother paused for breath. "And of course you enjoy dancing, Miss Mayhew?" he asked, just to shut the woman up. "You will, of course, be at the Halverson ball tomorrow. Might I reserve a dance?"

Given a chance, he suspected she would have told him exactly what she thought of that idea. One quick, panicked glance at her mother had her nodding her head. "Yes, my lord."

Grey shot a desperate glance at the mantel clock to see that for the moment he was rescued. He had reached the obligatory fifteen minutes. Setting the cup and the cake back on the piecrust table at his elbow, he rose to his feet.

"I thank you for your hospitality," he said.

The mother was on her feet. "But my lord. Don't you wish to spend a few minutes with our Priss?"

What was it with the royal *we's* lately, Grey wondered. Had he just never noticed them before? All he knew was that right now they annoyed him nearly into mayhem. He needed to get out of here before the woman standing before him had her hair pulled out.

"I fear not," he said, casting Miss Mayhew an apologetic smile. "Responsibilities at the House of Lords, you know."

A bit of a stretch, since he hadn't even been invested. Instead, he very much feared he would be forced to feed Sophie and Amelia's grandmother. Which might end up being worse than dancing with Priscilla or withstanding her mother's siege, but Grey couldn't leave that particular field of battle to the old harpy.

Not even old, really. Definitely a harpy.

"Thank you again," he said with the pro forma bow, not sure whether he was relieved or newly aggrieved that his fiancée looked so relieved at his going.

It didn't matter for the moment. The butler was waiting with his coat and hat, and the door was right there.

"Do you like dogs?" he asked suddenly, unsure why.

Both women stopped as if struck.

"Of course, she does," the mother trilled. "Such a comfort to have a sweet companion to sit in your lap."

His grin was genuine. "Not this one," he said as the butler helped him into his coat. "Irish wolfhound. Comes up to my waist."

Oh, blast. The chit was blanching again. For a moment he thought he'd have to toss hat and coat back at the butler so he could catch her. But she rallied just enough to cast her mother a terrified look.

"Of course," her mother said, not even looking the girl's way. "A beast like that would be kept in the stables, I'm sure."

His smile was unpardonably satisfied. "The breakfast room. And the salon. Oh, and the kitchen, come to think of it." Popping his hat on his head, he gave it a tap. "Ate an entire roast yesterday. Just grabbed it from the counter and ran off like a pickpocket in St. Giles."

Now the mother blanched. The butler was manfully fighting a grin.

Grey just smiled, gave another bow, and left.

He was just beginning to feel better when he climbed into his carriage to find Braxton waiting inside for him. "For the love of all that is holy, Braxton. Do I not get a minute without you?"

"We thought you should know, my lord. The young relations' grandmother has been delayed. Her carriage suffered a mishap to a wheel, we believe. However, Lord Drake is expecting you."

Grey stopped. "Drake? Why? I saw Lord Finch yesterday."

"There is new information, and possibly a need for you to leave sooner."

"Sooner?! Good God, they already have me on my way by the end of June."

"Our man in Paris came up missing."

Grey shut his eyes. "Gracechurch? How?"

"They aren't sure. But Foreign Office wants you to prepare to possibly leave sooner."

Grey started rubbing his eyes again. "Not until I'm safely married. I cannot leave the girls at the mercy of that...that..."

"Hag? Shrew? Virago?"

"Threat. All right. Let us see what Drake has to say, and then we'll tackle my marriage."

"To Miss Mayhew?"

"Good God, I hope not."

For the first time since Grey had climbed into the carriage, Braxton smiled. "We have been sharing information we garnered about the young lady's parents with our staff. It is believed that if you attached yourself to that family, half of them would leave."

"Would that include you?"

"One virago we might withstand, my lord. But this would invite a second into our happy home. It would be inconceivable."

~

WHILE GREY HAD BEEN WITHSTANDING the Mayhew women, Georgie had gathered the troops to draw up lists.

"Millicent Bickerling," Eddie said, hunched over the paper that already had five names on it.

Activities like this did not belong in the public rooms. So the cousins had made a strategic retreat to Georgie's sitting room, where they could come up with potential wives for the new marquess as they toasted cheese. Charlie toasted the cheese. Eddie kept the list at Georgie's desk. Georgie paced, unsure why this activity made her so uncomfortable.

Usually being in her rooms calmed her. Taking her inspiration from Mrs. Bauer's little sitting room, she had decorated in bright colors, overstuffed sofas, and soft materials, making her own nest, as she'd called it. For once, though, the sunny yellow walls, emerald-and-aqua floral Chinoiserie chintz cushions, and simple lines of the Sheraton furniture didn't soothe her at all.

"Isn't Millicent Bickerling the one with teeth like a mole?" Charlie asked from the floor by the fireplace.

As Georgie passed by, Charlie handed her a sample. Georgie nodded and took a bite. "I fear she is. We want to help Lord Coleford, not punish him. It isn't his fault his cousins were improvident. Besides, those little girls deserve a better mother than one who is constantly sniffling and reading improving tracts."

"Louisa Allen," Eddie offered, lifting her head.

"Too poor."

"Isabelle Stroud."

"Too rich."

Charlie looked up. "How can anyone be too rich?"

Georgie turned by the door and headed back across the Turkey carpet she had discovered on a town ramble. "The man is already suffering the humiliation of his cousins' folly. He shouldn't have to be shamed by his wife's wealth."

That even got Eddie's attention. "There are men who would be shamed by being rich?"

Georgie plopped down on the plump sofa and licked cheese from her fingers. "This one would."

"I know I shouldn't have to tell you this," Charlie reminded her. "But he has to marry someone."

Georgie waved her off. Kicking off her shoes, she stretched out on the sofa, looking up at the ceiling medallion and thinking of a man who would humble himself for two frightened little girls. A man with breathtaking blue eyes and an impressive line of scowls that could make a girl weak in the knees. "She has to be the right someone."

Eddie motioned to the tome open before her on the desk. "Which is why we are going over Debrett's."

"Does he have to limit himself to Debrett's?" Georgie asked no one in particular.

Charlie motioned to another piece of cheese, but the cousins shook their heads. "We don't know anyone *not* in Debrett's."

"Of course we do."

"I'm not counting the bastards, George."

Eddie huffed in distress. "Don't call them bastards, Charlie. It isn't their fault."

"But it is what they are. And we seemed to have had an inordinate number of them at our school, acknowledged or not."

"Should we scratch them off the list?"

"Not if they're rich."

"But not too rich."

All three girls shared rueful smiles.

"Which brings us back to the original problem," Georgie said, still considering the ceiling. "How are we doing on convincing Prissy's father, Eddie?"

Eddie sighed and turned to sharpening her quill. "Priscilla believes she can get him to the Halverson's ball tomorrow night."

Both Georgie and Charlie groaned. The Halversons threw the most stultifying entertainments in London. All pretense and no charm. And yet, mandatory for young ladies still on the market. Which, unfortunately, the Packham girls were.

"Eloise Chadwick," Eddie suggested suddenly, flipping pages.

Georgie opened her mouth to say *no*, and then realized that there was nothing really wrong with Eloise. She was rich, quiet, nice, pretty, a baron's daughter, and twenty-five. Which meant she could be amenable to suggestion. After all, no matter how nice you were, twenty-five was still twenty-five.

"Why isn't she married?" she asked.

"Eloise?" Charlie asked. "She was promised to a Guardsman, wasn't she?"

Eddie nodded. "He fell at Salamanca. She was devastated. They'd been childhood friends."

Georgie waved a hand. "Put her name down. She needs a nice husband."

"Coleford is nice?" Charlie asked.

Georgie scrunched up her nose. "Well, not...exactly. But he is honorable. And kind to little girls."

"And handsome?"

Georgie closed her eyes, his face still before her. "Not that either. Striking, I'd say. Compelling. But any one of our brothers is more handsome."

She opened her eyes to see Eddie considering whatever she'd written. "Then are you certain Eloise is right for him?"

Again, there was that catch in her chest. "Of course. Oh, and possibly Lilly Trent-Parker." Georgie caught Eddie exchanging quick glances with Charlie. "What?" she asked.

"Nothing," both answered a bit too quickly, which tipped her off quite neatly.

"No," she said, sitting up, since it was difficult to be threatening lying down. "Definitely not. If I see my name anywhere on that list, blood will flow. I have things to do." She waved at the list. "Put down Lilly. She is one of six and has four brothers."

Charlie nodded. "Proven breeder."

Eddie wrinkled her nose. "How complimentary."

"I'm only thinking the way a man would who is looking to secure his succession," Charlie protested. "If it comes to that, considering the size of our families, all three of us would fall into that category."

"Well," Eddie demurred. "Maybe you two. There are only Gabe and I for our branch."

Charlie waved that objection aside. "That's only because you lost your parents before they had a chance to add to the totals. And you do have Gabe, remember."

"True," Eddie mused. "We all have males in our families. That should be enough."

"And I certainly have the hips for childbearing," Charlie agreed with a grin, as she scooped up the rest of the toasting implements to put them away.

Eddie looked down at her lap. "I don't suppose I do."

Georgie grinned. "Women with less than you have managed quite nicely through the centuries. Look at Mother. And Grandmother, come to think of it."

At the word, all three stopped, looking stricken. "Grandmother," they all groaned.

None of them had managed to visit the old lady.

"Ooh," Charlie spoke up. "I just thought of someone. If we want childbearing hips, Petra Vincent."

The other two nodded.

"And she comes with vineyards," Eddie agreed as she scribbled.

"Well, if that is a bonus," Georgie said, "what about Margaret McEwan? She comes with a distillery."

Charlie laughed. "I'll marry her myself."

"Which reminds me," Eddie said, turning to face them. "We need an avowed rake."

Georgie blinked. "For who?"

"Whom," Eddie and Charlie corrected in unison.

Georgie waved them off. "Then why? And exactly how were you reminded?"

"Because Margaret McEwan didn't finish her last season due to an unfortunate association with Lord Havers. Her parents caught a whiff of, as they called it, 'unacceptable behavior' on her part—I believe she was sneaking out to meet him—and yanked her back to Scotland before Havers could cause further damage. I suspect that as focused as Priscilla's parents are about making the right match, any contact with a rake or real fortune hunter, they might think that it would be safer simply just to give her to her swain in the country."

"Brilliant," Charlie said. "Who do we know who might fit the bill?"

"Someone who owes us a favor and wouldn't hurt her in any way," Eddie added.

"So definitely not Havers," Charlie decided. "He has no scruples. And he plays for keeps."

"And he smells," she and Georgie finished together.

Georgie laughed. "The only good thing about that is that you can always tell when he's closing in. Who else?"

But they drew a blank. Nobody could think of one real rake

to approach. Certainly not one who would be considered trustworthy.

They were brought up short by the sound of scratching on the door.

"Come," Georgie called.

It was the maid, Minta. "'Scuse me, m'lady," she said, with a quick curtsy and a suspiciously bright grin. "You 'ave a visitor."

Georgie looked to the mantel clock to see that it was almost time for tea. "Good heavens. Who could be calling this late?"

"Says his name is Lord Coleford?"

Georgie froze on the spot. "Good God. Not at the kitchen door."

Minta giggled. "Lawz, no. Right through the front door."

Eddie and Charlie were already busy tidying their hair.

"Did he say what he wants?" Georgie asked.

The maid laughed. "Not to the likes o' me, he didn't. But yer lady mother joined him a few minutes ago."

Georgie jumped up to check her own hair. "Disaster," she groaned.

Charlie was laughing. "Don't forget the list."

"We don't know that is what he is here for. Does he have two little girls with him?"

"No'm. All alone, he is. And lookin' like a cat just landed on a griddle, if you pardon me sayin' so."

Georgie could just imagine. Throwing a shawl around her shoulders, she ran past the maid, her cousins on her heels.

They knew better than to arrive in such a hurly-burly fashion, of course. The minute they reached the main staircase, the three abruptly slowed like skiffs caught in a cross current and floated down the rest of the way, the perfect embodiment of English womanhood. Except for Charlie, who had limited capabilities for self-control.

"A crown says he runs after five minutes with your mother," she predicted.

"Nobody is taking that bet, Charlie," Eddie scoffed, smoothing her pastel-peach skirts.

"He withstood Marshall Soult," Georgie reminded them.

Charlie chuckled at that. "Marshall Soult is not nearly as determined as your mother."

No one could argue the point. But even as they stopped to collect themselves outside the South Salon door, they realized the situation had already developed into a full-blown disaster.

"And how did you meet my niece?" demanded a strident voice.

Charlie was already spinning back toward the stairs. Eddie and Georgie neatly caught her by the arms and turned her right back around.

"She's *your* mother, Charlie," Georgie hissed. "If we can stand it, so can you."

"They don't want to see me," Charlie hissed. "They want to see you."

Before Georgie could change their minds, Eddie and Charlie pushed her through the door.

"*Who* is not handsome?" was the last thing she heard from them as she tripped into the salon.

The first thing Georgie saw as she skidded to the edge of her mama's blue-and-rose Aubusson carpet was Greyville, sitting as rigidly as a defendant in the dock, a cup of tea on his knee, his expression that of a person who had been tossed into a bear cage. Trying to protect himself even as he struggled to decide what was going on.

Georgie could hardly blame him. Of course, no one just coming upon the scene would wonder why. He was dressed for a call in a chocolate-brown Bath superfine and buff inexpressibles, his cravat tied in a simple knot. Across from Greyville two absolutely identical women sat side-by-side on the cream settee, their aristocratic looks the mirror image of each other, from elegantly upswept blonde hair to commanding brown eyes to an attire of high-waisted, long-sleeve day dresses in identical soft periwinkle, adorned with just a touch of Brussels lace. It could throw anyone off.

Georgie quickly dipped a curtsy to her mother and her aunt, hoping the prompt arrival would gain her credit. "Mama, Aunt Berenice."

If Georgie were following protocol, she should have called her mother's twin Aunt Packham. But with all the female Packhams in the family, it had been decided the risk of confusion was just too great.

Her mother favored her with a quiet smile that looked just a bit smug.

Aunt Berenice glared. "You have a visitor," she announced, as Greyville got to his feet.

Once one heard Aunt Berenice, they never mistook her for Georgie's mama again. Georgie's mama was all refinement, subtlety, and calm authority. Charlie's mama could easily be mistaken for an artillery colonel. The problem was that one wouldn't recognize the difference until it was too late.

"Yes," Georgie said, hand out. "I see that." She allowed Greyville to perform the obeisances. "Lord Coleford."

He bowed. "Lady Georgianna."

"He was just about to tell us how you met," Aunt Berenice stated, her nose wrinkling a bit, as if she could smell Georgie's brain working overtime on a reasonable lie.

"In the park," Georgie blurted out, sure her brain was frying. "I was walking with the cousins and came across Lord Coleford and his own little cousins out for an airing."

"An airing?' Aunt Berenice barked. "They are not winter blankets, young lady."

"Yes," Greyville gently agreed, "but you cannot say that all children don't need fresh air."

Aunt glared at him. "It *was* a lovely day."

His smile was much calmer than Georgie felt. "It was."

"But how were you introduced?" her mother asked in her velvety company voice.

"Well, you see," Greyville said with a duck of his head. "Lady Georgianna not only saved the ball my girls were kicking about, keeping it from the Serpentine by no more than a kick of her foot—"

Georgie thought she might kill him. She would hear about unsightly behavior later.

"—but also, possibly my youngest little cousin Amelia, who went charging after the ball. It was a gift from her papa, you see. She has been known to sleep with it."

Good lord, Georgie thought, seeing the softening of his audience's expressions. *It's working. How dare he be so smooth?*

"Your cousin Peter's girls?" Georgie's mama asked, her expression completely unruffled.

"Yes, Lady Clevedon. I admit I am not proficient at childcare yet, having only returned home from the battlefield." Blast if he didn't look perfectly sincere. All the while he was igniting fresh chills just from the timbre of his voice. "The closest I've ever come to this kind of business has been keeping subalterns in line. I fear I wasn't watching closely enough. I am more than grateful that Lady Georgianna was. When I realized I had a few minutes today, I thought I would attempt a formal introduction so I might properly thank her. I hope you don't mind."

And then he unleashed a smile on the older women that would have melted brick. Georgie found herself wanting to stare again. Good heavens. How could anyone have teeth so straight and white? Especially someone who had been making do from one battle to the next for the last ten years. It simply was not fair.

It didn't help that as she assessed his teeth, she was running her tongue over her own left canine where it encroached on its neighbor.

"Consider yourself introduced," Aunt Berenice said with an imperious wave of her hand.

"Thank you, Aunt Berenice," Georgie said.

She was just about to sit down when she caught sight of two waving females through the garden windows. "Er, would it be acceptable for us to take a short walk?"

Georgie almost put her hand over her own mouth. Her mother had suddenly lit up like sunrise. Oh lord, how did she eventually tell her mama what they were really doing for this man? *Not that kind of walk*, she wanted to say. Not that it would make a difference.

"Of course," her mother readily agreed. "The garden is not big, but it is at its prettiest right now."

Rising, Greyville gave another brief bow. "Thank you. I have several messages to deliver from Sophie and Amelia."

Georgie was feeling ambivalent about going off with Greyville, and not just because her mother was certain to get the wrong idea. Because Greyville might. Even so, she acquiesced with the grace her mama and her aunt—to be fair, mostly her aunt, since her mama was so involved in her projects—had relentlessly impressed on her and took Greyville's proffered arm.

"Are those the famous cousins I saw out the window?" he asked as they left the salon for the garden door. "The Kings?"

"They are," was all she was willing to say until they reached them.

"Reinforcements?" Greyville asked, his voice dry as Georgie's throat.

She refused to feel bad. "Believe me when I tell you that you would rather meet Charlie and Eddie than suffer the interrogation from my aunt for being alone with me for more than five minutes," she said as she guided Greyville out the garden door to reveal Charlie and Eddie waiting by the rosebushes.

She didn't even get a chance to perform formal introductions before Charlie set the tone, hands on hips. "Well, no wonder Priscilla doesn't want to marry you," she said, giving Greyville a thorough examination, the only thing missing a lorgnette. "You'd frighten the daylights out of her."

Greyville's answer was no more than a raised eyebrow.

Georgie sighed. "My lord," she said. "May I present Miss Charlotte Packham and Miss Edwina Packham? Charlie, Eddie, I suspect you already know who the Marquess of Coleford is."

Both dipped perfect curtsies.

"Grey," he immediately intervened. "Or Greyville."

"Not used to being a marquess yet?" Charlie asked. "I imagine all the sudden bowing and scraping can be a bit off-putting."

Georgie wasn't certain Grey's eyebrow would ever resume its normal position. "Indeed."

"How did you fare with the Twin Terrors?" Charlie asked.

"If we are here to help him," Eddie interjected, "We might wish to start. The mothers will not give us much time. In fact, one of them is watching out the window even as we speak."

Georgie motioned to a well-placed arbor with facing benches surrounded by her mother's favorite iris in gold and purple and white, their blossoms nodding in a breeze. Georgie took in a calming breath, the iris scent settling her a bit. She always connected that scent with her mother, who spread calm like a balm.

Greyville settled Georgie on the bench and then sat beside her. "I had heard they were twins. The rumors don't do them justice."

Charlie chuckled as she took up her seat across from them. "What a lovely way you have with a euphemism, my lord."

"They do it on purpose," Georgie informed him, wishing there was more room on the bench. He was distracting her. "If they can keep people just a bit off-balance, they can more easily control a situation."

"Like an unmarried marquess appearing suddenly in their salon."

Charlie beamed. "Exactly."

But Greyville didn't seem to be paying attention. He was organizing himself, his focus on settling a jacket that looked just that much too big. Excellent material and tailoring, but hanging just a bit limply, which seemed to disconcert him. Old togs, Georgie suspected, from before the war. She imagined he would have felt far more comfortable in his scarlets. Still, Georgie found that she had trouble looking away from the elegant line of his hands as he shot his cuffs. He might only have been a marquess for a matter of weeks, but he had the dignity of it down quite well.

"How can we help you, Greyville?" she asked.

He looked up, surprised into another smile. "It is that obvious?"

"It is the only reason I can think you'd appear at a veritable stranger's door this late in the day."

"To be fair," he said. "That stranger showed up at my door first."

She nodded. "Point taken. I assume that this means you have visited with Priscilla?"

He scowled, taking a moment to choose his next words. "I have no taste for torturing innocents," he said. "Especially if they are to be my wife."

If her Aunt Berenice had not drilled posture into her head, Georgie would have slumped in relief.

"In that case," she said, "we might have some ideas. Can you be at the Halverson ball tomorrow?"

He looked up. "I have already secured a dance with Miss Mayhew."

Georgie nodded and pointed to Eddie who held up her list. "We have some other young ladies you might want an introduction to."

He was looking even more uncomfortable. "I cannot break off an engagement I agreed to."

Georgie grinned. "That's all right. If we are very lucky, we will have Mr. Mayhew do it for you. Can you make sure you are overheard bemoaning the fact that you'll have to spend an inordinate amount of time this next year putting the Welsh property to rights?"

He blinked. "Wales?"

"Is that not where the ducal property is?"

He looked between the three of them. "Well, yes. One of them. In the Black Mountains. I have never been there, though. I have no idea...."

"It matters not," Eddie said, leaning forward in her enthusiasm. "Priscilla was horrified at the mere mention of Wales. She is a homebody and would wither so far away from her family. And thankfully, so would her parents. Her mother relies on her attendance on her."

"It's Wales," Greyville retorted. "Not the Antipodes."

Georgie smiled. "Maybe to someone who has traveled farther from London than Oxfordshire. We have it on good authority that even her father would be horrified to find that his daughter would be taken so far away. I believe they assumed you would spend the majority of your time in London. Parliament and all."

Again, Greyville looked from one cousin to the other. "You

seem to be taking an unusual amount of enjoyment in my predicament."

Charlie shrugged. "We enjoy solving conundrums."

"Why?"

Georgie sighed. "A habit we got into at school."

"We were called the Fairy Godmothers," Eddie added.

"Still are," Charlie admitted.

For a moment Greyville sat very still. "Lady Georgina bearded the lion in his den," he said. "Miss Edwina seems to be the listmaker." He turned to Charlie. "What do you provide?"

Charlie's grin was delighted. "Just the right touch of chaos and mayhem."

His frown just grew. "Why do I not feel encouraged?"

Georgie started to put her hand on his arm, but stopped when he looked her way. Did he have to smell of cedar and something citrusy? She wanted to lean into him and just breathe. "What Charlie meant was that if you play your part tomorrow, she will make certain Mr. Mayhew knows exactly what he will be forfeiting if he lets his Priscilla be dragged to Wales."

Greyville stiffened all over again. "I will *not* be dragging anybody..."

"But you will imply it. If not, the plan fails."

He gave a considered look at all three of them. "You really think you can help me."

All three nodded.

Georgie handed him the list. "Study the names on that list. We will find a way to introduce you. After we have seen to Mr. Mayhew. Once he realizes how isolated his daughter will be married to you, we shall have a clearer way forward."

He commenced rubbing at his forehead. "I feel as if I've been tackled by a squad of skirmishers."

Charlie beamed. "And so you have. Just be happy it is friendly forces."

He gave a distracted nod and rose to his feet. "Halverson's."

Georgie rose with him. "It is important," she said. "We can only hold off the notices from the papers for so long."

That earned her a shocked stare. "They haven't gone in yet?"

Georgie grinned. "A small mishap."

He gave his head a slow shake. "Wellington could have used you lot on the Peninsula."

Georgie thought she was in the clear a few minutes later when she handed the marquess off to their butler to see him out. She hadn't noticed her mother standing in the shadows just inside the Chinese parlor.

"Whatever the three of you are up to," the Countess said, stepping into the light. "I would advise you to use care."

Georgie startled. "Of course we will."

Her mother's frown was at once gentle and unsettling. "This isn't a lost bracelet, Georgianna."

Georgie fought a sense of panic. "Why would you say that?"

Now her mother smiled, and that was even worse. "Oh, my dear. You aren't the only one who excels at gathering information. Just be careful."

"I will."

"Are you planning to take him from Miss Mayhew?"

Georgie laughed, finally relieved. "Oh heavens, no. We'd be at each other's throats in a minute."

Then her mother did the most confounding thing of all. Her smile grew until it looked conspiratorial. "Oh," she said very softly. "But sometimes that's the most fun of all."

And before Georgie could demand to know what she meant, her mother gave her a pat on the cheek and walked out.

5

———————

ob had warned Grey about the Halversons. Braxton had warned him. Even the assistant at Weston's, where Grey had gone to recover his brand-new formal togs, had warned him. Paralyzing, they'd said. A crashing bore. Old title, new money from the big-toothed wife with pretensions of taste. Grey should probably be grateful they had just married off their last daughter. He could have been caught in Halverson's maw instead.

He thought all of this in the time it took to climb the stairs to the receiving line in his new evening attire, the shirt points as stiff and unpleasant as his uniform collar, the coat cut so close Braxton had had to coax him into it like a corset. Grey wasn't quite certain that he could lift his arms high enough to defend himself if needed.

Just another uniform, he kept thinking to himself, even if he felt completely out of place in it, especially every time he looked down to see the severe black jacket he knew to be *de riguer*. But then, he'd been wearing the scarlet one since his seventeenth birthday.

"Stop scowling," Rob hissed alongside him. "Two debs are crying, and a footman just ran the other way."

Grey snapped to attention. It was already hot in this mausoleum of a house, his stomach was growling, and his feet hurt. At least his head was in better shape. He and Rob had only breached one bottle last night before admitting they were too old to play rambunctious youths anymore. He still wasn't certain how he felt about Rob's offer to help rid him of a fiancée. He was even more uncertain since Rob told him he knew the Packham girls quite well. Would that help or hurt?

He still couldn't believe he'd put his problem in their hands. He had been so relieved when Deevers had followed the news of his inheritance with the offer of help from the Mayhews. He'd been home no more than a week and had just finished verifying the extent of his cousins' mismanagement, which left him saddled with two frightened little girls, several entailed estates encompassing an enormous amount of land, any number of buildings, and no cash to support any of it. Marriage to Priscilla Mayhew had seemed a godsend.

And yet here he was trying to get out of it.

"Lord Adam Noah Ezekiel Robert Glenn, Earl Hexham!" the butler bellowed.

Grey was impressed. Rob didn't even flinch at hearing his name being shouted out like a fishmonger's catch as he stepped up to take the hand of a florid man with a taste in bright colors and eyebrows that bristled like white gorse.

"Lord Peter Prentice Philpot Marsden Greyville, Marquess of Coleford!"

Grey did flinch. It was the first time he had been announced at all, much less like a cavalry charge. The first of many, he was afraid. Funny how strongly a man could yearn to be back on a battlefield.

"My lord," the florid man with the gorse eyebrows and chartreuse waistcoat gushed in a voice that sounded like a creaky door and a smile that revealed missing teeth. "Such a pleasure to welcome you."

Grey forced a smile and took the snuff-stained hand. "My pleasure, Halverson."

Don't thank him for the invitation, Grey reminded himself. *It's his privilege to have you here.*

Maybe he should have the Packham chit give him a refresher in precedent. No one had ever thought to in the slapdash horse farm where he'd grown up, too far from the title to worry about inhabiting it. The only precedent the military had taught him was that a colonel could court-martial a lieutenant, but if he knew what was good for him, he'd leave the regimental sergeants alone.

He seemed to have passed some test, if the beaming smiles were any indication. Halverson turned to the lady next to him, a breathless powderpuff of a woman in puce and feathers that swayed well over the top of Grey's head.

"This is my lady, Coleford." Halverson beamed. "The new Marquess of Coleford, my dear."

Grey saluted the air above the woman's hand. Thank heavens for Rob, who'd at least brushed him up on those niceties, although they'd both been three sheets to the wind when he had. Thank God Grey remembered not to actually kiss her plump knuckles. He would have sliced his face open on those rings.

"My lady, a pleasure. Thank you for inviting an old soldier to your home."

She giggled, which didn't fit the partridge-shaped fifty-year-old frame very well. "Looking pretty spry in those breeches for an old soldier, Coleford," she trilled with a hard smack on his arm with her fan.

Which almost left Grey speechless. Glenn hadn't covered this.

"Well," he drawled, still holding onto his smile. "We old soldiers keep fit on horseback, ma'am."

He got another slap on the arm with her fan for that and quickly moved along before she went for his nose.

"You didn't warn me," he muttered to Glenn as they strolled away.

"Yes, I did," his friend answered a bit too smugly. "You didn't listen."

"Adam Noah Ezekiel?" he volleyed back. "Why did we never know that?"

Now Glenn was flinching. "Because you would have immediately started thinking of droll jests having to do with my parents' Biblical leanings."

"Are all of you similarly afflicted?"

"You mean like my sister Miriam Rachel Eve?"

Grey couldn't help it. He let loose a bark of laughter that turned heads. "At least they didn't decide on Bathsheba. Or Jezebel."

Glenn was still scowling. "I wouldn't go throwing stones, Peter Prentiss Philpot."

Grey sighed. "My parents were more enamored with alliteration."

They had breached the crowd, aimlessly wandering along the sidelines as a quadrille formed up in the center of the room. The room's decorations were a nightmare that reminded him that his own house could have been worse. Swaths of garish pink, purple, and green silk had been draped from the chandeliers, and tall grasses were stuffed in the over-sized vases that sat in between too few windows.

He was just about to go looking for anything resembling a Packham when Glenn stopped on his heel and turned to him.

"What do you mean you can't make it to Price's place?" Glenn protested just loudly enough to be heard over the musicians on the balcony.

Grey was so busy scanning the crowd for a familiar face that he almost missed his cue. Glenn wasn't shy about kicking him to remind him.

"Price's?" he blurted out with a shake of his head and a throbbing ankle. "Wish I could. Re-fight old battles, share a few bottles, murder some birds. Sounds like heaven. Can't."

"Why not?"

Grey let go a despondent sigh. "I have to go to Wales."

He hoped he sounded disgusted and despairing enough.

"Wales?" Glenn echoed, his expression almost comically horrified. "Good God, man. What did you do to deserve that?"

"I didn't deserve it at all. But that seems to be where the primary estate is. Evidently, I cannot begin to salvage the whole mess from the ravages of my cousins unless I am there. Supervising. The *Welsh*." With a silent apology to the Welsh and to the actual primary seat of the marquessate on the English side of the border, he scrunched his face up in disgust. "Do *you* know anything about the Welsh? M' solicitor couldn't even tell me for certain that they spoke English."

Rob shook his head, obviously having far too much fun. "Surely there's a Welshman somewhere who must speak English."

"The question is, do they at Llanthony Hall. It seems my cousins have let the place go rather feral."

Glenn waved a hand. "Well then, let it stay that way. What's it to you?"

Grey picked a glass of something off a footman's tray. A footman dressed as a jester, even to the bells dangling from his cap. If the lad hadn't looked so bloody uncomfortable, Grey would have burst out laughing all over again.

The urge died a painful death when he took a sip of whatever was in that glass. He damn near spit it in Rob's face.

"*That* I should have warned you about," Glenn said with a sly grin.

Grey was looking at his glass as if it had grown maggots. "What *is* that?"

Glenn chuckled. "No one is quite sure. It's Lady H's special punch."

"Well, I'd have to say that seven-eighths of it is gin."

"Probably. As for the estate, check it out and then meet us at Price's in Cambridge."

Grey scowled. "Are you mad? It takes at least five days to get to the Hall from London. Probably more to get back to Cambridge. Over Welsh roads. In spring, when I understand it rains. Constantly. Once I get there, I'm not coming back until the entire place is put to rights."

Which was when he recognized the tall, rather stooped man nearby making a show of speaking to another gentleman half his size, although his eyes weren't focused on his companion. They were flicking in Grey's direction. Mr. Mayhew himself, eavesdropping and looking a bit appalled.

Well. It seemed the Termagant knew what she was about after all.

Grey set his glass on another passing tray and returned his attention to his friend. "It's pointless to plan anything this year," he complained. "At least."

"A big project?"

"Evidently the original title-owners were marcher lords. With castles. The kind with arrow slits and moats and curtain walls that all have a habit of sliding into said moats."

Glenn was grinning like an idiot. "Sounds full of...er, atmosphere."

"Full of bats and mold, more likely. Oh, and reportedly one

of the early marcher lords who still hangs about the place terrifying the servants. Can't keep even the cook overnight. I plan on filling one of the wagons in our little cavalcade with barrels of whiskey. I suspect I'll need it."

"A ghost to boot?" Glenn demanded with a delighted gleam in his eye. "Maybe we'll all come there. I haven't had spectral chains rattled at me in ages."

"This one pushes people down the stairs."

Out of the corner of his eye he could see Mayhew's eyes getting even bigger. Good.

"Well, when you're finished putting the castle to rights, then," Glenn suggested.

Grey shook his head. "*Then* I have to begin working on the livestock. And crops. And drainage. Which I know damned all about."

Rob gave him another delighted grin. "Too bad nobody's laying siege to the place. You're an absolute whiz at sieges."

Grey sadly shook his head. "If you know anyone who knows the difference between borage and beehives, please. Invite them along. There will be whiskey."

Glenn obviously knew Mayhew was standing by as well. "Oh, I suspect I'll be too busy. Besides, I can get whiskey at White's. Much more civilized, my lad. Happy to keep your wife company here, of course, since you'll obviously be up to your boot tops in muck."

Grey was already shaking his head, uncomfortably aware that he, too, was beginning to have fun. "My wife? No, lad, she'll be right at my side. As bad as the fields are, the house is even worse. Once we get the roof fixed, she'll have to start from ground up. Oh, and did I tell you the village was too superstitious to allow their daughters into the house to fight ghosts for the brooms?" Grey gave a huge sigh. "I thought soldiering was hard. I suspect I'm going to be the first marquess who wants to give the bloody title back."

"Wait," Glenn said, brightening as he laid a hand on Grey's arm. "I know somebody who can help. Charlie! Come meet my friend."

Grey turned to see the entire Packham contingent headed their way. Amazing to think they were all so closely related. Miss Edwina should have been lovely with her pale, almost silver-blonde hair, sky-blue eyes, and tall, sleek form. Her dress was of a standard design with squared neckline and little puffed sleeves, a cream muslin with rose ribbons at her bust and hem, topped off with the obligatory string of pearls. But the entire picture ended up being rather vague, as if one needed to squint to better focus on her.

Miss Charlotte stood at least a hand shorter, her hair a distinct, gleaming red, her smile impish, her green eyes comfortably crinkled at the corners. She was a bit plumper than fashion, with dimples at her elbows and a lush bosom that was barely contained by her gold-colored gown, but somehow it all conspired to make a man want to smile when he met her.

And bringing up the rear was Lady Georgianna, whose easy smile was once again doing strange and terrible things to Grey's breathing. He couldn't have said why. She was no more beautiful than when she'd invaded his house. Her chin was still too strong, her forehead too broad. But that smile...not comfortable like her cousin's. Not vague at all.

Maybe it was the fact that it resided mostly in those sharp green eyes. He could look on them forever, he thought, even as his less honorable self wondered what she would look like disheveled and sated. In his bed, preferably.

Even perfectly coiffed and clothed, she inspired fantasies. She filled out her pale primrose silk dress quite comfortably, enhanced by a pearl collar that accentuated her sleek neck and little jeweled flowers tucked into her thick dark curls. Nothing dozens of other young women hadn't accomplished in presenting themselves at a ball. But she was…more. She didn't simply strike someone as memorable. She made a man want to stand up straighter, smooth out his attire, brush his hair back. Hell, if he'd had facial hair, he'd be pulling at it, just to earn her attention.

"Rob," Charlie greeted Grey's friend with what seemed to be sincere delight, striding over as if she were hiking the hills. "When did you get back?"

"About the same time my friend Coleford did," he said, bending over her hand.

"Greyville," Grey growled, tired of reminding people.

"You're going to have to get used to it eventually," the redheaded Miss Packham said with that impish grin of hers.

"I still have time."

Rob beamed as if he'd performed a magic trick. "You two are already introduced?"

"Yes," Grey said. "These ladies helped me save my cousin from sure disaster at the Serpentine the other day. Lady Clevedon was kind enough to make the introductions."

If he repeated that lie many more times, he'd start believing it enough to describe the squelch in his boots from wading into the water to rescue a ball.

"Miss Packham," he murmured bending over one hand, then the next. "Miss…er, Packham. And Miss…Packham," possibly lingering just a bit longer over Lady Georgianna's.

All three of them grinned at him. "It will save time and confusion if you simply use our first names," Miss Charlotte Packham said. "Everyone does. If you feel particularly starchy, you may add Lady or Miss."

He nodded. "Thank you. I believe I will."

"How are the girls?" Lady Georgianna asked, and damned if

Grey didn't think she meant it. Maybe he would be comfortable calling her Georgie after all.

"When they knew I might see you they asked me to give you their best wishes."

Her smile grew. "I can just picture Sophie doing that very thing."

He couldn't help grinning back. "While Amelia tugged on my jacket and Bark sprawled across my boots."

She nodded as if satisfied. "Well, please tell them that we shall be issuing formal invitations to tea this week. My mother is longing to meet them."

He scowled. "You're sure? They can be hard on your shelves."

Her chuckle was delighted. "Oh, yes. From what I've heard as we walked up, we need to visit before you drag them off to darkest Wales."

"You live on the Severn," Glenn spoke up. "What can you tell my friend here about the country across the river?"

She shook her head. "That it's too much trouble to cross the river to see it. Even from the Manor it takes at least at least two days, depending on the season. As unreliable as ferries are in the tidal currents, you must travel all the way up to Gloucester to cross over."

"We have made the trip a few times," Miss Edwina said. "We have some cousins near Abergavenny. I remember how pretty the hills were."

"I remember that it rained," Miss Charlotte added. "Constantly."

"Oh, yes," Lady Georgianna agreed. "Which meant it took *three* days to get there. And everything was damp." She lifted an elegant hand in exception. "Beautiful, mind. But wet."

"I think our work is done here," Lady Charlote murmured. "Prissy's father just hurried out of here as if the place had caught fire."

"I suspect he's looking for Prissy's mother," Lady Georgianna responded with a small turn of her head. "She tends to frequent the card room."

"Somehow I doubt she'll be so easy to convince," Grey said.

Lady Georgianna nodded. "We'll probably have to perform a second act," she said, "which we girls can manage. All we must do is share your sad news with my Aunt Berenice. She will provide all the outrage Mr. Mayhew will need to stoke his determination. She loathes Wales."

"Shall I see to it?" Edwina asked.

"Yes, please." Lady Georgianna shot her a bright smile. "You know how to handle Aunt Berenice better than we do."

"Everyone knows how to handle her better than *I* do," Charlie retorted.

"Eddie has patience," Lady Georgianna said. "Besides, you get along better with the fathers, Charlie."

Rob laughed. "That's because she can outride them all."

"I still say we need a rake," Lady Edwina said, her voice pitched low.

Rob leaned in. "You need a *what?*"

Lady Georgianna smiled. "Eddie believes that if a known rake shows interest in Priscilla, it would provide the final push needed for her parents to wed her to her safe neighbor. But we don't know any rakes. Well, not any who can be trusted."

Rob snapped his fingers. "Declan Bowdern."

Lady Georgianna perked up. "Is he a rake?"

"Worse. He's an *Irish* rake."

Lady Georgianna was beginning to look delighted. "Is he poor?"

Rob shrugged. "Nobody knows. My suspicion is that he does quite well for himself but just doesn't want to invite a notoriously anti-Irish *ton* into his affairs."

"But can we trust him?"

Both men nodded.

"Pulled my cods out of the fire more than once," Rob said.

"He was on the Peninsula with you?" Lady Georgianna asked.

Grey nodded. "Came home on the same ship."

Lady Charlotte tilted her head, her attention on Rob. "Aren't you enough of a rake for our purposes, Rob? I can't imagine you made it across the entire Iberian Peninsula in an unsullied state."

Grey was surprised to see Rob leveling a rather ferocious scowl on the petite redhead. "That'll be quite enough of that, young lady."

Which only made her laugh. "You *have* been gone too long."

"Not so long I can't turn you over my knee."

Now Lady Charlotte was scowling. "I'd like to see you try."

Her cousins took up position on either side of her. "So would we."

Suddenly Rob was leveling a blinding grin on the three. "Ferocious."

The returning smiles proved the point.

"Something to remember," Lady Charlotte answered. "Where is this notorious Irish rake? I'd love to meet him."

"Not you," Rob protested. "You don't want to frighten the man all the way back to Wexford before we can make use of him."

"If he's that easily frightened," Miss Charlotte said, "I doubt we'd have *any* use for him."

"Enough, children," Lady Georgianna intervened. "My lord," she said, turning those sharp green eyes towards Grey. "Have you spoken to Priscilla yet tonight?"

"I have not. I did reserve a dance with her."

She nodded. "That might be a good time to tell her about the girls."

He scowled. "It might sound just a touch overwhelming in public, don't you think? I'd prefer not to spend my evening catching swooning females."

"Possibly. But she'll thank you later. I promise. You can also tell her that we are devoting our every attention on freeing her up for her Timothy. She is over by the windows, Grey."

"In that case," Rob said, holding out his hand to Miss Charlie. "Might I have this dance, Miss Packham?"

She tilted her head. "You haven't called me Miss Packham since you were in short pants."

His grin was unrepentant. "I am quite the gentleman, now. Didn't you know? The Beau himself complimented me on my waltzing when we were bivouacked in Portugal."

Charlie tilted her head, her smile a gamine's. "Why would you waltz with the Duke of Wellington?"

Grey couldn't believe it. He found himself wanting to stay with these Packhams, these female kings who were so oddly like their ferocious brothers.

"Lady Georgianna?" he asked. "Might I sign your card as well?"

She handed over the dance card, and he signed for the last dance.

She nodded toward the windows. "Now go relieve the mind of your fiancée. I believe I have a hussar to enchant. Eddie, are you available to shadow Mr. Mayhew a bit? Let us know if we need to enlist Aunt Berenice."

Miss Edwina smiled, which should have been breathtaking. Why wasn't it? Grey wondered.

"I would be happy to," she said, tugging a bit on her gloves. "Better than standing by the potted palms with the mothers or dancing with...oh, bother. This dance is Lord Black's. Would you mind making an excuse?"

"Gladly," Lady Georgianna assured her. "Let him bore some-body else with his Tamworths."

Grey looked back and forth between the dramatically scowling cousins. "Tamworths?"

Georgie leaned in as if she was imparting state secrets. "Pigs. In fact, my Lord Coleford, it might not be a bad idea for you to take Eddie's place. Tamworths are nice hardy stock, cross-bred with Irish grazers by Sir Robert Peele. Might be perfect for a Welsh estate."

He couldn't help but blink. "Why do you know that?"

It was Charlie who laughed. "What I know about horses, Georgie knows about the estate. Especially livestock and the still room."

"Only because I'm teaching the boys estate management. All of them cannot run off to glory in a scarlet jacket."

"In that case," Grey said, holding out his hand to the increas-ingly fascinating Miss Packham, "would you allow me to put off speaking to my fiancée and do me the honor of this dance? I need to discuss livestock."

"You have other duties now, sir. Do not shirk them for the pleasure of discussing porkers."

He decided he was making progress when she laughed. He wasn't as pleased to realize that it was no longer enough. Blast. As if he didn't have enough on his plate. She put her hand in his and set off a jolt like cannon fire, and he very much feared she was not going to like what he wanted.

He wasn't sure he cared.

"WELSH PIGS," Georgie blurted out hours later as Grey led her into the final dance.

Drat. She should have anticipated her mistake. The last

dance at a ball was always the Roger de Coverly, which in the normal way of things was perfectly lovely...spritely, fun, and easy. What it was not was an easy place to share confidences, like how Greyville's meeting had gone with Prissy. Georgie had not seen the girl faint during or after their dance, so that was a hopeful sign. But because she and Greyville would be dancing figures with four other couples, she would have no real chance to quiz him on specifics.

No sooner had she thought that than the music began, a lively tune that set everyone into motion.

"You don't like the Welsh?" Grey asked as they spun about each other and retreated to their positions.

She had to wait until the next movement to answer.

"You were the one who asked about pigs," she accused.

Another round.

"Evidently I actually need cows," he said, catching her hand for a spin. "I have been conversing with some other landowners."

She couldn't help it. She started to chuckle. "I hope you weren't looking for a romantic moment," she said on next pass.

He grinned right back. "Oddly enough, I have never considered cows the least romantic."

But now the other dancers were obviously listening in.

"I like cows," the smilingly blonde Miss Swinton offered alongside Georgie, batting her eyes at Greyville.

He was grinning again when they met in the middle. "I stand corrected. Evidently cows *are* romantic."

Georgie spun under his arm and grinned. "Anything is romantic coming from the mouth of a marquess." she assured him.

They skipped in and out of the line and then around to hold their hands up, letting the other couples pass through.

He scowled. "Realist. Now, what were we discussing?"

"Cows!" the rest of the set chimed in.

They barely made it to the end of the dance without falling into whoops.

"Come," he said, slipping his hand under her elbow as the music came to an end. "Let us get some air while everyone else is saying goodbye."

She frowned. "Why?"

He bent his head towards her. "So I may give you a full report on the evening's progress. We have more to talk about than cows."

"You were the one who brought them up."

"The cows can wait," he said. "There are a few steps to be accomplished before we'll have a chance to rhapsodize over livestock."

"They are really lovely cows," she said, not moving.

His sole answer was a raised eyebrow. Georgie wished she could do that. Put him in his place. Although, truth be told, she didn't know where that exactly was. Just this silly back-and-forth was causing the oddest fizz in her blood. That and the scent of cedar and citrus.

"The Welsh blacks," she continued, just to goad him. "Great large eyes and sweet dispositions. And they would look quite artistic on those Welsh hills."

"English pastures," he corrected.

She let her eyes grow wide. "Well, that's silly. Who would put Welsh cows in England? People would think they'd gotten lost."

He huffed in impatience, but she could see the sly twinkle in his eye. "If we don't figure out how to manage my mess, I won't have a cow to wander anywhere, artistically or not. So, I would appreciate your letting me give my report so we can both go home and revisit things tomorrow."

"You spoke with Priscilla?"

"I did."

And then he turned her toward the window, and everything changed.

Georgie should have refused. She should have found an excuse of some kind rather than join him. She knew it the minute he cupped her elbow like fragile porcelain, setting off the most alarming reaction.

Chills, shivers, the oddest feeling that her feet weren't connected to the rest of her. A definite urge to get closer to him.

She did not want to become attracted to this man. Well, to be honest, she did not want to *stay* attracted to him, no matter how his touch sent chills skittering through unmentionable nooks and crannies in her body. It shouldn't make any difference that he smelled like starched linen, citrus, and pine, or that the feel of his hand on her arm, even though they wore gloves, both startled and settled her at the same time. Or the fact that he was humming the music they'd been dancing to, which was endearing. She did not *want* endearing. She wanted...she wanted...oh, bother. She was so distracted she didn't know what she wanted. Except more of this very enticing feeling, or that delicious fizz of matching wits with him. Or both.

"She took it well," he said as he swept the curtains aside and stepped out into the moonlight.

Georgie looked up to answer him and blinked, the sight of him stealing her wits. The gibbous moon sent bright light washing over Greyville, limning his hair and casting shadows that sharpened the angles of his face. Hard, suddenly, strong. Solid but not threatening. Compelling in a way Georgie hadn't really noticed before, which she should have anticipated somehow, considering the records of his courage she'd been reading for years. Somehow his features fit his heroism, as if he'd been cast in a play about brave soldiers.

For a moment she couldn't think at all, she was so struck by it. By the almost spectral look of him contrasting with the very solid feel of him. By the confusing, exciting lightning set off by no more than the touch of his gloved fingers.

She had been attracted to other men before. She had sneaked off for a kiss or two in shadowy gardens. But never had she been struck literally dumb.

It was when she looked into his eyes that she realized she wasn't the only one affected, and that set off new, even hotter sparks all along her skin, deep in her belly, robbing her of breath. Places she had never so much as acknowledged, much less understood, suddenly demanded attention.

Was it better or worse that she could sense the same confusion in him? He was staring hard; his fingers tightened on her arm. She could feel the brush of his breath against her hair. And she wanted....

"She took it..." she stammered, trying to pull her wits back together again. "Oh, yes. Priscilla."

Still staring, he licked his lips, which unnerved her even more. "Pri..."

"Priscilla. You, uh, spoke to her."

It still took him a moment to respond. Georgie wasn't certain if that was better or worse.

"Oh. Yes." He nodded abruptly, removing his hand to take a step back, which should have made things better. It should have made the night cooler.

It didn't.

"You told her about the girls," she said to him, her palm pressing against her own chest, as if it could quell the sudden thundering of her heart. "Amelia and Sophie."

This made no sense. She had been with him twice, had had perfectly normal conversations both times. How could she so suddenly feel as if she was flying apart, just from the heat in his eyes, the strain in his voice?

He nodded, his movement jerky. "Indeed. Priscilla knew. She

sends her thanks for your efforts. If those don't work, she is considering an elopement."

"Oh, no," Georgie protested, struggling to pull her thoughts back to order. "That will not do at all."

"Exactly what I told her. I told her that impulsive decisions rarely end well."

His words were a warning, and Georgie wished she could have attended better. But he was looking at her again, and Georgie was feeling it right down to her slippers.

She was twenty, for heaven's sake. She had met this man twice without incident. Oh yes, she'd been attracted to him, but what wickedness was the moon causing? She suddenly had images in her head, and they were none of them polite. But oh, they were tempting.

She licked her own lips and found his gaze focused there. More blasted chills, chasing up and down like lightning. "Eddie...uh...." She cleared her throat, struggled for coherence. "She said that Prissy's parents were in the middle of a full-scale whispered dispute. I'm sorry your friend Bowdern isn't here. He might have put a coda on the business."

"And then what?"

Was he standing closer? She was feeling crowded, and she swore he wasn't intentionally looming. But he was...close. Too close. And she had nowhere to move.

"Did you manage to talk with the young ladies on the list?" she blurted out.

He turned away for a moment, his left hand clenching and unclenching down by his leg. Georgie found herself mesmerized by it.

"They were..." He paused, drew in a breath that sounded a bit shaky. Shook his head. "Pleasant."

Georgie flinched. *Pleasant* was not exactly a ringing endorsement.

"Well, it was only your first meeting," she demurred.

He turned back to her, and the last word she would have been able to use about his expression was *pleasant*. Hot. Hard. Seething. Mesmerizing. And she simply couldn't look away.

She was struggling to pull herself back together when he reached out a hand and tucked a stray strand of hair behind her ear. She found herself closing her eyes.

"I don't understand...."

"I'm afraid I do," he growled, and she felt his hand on her shoulder.

She couldn't help it. She leaned in, as if starving for his touch. She opened her eyes finally, to see that the moonlight had reached his eyes and set them gleaming. She heard his breathing quicken. She swore she could sense his heartbeat just through his fingertips.

"What?" she whispered.

He shook his head again. Clenched his hand. "I don't want *pleasant*," he said.

And before she could draw breath to answer, he was kissing her.

Kissing? More like devouring, his arms tight around her, his mouth coaxing hers open, his heart thundering against her breast. He stunned her, swamped her senses with the unbearable silk of his lips, the insistent invasion of his tongue, the tender strength of his hands, that were the only thing holding her up when her legs went weak.

She couldn't believe it. She, who prided herself on her control, had her fingers threaded through his delicious soft hair, her body pressed to his, her back arched so she could feel the sleek wall of his chest against her suddenly sensitive breasts. She lost her purpose and jettisoned any good sense that remained, wanting nothing more than...*more*.

She was so lost she never heard the steps approaching from

the other side of the curtain. She barely heard her cousin rasp out, "Georgie, 'ware!"

Instinctively she tried to pull away. Grey held on tighter, his hand cupping the back of her head, his arm a steel band across her back. She almost lost herself completely.

It took the stentorian condemnation in her aunt's voice to haul her back.

"That will be *quite* enough of that!" A clarion call sure to be heard all the way to the foyer. "Georgianna Alice Elliott Packham, stop that at once!"

Grey startled upright, and the rest of the world came crashing back in. Literally. Georgie didn't look, but she could hear the shocked murmuring of more than one attendee, the tone as salacious as the gossip would undoubtedly be by morning. She was certain she should be stunned, ashamed. Something. All she could think was that she felt suddenly cold without Grey's arms around her, and it made her angry. She didn't want that. She *didn't.*

"Explain yourself!" Aunt Berenice demanded.

She couldn't. She even managed to open her mouth, but words simply wouldn't form.

It was Grey who responded, settling his arm around her shoulder and smiling at her aunt. "You may wish us happy," he said.

Georgie startled so badly that only Grey's arms kept her from falling backwards. "What?!"

And then she heard Eddie's soft voice behind her and knew that her disaster was complete. "I don't think we're going to need that rake after all."

6

Georgie wished she could have been oblivious to the next few minutes. She wished she could simply have walked off that balcony and into the night, or for once in her life managed a graceful swoon. She fervently wished she'd never done Priscilla Mayhew a good deed.

But never let it be said that her Aunt Berenice would allow any person to escape the consequences of their actions. Not one to settle for a whisper when parade ground volume would do, Georgie's aunt made sure everyone along Bruton Street would know that there was a disaster brewing.

And she was doing it while Georgie was desperately trying to regain her composure, even as the fire Greyville lit in her still raged. Her mouth tingled. Her fingers tingled. Places in her body she had never even acknowledged before positively throbbed like hot embers. All she could think about was the taste of Grey's kiss, his scent. His smile. And her aunt was busy destroying Georgie's reputation.

She had to focus.

If only Greyville wasn't still standing so close, his scent tempting her all over again.

"Well?" Aunt Berenice trumpeted for the second or third time. Georgie wasn't quite sure.

"Aunt Berenice," Eddie whispered, grabbing her aunt's sleeve.

"What?" Aunt Berenice demanded, whipping around.

Eddie tilted her head to include the small crowd that had gathered at their end of the ballroom when they should have been in the foyer donning cloaks and looking for their carriages. "Not here."

"This is no business of yours," Aunt Berenice accused them all, the feather in her gold turban quivering with her outrage. She made shooing motions with her arms. "Go along. Don't let your horses be kept standing."

There were some knowing smiles, but about half of them bowed to Aunt Berenice's glower and faded away. The rest wouldn't be moved by anything short of cannon fire.

"Now," Georgie's aunt barked, turning back to her prey. "What is this all about?"

"As I said," Greyville said with a smile and a slight bow. "You may wish us happy."

"You may *not*," Georgie insisted under her breath, panic exploding in her chest. At least it cleared her head, not to mention the uncomfortable throbbing.

Her aunt leveled the kind of glare that should have melted Georgie's pearls. "Oh, I believe we must," she declared. "But we shall do it at home like civilized people. Coleford, you may follow us there. Lady Georgianna's father will be delighted to speak with you."

"No, he *won't*," Georgie retorted, her voice thinning with distress.

She got another glare. "Don't be ridiculous. Now, come along."

"Might I speak to Georgianna for a moment first?" Greyville asked.

"No!" both Georgie and her aunt snapped.

"What happened?" Charlie demanded, skidding to a halt by her mother.

Eddie frowned. "Evidently Georgie's engaged."

Charlie frowned right back. "But he called her Georgianna. Why in heaven's name would a fiancé do that?"

Eddie just shrugged. Georgie, growing more frantic by the minute, saw the doubt in her cousin's eyes and felt even worse.

"You will meet us at Packham House, young man," Aunt Berenice declared, sounding rather like a judge delivering sentence. "There will be quite enough time to speak with Lady Georgianna *after* you have spoken to her father."

Only Aunt Berenice could diminish a blooded marquess to 'young man' in quite that manner. Georgie was more than a little surprised to see Greyville look a bit abashed.

He gave another small bow and stepped away from her. "Of course, ma'am. I look forward to seeing you there."

For that he got a baleful assessment from Aunt Berenice before she simply turned on her heel and led the cousins like ducklings through the remaining guests.

Before they could escape back out into the night, Lord Halverson came trotting up, his color high.

"Everything all right?" he asked.

Aunt Berenice looked down her nose. "Quite. Thank you for a lovely evening."

Georgie almost choked. Even so she dipped a fleeting curtsy along with her cousins, only to be rewarded with the sound of Lady Halverson's chirping. "Our ball has just become the success of the season."

And then Eddie sighing. "I do wish I could have met the rake."

GREY SHOULD HAVE BEEN FEELING a lot worse. He hadn't meant for this to happen. He could never have anticipated it; not here, not now, not her. But there was no question that it had. It took him several minutes before he could turn from the cool dark night on the balcony to face his contemporaries. And even then he was fighting the most unsettling distraction. Not to mention an unholy urge to smile.

He damned near laughed at himself. Distraction. Was that what he was going to call it? It had probably been a good thing the aunt had swept in like an avenging angel, or she might have witnessed far worse.

If Lady Georgianna—oh bloody hell. *Georgie.* After what had just transpired out on that balcony, it was difficult to hold onto a polite distance. If she had not so enthusiastically participated a moment ago, he would have felt ashamed. After all, he had compromised her about as thoroughly as a man could and keep his clothing on. But he couldn't help but think that that moment had revealed a real connection, one that could, with work, develop into something more.

And yes. He admitted it. Selfishly, he was relieved. He had walked into this ball a harried man, caught between a sudden family, a financial crisis, and a relentless government. Completely upended from the wandering life of a soldier where he'd known his responsibilities, his limits and his rewards. Now, he admitted that even with the girls he felt like a nomad settling for a visit.

After this, at least he knew his girls would be protected no matter what happened. He knew from only two meetings with her that Georgie had an uncanny ability to create order out of chaos, a home for a wanderer. Mostly, right now, he knew his house would be transformed into a place of at least comfort while he was stuck in Paris. And then, when he got home, maybe Georgie could actually help him create a home out of the peeling wallpaper and overwhelming responsibilities. Someplace he could finally feel settled after ten years of war.

Halfway across the dance floor toward the foyer, he stopped dead in his tracks. His girls. *His* girls. He smiled. So they were. And Georgie was just the woman to keep them safe and happy while he was away. To mold them all into a family. Which meant he would be free to go. Well, he would be right after he made Lady Georgianna Packham the next Marchioness Coleford.

Deciding that the best plan was to get things over with as soon as he could, he waved at Rob who was busy in a rather intense conversation with a well-endowed heiress, bowed his farewells to the gloating Halversons, and made for the front door.

"Was that intentional?" he heard behind him and didn't even have to turn to know who it was.

"What are you doing here?" he asked, finally facing his friend and unofficial superior, Marcus, Earl Drake.

Drake's smile was as enigmatic as the rest of him. Blond, blue-eyed, and flawlessly elegant, Drake had a knack for knowing more than he should and saying less than one expected. But right now, Grey suspected he was looking for answers.

To that end, Drake laid an arm over Grey's shoulder and led him through the open door out into the night. "I am an earl," he answered easily as they descended the steps to the street. "I am seen everywhere. What of you?"

"I am a marquess," he reminded his friend. "And I am on the marriage market."

"No longer, it seems."

Grey cast a suspicious look at him. "You saw that?"

Drake smiled. "Oh, my dear, I believe Lady Berenice made sure everyone but the Prince Regent saw that. I thought you were to marry the Mayhew chit. Was I mistaken?"

It was all Grey could do not to shrug off Drake's arm. He didn't like being manipulated. He didn't like to feel boxed in. He felt both right now, even as he spared a flash of regret that he was doing the same to his probable fiancée.

"Miss Mayhew's parents decided that she and I have decided we didn't suit," he said. Thank God they had caught him on the way out and pointed that out. "Anything else?"

"Which Packham chit is it?"

Grey found himself staring at his friend. "You don't know?"

He got another lazy smile. "All three were crowded in that doorway. The aunt didn't specify."

"Lady Georgianna."

Drake's left eyebrow rose. "Indeed. Interesting choice."

Grey came to an abrupt halt right there on the walk, with other guests parting around them like a stream around boulders.

"It wasn't a…" He shook his head. There was no point explaining. Lifting Drake's arm, he took a step away. "Why exactly is it an interesting choice?"

"Share a glass at the club?"

"No. It seems I am due at the Packham abode."

Drake nodded. "I'll walk with you. It's not far."

"I know. What were you implying?" he asked as they turned down the walk toward Brook Street.

Around them Mayfair echoed with late evening entertainment. Carriages rumbled down the street, the faint hum of strings drifted from more than one home, and lights spilled from myriad windows. The night was mild, relieved by only a lethargic breeze, and clouds skimmed low in the sky. A perfect night for a walk and a think. He was just afraid Drake wasn't about to allow him that luxury.

"She will be perfect for your little cousins," Drake mused. "She certainly has the experience, having grown up in that madhouse they all call a home and taking on some of her mother's social duties. And she must have extraordinary patience, or her aunt would not still be breathing."

"But?"

Drake blinked at him, as if just coming awake. "But? Nothing. I approve of your choice. The question will be whether she does."

Which lazy observation sent another flash of guilt stabbing through Grey. "No," he said, turning again toward the over-sized rowhouse on Brook Street that held all the myriad Packhams. "It was not intentional."

Drake nodded amiably, lifting a hand in greeting to a gentleman strolling the other way. "She is a lovely girl."

Drake stared at him. "Girl? That is no girl. That is a whirlwind."

Another lazy smile. "You will have to either enjoy being managed or come to some mutually agreeable compromise. After all these years being in control of the clans, she will naturally take charge."

"If she can make those little girls happy, she can take charge of anything she wants." He found himself grinning. "I may also let her take charge of the livestock."

That merited another raised eyebrow. Grey refused to explain.

"The other excellent benefit of tonight," Drake mused as if continuing a thought, "is that she is more than well-set-up. She is, in coarse parlance, filthy rich. She will be everything you need if you're smart enough to hold onto her."

Funny. He hadn't even considered that. "Thank you for the

endorsement. Now, why else are you acting the limpet this fine evening? There are at least four other balls, a musicale, and Covent Garden to be enjoyed."

Drake smiled again. "I am not allowed to support a comrade-in-arms?"

"I have never known you to perform an altruistic act that did not also involve a bit of hugger muggery."

"No, no. Nothing of the sort. I just wanted you to know that I approve your choice, since she can quite easily manage your home while you are away. Next week."

Grey slammed to a stop. "No."

Suddenly Drake wasn't looking quite so sanguine. "I wish I could send someone else. But I fear our friends in Paris are already too well-known. A military attaché liaising with those involved in the peace preparations will barely be worth a notice."

"I understand that. But I will not leave so soon. If you want me there, those are my terms."

"Even if Gracechurch is dead?"

Grey caught his breath. "Is he?"

For the first time Drake hesitated. Turning away, he lazily swung his quizzing glass as he considered the leafing trees in the square. "We don't know. I have a bad feeling, though."

"As harsh as it sounds, he won't be any more dead in three weeks. Give me a chance to settle in with my family before I leave, or I suspect my new wife will make me pay for the rest of my life. And you, if she finds out you are involved."

"A wife who has not accepted your hand yet."

Drake scowled at him and started walking again, hands in his pockets. "I'm afraid after the spectacle her aunt put on tonight, she'll have little choice."

"I'm not so sure," Drake mused, strolling along beside him. "She also has a rather charming streak of independence. "

Grey scowled at him. "In what way?"

"Well, every Friday while the rest of the house naps in preparation for their active social life, Lady Georgianna disappears."

Grey came to a halt. "Disappears? Where?"

Drake shrugged. "Her maid calls her a hackney back by the mews and they leave."

"And why do you know this?"

Drake looked at him like a particularly slow-witted first former. "Her father is on the Privy Council. Her brother and cousins are performing a bit of extracurricular governmental service much as you have. She was a student in that particular boarding school so she could be protected from people who would try to use underhanded methods to influence the men in her life. It is my job to know."

"But you don't know where she goes."

Now Drake was smiling, that infuriating smug quirk to his mouth that made Grey want to punch him. "I thought it might be a bit more appropriate—and judicious—for *you* to."

After a moment's consideration, Grey started walking again. "You're an ass."

Drake nodded pleasantly. "I know. But I am the King's ass."

"Don't be a ninny."

There was something about that strident voice that made Georgie want to rip the feathers out of her aunt's headdress and stomp on them, just so they would stop bobbing in her face every time Aunt Berenice made some ludicrous declaration, like, "You could do worse."

For the sake of household peace, Georgie chose to pace instead. She certainly couldn't admit that her aunt had a point. She *could* do worse than the Marquess of Coleford. Much worse.

But for once, just this once, she had hoped they would listen to her and understand. That maybe they would admit that she could do better. That she *should* do better.

She was so frightened.

"For once," he aunt snapped, "Think of this family."

And there it went. The very last shred of her patience with her frustratingly righteous, autocratic aunt. Georgie even heard a hiss of breath from one of her cousins.

It did not deter her. She suspected her face was bright red as she pulled herself to her not-inconsiderable height to face down her godmother for possibly the first time in her life. But correcting her aunt had never mattered so much before.

"Think of this family?" she echoed in the kind of hushed tones one hears a fuse make before the explosion. "Think of this *family?*"

Her hands were clenched, her heart thundered. She swore she saw a red haze before her eyes even as she struggled to control the temper that was astonishing her even more than it was her cousins, if their wide eyes were any indication. She never lost her temper. She prided herself on it, the ability to remain calm in the face of the chaos that seemed to regularly break out in this house, not to mention society as a whole. She was famous for it. Relied on because of it. But it was disintegrating fast.

Her aunt meant well, she kept thinking. Her every aim was to protect the Packham reputation, the Packham history. The Packham status as one of the premier political families in Britain. And truly? No single person lived up to her expectations.

But being the oldest daughter in the entire family, Georgie had spent her life bearing the brunt of those expectations, demands, and coercions. And she was so *tired* of it.

"Tell me, Aunt," she all but snarled, her fists clenched,

"Exactly when have I *not* thought of the family? Please. Any incident will do. Was it when I was teaching my young cousins, or doing menus with Cook, or helping my cousins shop and decide on wardrobes, or maybe when I organized the move to the Castle and back this year? Again?"

Her aunt looked as if Georgie had struck her. Georgie suddenly didn't care.

"My pardon, ma'am, my lady."

Georgie almost sobbed with the effort to rein in her frustration. "Yes, Reems," she said, not even turning to acknowledge their butler who undoubtedly stood in the parlor doorway like a Guardsman on parade.

He cleared his throat. "Lord Coleford has arrived. Shall I tell him...."

"Chinese parlor," she said. "Maybe he will enjoy communing with a dragon or two for a moment."

"Tea, my lady?"

"Of course. We are a civilized family, after all." She was still eyeball-to-eyeball with her aunt. "And Reems, when my parents arrive, please direct them here."

"Not...?"

She didn't even bother to shake her head. "Here."

"Of course, my lady."

"Oh, and please send for Preston. I will meet her outside the Chinese salon."

She saw her aunt bristle and couldn't be sorry, even as she heard Reems quietly close the salon door. But truth to tell, Aunt Berenice would never think to direct the staff. That, she said more and more frequently, was a task Georgie should learn. Georgie was becoming hard pressed to keep from telling her aunt that she had thoroughly learned the task by her twelfth birthday.

"Your parents are due home from the embassy any minute,"

Aunt Berenice warned. "You would not add further distress to your father's burdens."

Georgie continued to face off with her aunt, which she realized with a surprise, she was actually enjoying a bit. "What happens between my father and me is between us alone."

Aunt Berenice snorted like an overheated horse. "Not—"

"Between," Georgie repeated, "us."

And all she could hope for was that she could talk her service-minded father into understanding that his oldest daughter, who had lived her life as an obedient oldest daughter, had finally had enough. She had hoped...

She had planned....

She shook her head. No matter to give voice now. She would simply confuse her aunt and worry her cousins. But the chaos that was upending her plans swelled in her like lava rising in a volcano, threatening to scorch the earth beneath and send everyone fleeing.

And yet, still, she couldn't discount the lingering delight from that kiss.

Blast him.

"It would seem, Aunt," she said, finally pulling at the fingers of her gloves, "I do have time to speak to the Marquess before my parents arrive home."

"Do not be absurd," her aunt protested, feathers bobbing again. "Haven't you caused enough talk for one night? You shall wait for your father."

"No, Aunt," Georgie disagreed, pulling off her second glove and laying both on the secretary, her voice gentling. "I need to speak with the Marquess before a formal offer is made or my voice will never be heard."

Her aunt spun around, those pernicious feathers bobbing and swaying. "What do you have to say to the matter? Especially after that display you put on tonight?"

A display no one would have seen if her aunt had not broadcast it like a town crier. All Georgie could do was walk over, give her aunt a kiss on the cheek and continue out of the room. She had a real confrontation to face.

7

Georgie was standing outside the door to the Chinese salon trying to screw her courage to the proverbial sticking post when the sisters' maid trotted up and took a moment to consider her, head tilted like a curious bird, her hands filled with the ubiquitous knitting she did for the village poor.

"Got yourself in the suds, did ya?"

All Georgie could do was nod. She didn't need to ask how Preston knew. Preston knew everything almost before it happened.

Preston nodded right back, her greying blonde hair not moving an inch from its ruthless bun. A comfortably plump fifty, Preston had been assigned to Georgie and her cousins on their seventeenth birthdays when they came down from what she and her cousins fondly called the Last Chance Academy, where they had allegedly learned the basics of being a lady. Preston's job had been to polish the edges and watch for trouble. Too bad she hadn't been at the ball tonight.

"Is he at least easy to look at?" the older woman asked,

considering the door much as Georgie was, as if she could discern his features through wood.

Georgie shrugged. "Compelling," was all she would allow, even as her heart picked up speed again in anticipation of seeing him. Her ridiculous heart that didn't know what was good for it.

Blast him.

"Well, you're not gettin' anything done standin' here. Wait much longer and yer auntie will be goin' in before you do."

An excellent point.

Taking a last moment to wipe her damp palms against her skirts and draw in a steadying breath, Georgie opened the door and stepped through to find the Marquess standing over by the display case in the corner, hands clasped behind his back, head bent forward, evidently perusing the collection of jade dragons that inhabited the shelves.

"Exquisite," he said without turning.

She stopped inside the door, hand still on the latch. "My parents are well-traveled."

Finally, he turned, wearing a half-smile. "And you? Are you well-traveled?"

That caught in her chest like a shard of glass. "Not as much," was all she would admit. She would *not* tell him of her dreams delayed that involved time on the Continent, the subcontinent, maybe a continent to the west. Dreams she had only recently allowed to crystallize.

"Won't you have a seat?" she asked as Preston carried her knitting over to the conveniently placed chaperone's chair by the window.

As if on cue, there was a scratch on the door.

"Come," Georgie said, approaching the scarlet settee and easing down as if she were practicing etiquette back at school.

The door opened to admit Reems and two perfectly turned-out housemaids laden with tea fixings. Flipping his tails, Coleford sat in the opposing settee and laid his hands on his thighs. Beautiful thighs. Horseman's thighs. Strong, sinewy hands.

Blast him.

"Or would you prefer something stronger?" Georgie asked on seeing Coleford's raised eyebrow. She didn't even wait for an answer. "Reems?"

The butler silently retreated to the corner where her father kept the room's supply of spirits and measured out a tot of brandy. Georgie saw Coleford open his mouth to possibly decline and ignored him, focusing instead on the ritual of tea. A plate of little cakes for him, one for her. Her own cup of tea prepared to her exact specifications. At least she could control that, she thought, proud that her hands didn't shake as she dropped in a lump of sugar and poured in a bit of milk.

She still had no idea what she wanted to say, except that she wanted to tear at his hair and scream epithets for not letting go in time to prevent this. For making that kiss so all-consuming she had found herself in this position at all.

Coleford accepted his snifter from Reems with a nod and waited as the butler ushered the maids out.

Georgie gave her butler a smile. "Thank you, Reems. That was kind of you all."

Preparing tea at two in the morning. Because they were a civilized family. Reems bowed the maids out, and Georgie took a sip from the cup from the second-best Sevres china.

Coleford took his own sip of brandy, his eyes going wide. "Your parents traveled to France quite a bit as well?" he asked, lifting the glass to peer into the rich golden depths of the liquor. He had taste, did the marquess. That brandy was twenty years old. Georgie wished she had the nerve to pour her own.

"No," she said. "My second brother is a smuggler and two cousins run guns."

Well, at least she got his attention. She almost laughed. He actually spent a moment considering her words.

"You can find them plotting their next run up in the nursery," she finally conceded, taking another sip.

She earned a bark of laughter for it and hated him even more right then for sounding so gleeful and delighted. Because he made her want to smile, too.

"How did you get me alone before your father had his way with me?" he asked.

She took a sip. "I tied my aunt to the servants' stairs and barred the front door."

He was still smiling. "Should you be the one I list my assets for then?"

"I know your assets. Two young girls and at least four estates with no money to support any of them. Oh. And ermine robes that are perfectly useless for day-to-day wear."

"And all my teeth," he retorted, displaying them for her.

She nodded. "They should come in handy for gnawing on roadside roots and berries when you run out of funds."

"But...."

He stopped just short of saying what they both knew he was thinking. *But he wouldn't.* Not now. Not with her dowry and her portion of Grandmother Breslin's inheritance. The pressure in her chest swelled.

"Would you like to rail at me now?" he asked, more gently than she could have credited.

Georgie admitted she stared at him. "What?" She even forgot to be polite.

His smile was rueful. It was still breath-taking, damn it. "For what it is worth," he said, "I'm sorry." He gave a brief look back at his drink, then faced her again, which impressed her too much. "It is not how I would have had this happen."

She wished again she could manage to raise a single eyebrow. "This?"

He sighed. "Your aunt neatly removed our options. If we aren't married, you will be ruined."

"And how would you have rather it happened?"

He shrugged. "I would have asked you like a gentleman."

She didn't even hesitate. "And I would have said no."

That seemed to surprise him. "Why would you do that?"

For a moment all Georgie could do was stare at him. "Are you truly that arrogant, or simply that oblivious?"

He tried another smile. "I have all my teeth and five houses, actually. One is a horse farm in Ireland."

"Then you should have proposed to Charlie. I have my own teeth and four houses of my father's I can visit."

"Visit. Not be in charge of."

That got a very dry laugh out of her. "You think so? You have obviously never been the oldest daughter of a busy earl."

"Don't you want your own home?"

Down went the teacup. Up went Georgie. She had no idea why. She simply needed to move. She'd forgotten that if she stood so did he. They ended up almost nose to nose.

And blast it, he stood too close. She could feel that odd energy spark again. She was suddenly beset by an urge to get closer. To rediscover that thrumming heat that seemed to live in his hands, his mouth.

She saw his nostrils flare, just a bit; his eyes darkened. So he felt it, too.

"This is not the time to get into the hard facts of women and ownership of homes," she said. "Suffice it to say that the matter of a home is not high on my list of frustrations."

"Then what is?"

She glared at him. "You never thought to ask me if I *wanted* to get married."

Again, he seemed sincerely bemused. Setting down his snifter, he returned to the fray. "What else is there?"

She couldn't help it. She laughed. He must have heard that it wasn't an amused laugh, because he frowned.

She tried to calm herself. "You truly have no idea."

"Of what?"

She briefly closed her eyes, but that didn't help. She could still smell him, that sharp pine scent. She could feel him, like standing too near a fire. "How did you come by the marquessate?" she asked.

She seemed to have flummoxed him again. "You know perfectly well. My cousins died."

"Which means you had no notion of ever assuming the title."

"Not one."

"And your father was an army man?"

He was looking completely confused. "Well, he bred horses for the army, but that's as close as he came."

She nodded. "Then why aren't you breeding horses?"

His grin was perfectly comfortable. "I'd be shown out on my ear. To tell the truth, my sister's husband is better at the task than even my father. My contribution is to ride one of our stallions around and make other officers want a horse just like him."

"Then how did you end up in the army? Are you the second son?"

"Only son. Four sisters."

"Then why the army?"

He shrugged. "I've been army mad since I can remember. Finished my studies and took my chance. If it weren't for this blasted title, I'd still be there with the gentlemen of your family."

She nodded, focused a moment on the darkened windows. "And no one thought to say to you, you are the son of a horse farmer, and that is the only thing you have a right to be until the day you die. Because it is your only choice."

That seemed to merit silence. He shook his head and took a step forward. "I don't understand. Are you telling me there is something you'd rather do than marry?"

"Almost anything."

He opened his mouth and ended up closing it again. "You'd rather be a spinster aunt? I have not heard many positive assessments of that vocation."

"Most of those women didn't have a choice. I do."

"And you'd rather live without a family? Without children?"

She realized she was about to shout. He expected a pat answer. He expected what every man expected to hear. *Of course, I want children. Children of my own I can nurture and guide and teach. Heirs, which is what is important.*

But she'd spent her life nurturing her mother's children, her aunt's children. She had begun to see her way clear from constant responsibility, and then...*him.*

She was still hashing those inchoate thoughts when she realized that he'd stepped even closer. She realized it because her body began to thrum again. Her heart picked up speed. She swore her breasts grew heavier.

She looked up to see that he was lifting his hand as if to swipe back a loose curl, except her curls never broke loose. Not the Countess of Clevedon's daughter. Even so, he stroked the hair right above her ear, sending shivers cascading through her. She might have stopped breathing entirely. She wasn't certain. But she was so very *warm.* So anxious. She wanted to take hold of that hand of his and see if he had calluses, and that was the very last thing she should be thinking of.

"You can't say you don't want me," he challenged, his voice like dark honey.

She blinked, and the air came rushing back into her lungs. "What does that have to do with anything?"

He took another step forward. "Don't you want to see where tonight would have gone?"

That absolutely froze her. It was all she could not to haul off and box his ears. She stepped back, feeling the settee hard against her legs. "So, I should sacrifice my entire life to, how do you gentlemen put it, scratch an itch?"

She was so delighted by his shock at her words that she might have gone further, but from the window she heard a definite throat-clearing.

Good Lord, she'd even forgotten that Preston was sitting there. If she'd been able to blush, she would have been red as Charlie's hair.

"It might be a better attitude to make the most of the situation in which we find ourselves," Coleford said, and Georgie wasn't sure whether he was challenging, apologizing, or negotiating.

She didn't get the chance to find out. Suddenly the door flew open, and her parents strode in, both of them smiling like pirates.

It was bad enough that her father was rubbing his hands. "I hear we have a wedding to prepare for."

"Now, Clevedon," her mother cautioned, stepping up beside him. "You haven't even been introduced yet."

Her father's laugh was sharp. "Georgie knows him, obviously. Knows him well enough to warrant a wedding. Isn't that right, girl?"

"No, sir."

Her parents gaped. At which point, of course, it got worse.

Aunt Berenice stalked in right behind them. "I told her there was no other option."

And behind her Eddie and Charlie all but tumbled into the room like Astley's clowns. "We tried to keep her out," Eddie protested.

"You shall do no such thing," Aunt Berenice insisted, turning on them like a fury. "This doesn't concern you."

"It doesn't concern you either," Charlie accused her own mother, which made Aunt Berenice choke on her own ire.

And all Georgie could see was the way Greyville looked at the windows as if planning an escape.

"Stop," she said.

"Why don't I talk to the young man," her father said.

"Once you've been introduced," her mother said in that velvety voice that belied the underlying steel. "Yes, Georgianna?"

"I'll introduce you," her aunt offered, her voice even more strident.

"Stop," Georgie insisted a bit more loudly.

"No," her mother said, "Georgie should do it. He is her fiancé after all. At least that is what the guests at the Embassy Ball were saying."

And all of a sudden everyone was trying to talk over each other, and Greyville looked as if he were being attacked by hornets, and Georgie couldn't tolerate another minute.

"*Stop!!!*" she screamed.

And amazingly, they did. For at least enough time for her to speak.

"Father, may I introduce you to Peter Greyville, the Marquess of Coleford. Greyville, you already know my mother, Countess of Clevedon. My father, the Earl of Clevedon. Who haven't yet noticed that you look as if you are frantic to escape this madhouse. So I will tell you right now that no, we are not engaged."

"I asked," Greyville offered with a rather winsome smile.

"And I said no," Georgie said.

He turned to her, that mischief still in his eyes. "You did?"

She glared at him. "I am now." Facing him fully, she dipped a quick curtsy. "Thank you for the honor you do me and all that," she said, so frantic that her voice sounded thin and fractious. "But I do have another option. Thank you for the offer. My answer is no."

"What option is that?" her aunt demanded.

Georgie didn't stop walking. "The convent, if it comes to that."

And before Aunt Berenice could wind up for a good scolding, Georgie strode from the room, the last thing she heard being Greyville's voice.

"I didn't know she was Catholic."

And damn him, she wanted to laugh.

WELL, Grey thought, standing in the middle of the room like the interloper he was. What do we do now?

Oddly enough, Lord Clevedon acted as if nothing had changed, smiling and clapping his hands. "Coleford, eh?" he all but sang. "Colonel Greyville of the Dragoons, if I don't miss my guess."

"Retired, sir."

"Precipitously, I should think, once word of the title came down. Good, good. We need to have a chat, don't we?"

Grey had no idea how to answer. Hadn't Clevedon heard his daughter? Or did he bother to listen to her at all?

He knew the Packhams' type—well-fed, well-shod aristocrats who bore the classic stamp of power and privilege. The Earl was white-haired, squared-off and solid, his tailoring perfect, his signet sleek, his voice the honeyed tones of an experienced orator. He radiated bonhomie, but Grey strongly suspected one shouldn't take that hail-fellow-well-met attitude at face value. This man had negotiated some very complex treaties and stood up to Prinny on more than one occasion.

Grey already knew his wife, so he bowed to her like the gentleman he was purported to be. She stood just outside her husband's shadow, her attire this time different from her sister's. She wore gold and scarlet, with diamonds and rubies in her elegant blonde hair, and a parure that had probably once graced a royal neck embellishing the rest. Of the group of them left behind in that overwrought room, he suspected she was the only one who comprehended the level of her daughter's distress. The rest of them were still milling about the doorway, as if Lady Georgie had taken their direction along in her wake. He couldn't help it. No matter what happened, he thought she was magnificent.

Her aunt was obviously not so enamored, nor with her own daughter's behavior. Her voice rattled around Grey's head like shrapnel as she pushed the remaining cousins out.

Grey was distracted by the departing winks the girls gave him and almost missed the Earl holding out a manicured hand. "Welcome to the family, son."

Grey shook like a gentleman, but his attention was all on the void left by Lady Georgie's departure. "I wouldn't be so sure about that, sir."

Clevedon waved at the settees. "Nonsense. Sit, sit. We'll discuss the situation. I see you've already got yourself a bit of courage. Think I'll get a bit myself."

And before Grey could answer, the older man was over at the drinks table.

"Girl has no sense," the aunt snapped, setting the feathers in her toque wildly bobbing. Grey could hardly take his eyes off them. "She needs to admit the truth."

"Berry," Lady Clevedon said, her voice like silk.

Oddly enough that seemed to stop her sister in mid-flight. "Well, she does," she insisted. "But obviously you don't wish to hear from me on the subject."

The Countess smiled. "We can have a coze later, yes? Why don't we get the Marquess on his way. We can revisit all of this in the morning after I have a visit with Georgie."

"You want to get that girl to do anything," the aunt insisted, "you should leave her to me. Stubborn as a shrike."

This time the Countess didn't even speak. Just leveled a look on her twin that sent the woman bustling from the room.

"And please leave Georgie to herself," Georgie's mother suggested. "You know that hectoring doesn't help."

The only answer she got was a huff of impatience and the sharp click of the door.

"Preston, thank you," the Countess said while smiling at Grey. "I'm sure Georgie can use your help about now."

Grey admitted that he was startled. He'd forgotten the maid was still there. At least he knew where Lady Georgie got her unshakable air of command. Her mother had routed everyone with the dispatch of a seasoned general. And Grey suspected it was hard to do with that sister of hers.

Even as the servant gathered up her yarn and gave a quick bob in the general direction of the Countess on the way out the door, that august lady was giving Grey a quiet but thorough assessment.

"I suspect you have had quite a long enough day, my lord," she said. "We certainly have. Embassy balls are more effort than they're worth, I often think. Would it be better for you if we reconvene in the morning?"

Which was how Grey found himself back out on the walk wondering who the diplomat really was in that family. Nothing had been settled at all. Nothing except the fact that it wasn't settled. Although it would be easy to take Lady Clevedon's parting words as a promise. "Georgie is no fool. She knows what her duty is."

Not exactly the encouragement Grey had been hoping for. He was developing the very strong suspicion that the last thing he wanted from Georgie Packham was duty.

8

———

Georgie was not encouraged by the fact that her mother did not come to see her all night. It as a favorite tactic of her mother's, delaying the confrontation in order to strain one's nerves. Capitulation came much more easily that way.

She dressed carefully for breakfast, even resorting to a little rabbit's foot to hide the ravages of a sleepless night. But it didn't give her any confidence when she arrived at the breakfast table to find only her parents before her.

"Good morning, my dear," her mother said, not looking up from the ubiquitous correspondence at her plate.

"Mother. Father."

"I like him," her father said with a definitive nod.

He didn't say another word. Just got to his feet, gave both Georgie and her mother a kiss on the cheek, and walked out.

"Eleven o'clock," her mother said at his leaving.

His only response was a wave of his hand that still held a piece of toast.

And then he was gone, and Georgie was left behind to once again envy him that freedom. What she wouldn't give to simply

119

walk out the front door without notifying half a dozen people, settling a half dozen more squabbles, answering staff questions, holding tearful toddlers, dragging a reluctant maid or footman along. Or facing a mother who had a terrible knack for getting what she wanted.

And here was her mother about to tell her that she was to exchange one household's responsibilities for another, without ever having had time to do something merely for herself.

"I'm afraid you were rude last night, Georgianna."

Ah, the punishment of disappointment. No matter what, it was familiar. It worked. Georgie felt as if she had worms crawling in her belly.

"I suspect Greyville will say he wasn't surprised."

"It still warrants an apology. And one to your father and your aunt."

Maybe she could go back upstairs and come back down later when the dining table was empty. Of course, the food would also be gone, and if there was one thing Georgie couldn't miss, it was a meal.

So, she stood to collect her eggs, bacon, and toast from the sideboard. "Of course, Mother."

"Your young man will be here at eleven to speak to your father."

More worms, these of dread. "I wish he wouldn't."

Her mother waited until Georgie had settled back in her seat. "Is there something we should know that would make him ineligible?"

Georgie almost lied. He was a deserter. He beat his wards. He enjoyed abnormal bed sport that involved whips and cheese.

In the end, though, she couldn't. He didn't deserve it. "Not that I am aware of."

"And you get along with his little wards?"

Georgie sighed. "I do."

But she didn't ask if Georgie got along with their guardian. She didn't ask if Georgie *wanted* to get along with their guardian. But then, Georgie suspected that wouldn't have helped. She would have to tell the truth about that as well.

Her mother put down the letter she'd been reading and considered Georgie rather as she had back when Georgie had tried to skip French lessons. "Then what reason could there be to refuse a marquess who is also a war hero his request for your hand?"

"Reason?" Besides the fact that she had dreamed of escaping for years, which her mother would not understand? "I don't know him."

Her mother, who knew all about the dispatches that had been pored over, simply raised an eyebrow.

Georgie huffed in frustration. "You know perfectly well that competence at war does not necessarily indicate a good character."

"Then how did you come to introduce him to your aunt and myself?"

Georgie sighed in frustration. "I have met him a sum total of three times, Mother."

Her mother's smile was too knowing. "You seem to have gotten along."

Again, Georgie was relieved that she didn't blush. "That is not a compelling enough reason to marry."

Her mother shrugged. "It doesn't hurt."

For a very long moment Georgie and her mother simply considered each other. "Am I to have no say in this?" Georgie finally asked, feeling as if her insides were being hollowed out.

Her mother's expression never changed. But her mother had decades of practice at that particular skill. "Go see your grandmother," she said. "The two of you have always sung a similar tune. Besides," she said with a long-suffering sigh. "She'll wish you to make the announcement."

Georgie gave herself away with a smile.

She should have known better.

"After you have accepted the Marquess's proposal."

"Must I?"

Getting to her feet, her mother collected her correspondence and gave Georgie one last smile. "Convents are dismal. You wouldn't like it there."

And that was it. Georgie was trapped.

IT BECAME official two hours later. Grey didn't see Georgie when he was ushered into the house by the very correct butler or when he was led up to the Earl's study. In fact, he saw no one as he waited for the Earl to put in an appearance. At least Reems knew to bolster Grey's courage with another snifter of brandy.

"A little early," the very precise butler allowed with a perfectly straight face. "But it is a portentous day. We on the staff only wish the very best for our Lady Georgie."

And damn if Grey didn't suspect he'd just been warned to behave. "I do as well," he responded, wondering if he could empty and refill his glass before the Earl arrived.

The butler nodded as if dispensing a blessing. "Your home will prosper under her hand."

And that was that. The butler processed out and Grey waited another twenty minutes, enough time to peruse from his seat the shelves of books behind the desk. If he wasn't mistaken, there were some very valuable books keeping company there. There were more under glass in the corner away from the light that appeared to be illustrated manuscripts. Grey didn't have the courage to get up and wander to verify his impression. But the sight of the collection intrigued him.

He had just taken his first sip of brandy and set the glass on the mahogany desk when the door opened.

"A little early, what?"

Grey fought to urge to jump to his feet. He rose with decorum to face the man he was more and more convinced would be his father by marriage.

"Your butler seemed to think a celebration was in order."

The Earl positively beamed. "And so it is. Sit, sit. I believe I'll join you. Not every day a man fires off his oldest girl."

"She hasn't accepted yet."

The Earl bestowed another beaming smile as he poured a healthy portion and settled himself behind the desk, snifter at his fingers. "Her mother is right. She knows her duty."

Grey sat across from him. "That doesn't evince enthusiasm, sir."

"Enthusiasm? Our Georgie? She's the steadiest creature alive. In fact, I suspect we're about to miss her a great deal. She has helped her mother, you know. And her aunt, I suppose. We have three families crammed all higgledy-piggledy in one house. Wonderful for the children. A bit confusing for adults sometimes. There have been occasions I've claimed the wrong brat. Not Georgie. Frightening command. Knows this house better than I do, and I was born in it. Oh, and I hear you have young wards. Perfect, perfect. Nobody better with the little ones. She'll raise your heirs right, I can guarantee it."

Grey listened to the growing store of accolades and realized that it was weighing him down. Everything the Earl said about his daughter spoke of responsibility. Good God, the way the man talked she'd been in charge of the children since she'd turned five. It was no wonder she wasn't that interested in pursuing it with him.

"What hobbies does she have for herself, sir?"

The earl blinked as if Grey had spoken a foreign language. "Hobbies? Georgie?" He paused, obviously digging for some memory or other. "Not quite sure I know. Suspect she doesn't have time for frivolity."

Oh, better and better, Grey thought morosely. *No wonder she had the look of a spooked horse when he'd mentioned marriage.*

What did he do now, though? How did he mitigate a disaster in the making, when he had no choice but to carry on?

"Talked to Marcus Drake this morning," the earl was saying.

He opened a case of cheroots and offered Grey one. Grey shook his head. It was one habit he'd managed to avoid during his time in the military.

"Soothes the nerves," the Earl said with a grin. "Drake admitted that we needed to get you on the road as quick as can be. Means we won't have time for banns. Might get some push-back from Georgie. Insist. She's a good girl. She knows how to go about. And obviously you don't have to worry about leaving your house in her hands."

Grey admitted he was surprised. "You know Drake?"

The Earl waved a hand. He seemed to do that a lot. "'Course I do. On the Privy Council, aren't I? He's of incalculable aid to the war effort."

The war that was over. Supposedly. Grey imagined that the need for him to decamp to Paris wouldn't be so urgent if important people really believed that.

"And you will make certain Georgie and my wards are well-protected while I'm gone?" he asked.

The Earl blinked in surprise. It had obviously not occurred to him that by leaving his house for Grey's, his daughter could be putting herself in danger. "Girl can take care of herself."

"Not in this case, sir. Either make sure the protection is there or there will be no vows. And no trip."

Another wave of the hand. "I'll notify Drake, although I suspect he's already ahead of the game."

Grey did, too. But he wanted the Earl to do more than dismiss his daughter as domestic help.

"Had my solicitor draw up the papers," the older man said with a clearing of the throat. "You should be happy."

Gray must have betrayed his surprise. The Earl waved that hand again. "Actually had them for a bit. Just in case, you know. I can't think they need to be altered. Let me know if they do."

Grey accepted the document the Earl pushed over and wondered what it was that compelled the Earl to be so efficient in firing off his daughter. Was there something Grey should know about her that might make this marriage imprudent? An opium habit, or too many toes? Maybe a less than pure background? Not that he cared, particularly. He hadn't expected this title and didn't particularly want it. He couldn't see losing sleep over where it went next.

Then he caught sight of the terms of the contract and almost choked on his brandy. Over a hundred thousand pounds would be his the minute he said his vows if he didn't challenge this. One. Hundred. Thousand. For the first time since he'd gotten that damnable message about his inheritance, he felt some of the weight lift from his shoulders.

"It is exceptionally generous, Clevedon," he said, pushing it back. "But I cannot accept it as is. There is no provision for Lady Georgianna."

There went that waving hand again. "Pin money's up to you."

Grey lifted an eyebrow. "Are you telling me your daughter doesn't know how to keep her accounts?"

That evoked a bright laugh. "Georgie? Girl's a whiz. Learned it from some friends at school. Once corrected the Astronomer Royal on his calculations. Frightening mind."

"In that case, she would be responsible enough to handle

money of her own. Set aside a third of these funds to be under her sole control. Name my solicitor as executor. I trust him. And add one of my unentailed estates." He thought for a moment, took a sip of brandy to enjoy the flummoxed look on the earl's face. "Ah. I have it. There is a lovely place in the Cotswolds. Painswick Park. Welsh blacks will look lovely against those hills."

This time the Earl just blinked.

"These points are non-negotiable. I would also need iron-clad trusts for my wards and any children, of course."

"Are you saying we cannot trust *you*?"

Grey used the trick of raising one eyebrow. He vaguely wished he had a quizzing glass for more impact. "I'd think you would be glad to find a husband for your daughter who seeks to protect her interests."

There was a nervous clearing of the throat and another wave of the hand. "Quite. Quite." Rising to his feet, the Earl held out a hand. "Again. Welcome to the family."

Grey took that hand. "Only if she says yes."

That got him a laugh. "Of course she'll say yes. What girl wouldn't?"

Which told Grey everything he needed to know about how well the Earl knew his daughter. It did not improve his own self-respect to know that just yesterday he'd known just as much. Or as little. And that even so, he would make sure she said her vows.

GEORGIE'S MOTHER had directed her to the East Salon so the sun could cast a warm light on her, evidently a benefit in proposals. Charlie and Eddie had been sent off to the modiste's to make certain they would not interfere, and her father had returned home just in time to closet himself with his prospective son-in-law. For Georgie's part she sat quite properly, back straight, feet on the floor, perfectly aligned on the lemon-yellow settee listening to the *clack clack* of Preston's knitting needles.

"He's been in there quite a while," the maid offered.

Georgie refused to answer.

"Knowing your father, the brandy bottle's been broken out and all."

Silence. Georgie was too busy keeping the bile from rising in her throat from imagining what exactly her father and Grey were discussing. How they would decide to 'dispense' with her.

Then Georgie heard footsteps in the corridor. Heavy, measured ones, with a very slight limp, the kind heard by a soldier on parade. Georgie was disgusted when her body recognized his tread before the rest of her and began to react in now-predictable ways. Her heart, her palms, her breasts. She felt as if her body were straightening and preening itself in preparation for showing off completely without her permission. And yet she found herself smoothing out the skirt of her blue-and-white striped muslin morning dress, which was a lady's way of drying her sweaty palms. Again. She seemed to do that a lot around him.

"And don't ever tell me again that he's...what, compelling?" Preston gave a scornful sniff. "What a paltry word."

It was, Georgie had to admit. But if she acknowledged how much he affected her, she wouldn't be able to hold onto what was left of her sanity, much less her autonomy. And she had a strong suspicion she was going to need every bit of both.

If only she could see Grandmama before having to face Greyville. Maybe Grandmama would give her sanctuary like a medieval church. Maybe she could spirit Georgie out of the country. The Continent was open. America. South America. The Antipodes.

Except exile wasn't what she wanted either. She just didn't want *this*. Especially with a man she suspected could compel her right past the point of self-respect.

He was still only halfway down the hall when she got to her feet. She wasn't about to face him from a subordinate position. Preston was gathering up her knitting, since there was no question Grey would ask for a few minutes alone. Georgie was once again wiping her hands on the sides of her skirts. She so hated this feeling of uncertainty. Of anticipation. Of pending disaster.

And then he was in the doorway, and she couldn't breathe. *It could be worse indeed*. He was so solid, so *compelling*, dash it. And he was looking at her as if she were a puzzle to be solved.

Oh, excellent.

"My lord?"

He shook his head. "You know better. Is there actually any privacy in that back garden? We need to talk."

She looked about the room as if he wasn't seeing it.

"Where the staff isn't listening in," he clarified.

That kicked her heart rate up another notch.

"I'm leavin'," Preston assured him as she dipped a curtsy and stalked by him with a quick assessing look that didn't bestow much approval. "Can't speak for anybody else. They all feel a bit protective."

"Yes," Greyville said with a faint smile. "I know. Somewhere private, Lady Georgie?"

"I assume it's solely a matter of not wanting to be overheard, not wanting to ravish me in the bushes."

His smile grew at the very distinct huffing noise coming from Preston as she walked past him.

"While the second does sound appealing, I'm afraid we just don't have the time right now."

Georgie nodded as if it were as easy as a quip, while her heart thundered and her less public parts started that infuriating humming again. "Then come with me. Preston, you come too."

Greyville's expression was rather comical, but Preston fell right into step as Georgie led them past her father's office and her mother's morning room to the side of the house and the room many people overlooked. Halfway down the corridor they ran into Reems, who bowed.

"We are going to the conservatory, Reems," she announced. "Which you know nothing about. Especially if my aunt asks."

"Indeed, Miss Georgie. I believe I have pressing business in the wine cellar."

She gave him a grin. Reaching the door, she motioned for Preston to sit outside and then led Greyville into the conservatory where they could, indeed, be seen but not heard.

The warm moist air that rolled out of the open door immediately threatened the hold of every pin in Georgie's hair. But this was more her room than anyone else's, both from interest and from attention. Drago and fishtail palm trees lined the walls, giving the mostly glass room a sense of privacy, and crimson mandevilla climbed several trellises. But the center was devoted to not only English plantings, but several exotics as well.

"Good heavens," Greyville breathed, heading straight for the small tree tucked into the back corner, where the entire wall was glass to let as much light in as possible. It was Georgie's favorite, with its glossy leaves a backdrop for star-shaped flowers that shaded from cream to faint pink to yellow and perfumed the room with a scent too exotic for England. And yet, here it was.

"Frangipani," he marveled, looking back at her. "Where in heaven's name did you get this?"

"You know frangipani?" she asked, joining him until the delicious scent enveloped them both.

Taking in a slow breath, he nodded, reaching out to stroke

one of the flowers with unspeakable gentleness. Somehow that one motion shook Georgie's determination.

"When we were in India," he said, sounding reverent. "Oh, the scents in that country. Incense, spices, coffee, tea, flowers of a thousand kinds. There were quite a few scents that were not as pleasant, but those aren't the ones you remember. But this was always my favorite. Where did you get it?"

She smiled. "A good friend from school is Anastasia Dunn. Her father is Wilbur Dunn, the Soap King. Stasia has been helping him expand his empire. She hopes to become his perfumer. I talked her into a cutting."

He shook his head. "It's a delightful surprise in this usually cold and rainy climate."

"Did you like India?"

"Yes and no. It is overwhelming. So many people, so much strife, but so much beauty."

"I have always wanted to go. Michael hated it. The heat, the noise. Would you go back?"

He shrugged. "Not much chance with my new responsibilities." Before she could follow up, he pointed to the black wrought iron bench tucked in among the fishtail palms. "Speaking of which...."

Excellent. Now she was a responsibility. She couldn't think of a better way to woo a woman. And that quickly, the bubble of anticipation burst. Georgie sat and laid her hands in her lap to hear her sentence.

Greyville didn't sit right away. He paced, which made her feel worse. She was not feeling any more enthusiasm from him than she was from herself. She was plagued by the suspicion that they were walking straight into disaster. And she hadn't even heard his proposal yet.

Georgie knew what her opinion was, but she pulled in a

deep breath and clasped her hands and waited. Greyville kept pacing.

"Unless you intend to ask your questions of the palm trees," Georgie finally said, "could we get on with it? I have a busy day ahead of me. And now I must go out to my grandmother's and tell the bees."

Well, that got his attention. It even got him to stop and turn. "I beg your pardon."

She spared him a wry smile. "Sit down and I'll tell you."

He sat. Far too close, but there it was.

She sighed and held her position. This always made perfect sense to her, possibly because Grandmama had been telling her since she could remember how the bees that Grandmama raised were part of the family and deserved the same respect. When Georgie had been seven, she had quite archly told her grandmama that considering some of the people in her family, the bees probably deserved more respect.

"It is an ancient custom," she said, purposely leaving out her childhood. "Grandmama grew up with it from her Irish grandmother. If you have bees, you must alert them to every major life change. Especially death. They must have the option to leave if they want. Although they never have."

"You've done this before." He did not sound as if this made sense to him. Georgie could hardly blame him. On a bad day, it was just a bit too much like a fairy tale, even for her. And she had been sitting on that little bench before the bees ever since she could remember.

"I have. It is very precious to my grandmama, and I will never do anything to hurt her."

He nodded, as if that was all that needed to be said.

"You know we have to marry."

This time she did not answer.

It was his turn to sigh. "When we marry, we will have a

comfortable life. Your father is making certain you have a sizable dowry under your control."

She squinted as if he needed to come into focus. "My father. The short man who waves a lot."

His smile was wry. "Yes."

She actually smiled back. "I love my father, but it would never naturally occur to him to give any woman such an option. I'm still not certain how my mother manages it."

"Well, he did this time. You'll want for nothing."

"Except a breath of free air."

"I don't follow you."

She sighed, collected her thoughts, struggling to make him understand what no man truly could. "I have been in charge of the day-to-day running of this house and two others when we're there, since I was fifteen. I also do most of the parish visits, the church committees, the governess and tutor interviews. My entire life I have been responsible for quite a few people, even my parents. Do you know what that's like? And please don't say yes."

His grin was a bit sheepish. "I was merely a colonel in the Dragoons. Does that count?"

"You've served with my brothers. Do you think so?"

She was gratified to see a scowl.

"There are five more just like them under the age of twelve in this house," she said. "Not to mention the three girls. And that doesn't even take into account the parents and staff. Or Charlie and Eddie."

"There are only two little girls at my home," he said, as if it would answer everything. "Much easier."

That once again brought her to her feet. Why didn't anyone understand? Why didn't they ever understand? The girls only made it so much worse, because she could so easily love them.

"I can't!" she said, surprising herself.

Inevitably he came to his feet as well. "Why? Are you afraid? You're obviously skilled enough. After seeing what you do here, your change to my home would seem a vacation."

She was shaking her head, the panic rising in her throat.

He shrugged. "It could be—"

She spun on him, leveling an accusing finger. "Do *not* say it could be worse. Not if you want to leave this room in possession of all your teeth."

Of course, she surprised a smile from him. What else did she expect?

"Don't you understand?" she demanded, hands clenched, back so straight she feared she'd crack. "It is what I tried to explain last night. I have never been given a choice or an option. I have never been able to do what *I* want. My entire life has been spent at the service of my family. And now, it will be *your* family."

"But what do you want?"

"I don't know! But something that is *mine*. Now I will never get the chance to even look! I've gone from being a little mother to a big mother. I've never been just Georgie."

When she looked up to see if he was finally beginning to comprehend what every woman did, she found herself caught tight by his expressive seawater eyes. Pain, she thought. Frustration. Caring. He was trying, she realized.

With a sigh of his own, he reached down and captured her hands. His fingers were callused, long and elegant. A real gentleman's hands. Hands that should have played the pianoforte, not wielded a weapon. Hands that nonetheless held hers as gently as a whisper, so that she didn't feel threatened or overwhelmed. So that she felt...cossetted. Comforted. Even as her body once again sang with a life she barely recognized as her own.

Oh, how frustrating! That this was the man who would steal her only chance at escape, and she could see that he regretted it.

Not enough to throw over the traces and let her go, of course. She saw it in his eyes long before he knelt down at her feet.

She immediately frowned and pulled at her hands. "Stop that."

Looking up, she made sure Preston was looking the other way. She did not need this bruited about below stairs. She tugged again at Greyville's hands, but he was suddenly immovable. He was also smiling, albeit one that was rueful and wry.

"Lady Georgianna," he began, pulling her hands to his chest, which meant she went neatly along.

Too close. Too blasted close. She couldn't think when she was this close.

"I am sorry," he said, which helped clear her head. "I wish I could give you your wish. But you know that it's been too late since your aunt stepped onto that balcony."

The panic was building again. He was boxing her into a corner, and doing it in the kindest way, and she saw the door to escape closing before her eyes. And worst of all, she was so afraid that she would end up hurting this kind man because her frustrations would simply pile up like dirty snow and freeze her. She was even more afraid that she might come to love him and his little girls more than herself, which would take away her last choice.

She tried pulling again. "What about Priscilla?" she asked. "Last I heard, you were still engaged to her."

He held her hands right against his heart. She could feel it speed up, as if he were as afraid as she.

"Your subterfuge seems to have been successful,' he said. "This morning the Earl sent a notice to papers. Evidently the entire family is loath to visit Wales."

She nodded and couldn't think of a thing more to say. This time she wished she hadn't been quite so successful.

"We must wed," Grey said. "But even though I would be

heartsore, what if we give it our best try for four months. At the end of that time, if you simply cannot abide me, I can arrange for a separation."

That made her even angrier. "And what about the girls? Are you intending to have yet another mother desert them?"

"Well, my cousin didn't exactly..."

She managed to get her hands free this time and punched him square in the chest. "They were abandoned. That's all they know. That is all they would know if I left again. Maybe you are that much of a beast, my lord, but I. Am. *Not.*"

"And so, what do we do?" he asked, rubbing at his chest.

She could only close her eyes. He was a good man, wasn't he? He wouldn't hurt her. Would he?

But it was the rest of her life.

"What about this idea?" he finally asked, once again catching her hands and pulling them to him. "What if we look for Georgie together?"

She found herself blinking. "What?"

He insisted on overwhelming her manners. Worse, he grinned when he did it, and her own heart began to stumble about.

"I cannot take away the responsibility," he said, his eyes distressingly sincere. "I can give you all the help you need. And the support to find what it is that belongs only to you." Another grin. "Unless it's gunrunning. I'm afraid I cannot support that, no matter what your brothers want."

He surprised her into a burst of laughter. How could he do that when she felt the world collapsing around her?

"I sincerely doubt gunrunning will be involved. I tend toward seasickness."

"Does this mean a future trip to India would be out of the question?"

"Absolutely not. I would overcome. But your responsibilities are here."

He shrugged. "We will have quite a bit of money to cushion life's blows, especially once I get the estates to be profitable again. I imagine it could also secure me a competent manager in time. The girls will be in school in a few years."

She almost pulled her hands back again. "Do not even think of it. I told you. Wherever we go, those girls go. I will not have them deserted again, even for the chance to explore the world."

He didn't answer right away. Just gazed up at her, his hands cradling hers, his smile seeming to encompass her. "Is that a *yes*, Lady Georgianna?"

She battled an overwhelming urge to cry. "I'm afraid so."

"Why afraid?"

"Because I have been told I am not a restful person. And I am being inflicted on you."

"I have been a soldier for fifteen years, my dear. Not restful is my specialty."

"I will demand a voice in our affairs."

"I will be happy to listen."

"And the chance to try new things."

"Except gunrunning."

"Except gunrunning." She drew a shaky breath. "And I insist on honesty, Greyville. I cannot imagine surviving this without it."

"Yes ma'am."

"Your word."

"My word. May I get up now?"

"I told you to get up ten minutes ago."

He did, finally, managing to make it seem like a dance move, smooth and elegant, even as he flinched with that leg. Left leg, she realized. She wished she could curtsy half so well. He was so smooth he had his arms around her before she knew it.

"Would a kiss be acceptable?" he asked, his face so close she could see the creases fanning out from the corners of his eyes.

"Tell me anything I should know first."

He frowned. "About what?"

"Anything. I shall tell you, for instance, all holidays for the foreseeable future will be spent at Clevedon. That I shall spend an inordinate amount of time with the other kings. That I have a schedule of meetings coming up I cannot cancel, and that you will likely go into debt over my library subscription."

He smiled. "I'm afraid I have nothing nearly as interesting. I have a batman named Braxton who believes he is really the marquess, two little girls who confound and delight me, and a new fiancée I cannot wait to get to know. Now what about that kiss?"

She could feel the hard wall of his chest against her breasts and his arms encapsulating her. Those troubling reactions were firing again all along her limbs, into her chest, her belly. Deeper where she didn't have a name, heating her. Making her impatient, urging her to move even closer. Pushing her up on tiptoe so she could meet his mouth.

The kiss was different this time. Softer, deeper, sweeter. A greeting and a promise rather than a connection. A symphony of sight and sound and scent, pulling her in, sending her spinning. Imbuing her with the oddest sense of homecoming.

She felt his hand against the back of her head and rested against him, for the first time in her life giving herself up to another. For the very first time wanting to follow the path he was blazing. Wanting to lay her trust in his elegant hands.

Which meant it was inevitable that the door to the conservatory would swing open and her mother and father sweep in.

"I tried," Georgie heard from Preston and thought she should have locked the door against them. Nothing else would have kept them out.

She made it a point not to jump back but to separate herself with as much dignity as a woman could whose hair was mussed and whose lips felt tender and pleasured.

"I do hope this means we can plan the wedding," her mother said, smiling.

"Indeed, it does, ma'am," Greyville said, his arm now around Georgie's shoulder.

She instinctively wanted to buck at such a gesture of possession. She held still.

Her father was rubbing his hands again. "Excellent, excellent. I can have Charles whip up a special license by the end of the day. Cousin, you know. Owes me a favor from when were at Cambridge together. We can have the thing done by week's end."

He turned to consult with his wife, who gave him a calm nod.

Georgie wasn't feeling quite so sanguine. "This weekend? Won't that make the scandal worse?"

Her father gave one of his hand waves. "Might. But this way we can have Coleford here off on his trip by next weekend."

That quickly, the exhilaration Georgie had been flirting with died a terrible death.

"Trip?" she asked, turning on her brand-new fiancé. "What trip?"

Her father looked at her as if she were slow to catch up. "Why, the reason you're marrying so soon. So you can take over his house while he's gone."

Georgie didn't say another word. She simply turned away from them and walked out the door. The last thing she heard was her mother's faintly chastising voice. "You didn't tell her?"

9

It took him half an hour, but he finally tracked her down, in the kitchen of all places, kneading bread dough. A full apron tied around her pretty blue-and-white striped morning dress and her hands dusty white with flour, she didn't look up, although he knew she would have guessed he'd arrived just by the gasps and curtsies from the kitchen staff. He gave them all a nod of the head and tried his best to ignore the collective hostility directed his way. He suspected they had no idea why their mistress was upset. He also imagined they didn't need to know. All it would take was one look at the stark betrayal in her eyes and the furious beating she was giving that dough to tell the tale.

"May I explain?" he asked her.

She closed a fist and punched the dough right in the center. He suspected she was envisioning a particular person's body part.

"Please?"

With a sigh and a glance up at the very large man across the room in white who was cradling a meat cleaver in his arms,

139

Georgie cleared the room quite efficiently. That didn't mean she stopped pummeling the dough.

"Interesting hobby," he ventured, stepping closer.

She gave the dough another solid punch. He swore he felt it in his gut.

"It has saved the life of more than one family member," she finally said, folding the dough and folding it again before sprinkling flour over it and covering it with a towel.

"I imagine I should be grateful it was convenient as well."

"I suspect you should."

She had a smudge of dust on her cheek. He fought an urge to wipe it away. No, he admitted, trying to ignore his suddenly very interested cock, he wanted to *lick* it away. This shouldn't be the moment he realized that he would do anything to keep from losing her, but suddenly he knew that it wasn't at all about the girls' safety or the mission or the fact that Georgie could bake her own bread if need be. It was about her.

In that surprise burst of honesty, he realized that he suddenly couldn't imagine his life without her in it anymore, and it had only taken him a week to realize it. He just didn't think she would believe that right now.

He was feeling hopeful for a positive outcome until she finally lifted her eyes, and he saw not rage, which he'd expected, but devastation. Her eyes were dry, but they seemed to hold a world of pain and disappointment. Walking over to the sink, she washed the flour off her hands and very deliberately dried them before hanging the towel back up.

He couldn't seem to move, that pain cleaving his own chest. "I was about to tell you," he said.

She turned back to him with eyes that were once again bland and passive. He suspected she had a lot of practice covering her reactions.

"Were you?"

He saw it so clearly then, especially after speaking to her father. Everyone in her life had done this to her. Just assumed that Georgie would handle whatever they threw at her. That Georgie would pick up the slack, cover the mistakes, supervise the mess somebody might have left behind on the way to whatever pastime they wanted to follow instead.

And she had.

Which made him even more uncertain how to go on. Because if he told her he understood, he suspected she would simply haul off and punch him like a half-risen lump of bread dough.

"Could we go somewhere to sit?" he asked. "I imagine your cook would like his counters back. And I would like to speak frankly, which I cannot do with the audience I suspect is waiting around the corner armed with cooking weaponry."

For a long moment she just stood there staring down at the lump of dough and the towel that protected it as if waiting for it to advise her. Trim and tidy, her hair sleek as silk, her posture impeccable, her blue-and-white striped gown—even the apron —flawless, and yet somehow, she made him think of a child who had just been left on a street corner. He realized he'd lifted a hand toward her, as if to really pull her close. He let it fall.

Finally, without a word, she untied the apron and pulled it over her head. Hanging it up on a nearby hook, she called a name, which he suspected belonged to the cook, and led Grey out the kitchen door to the garden he'd first visited only a few days ago. Heading straight for the little arbor where he'd met her cousins, she sat and pointed him to the seat opposite. Not alongside.

He sat.

She settled, hands clasped primly in her lap, posture not an inch less rigid, her gaze unflinching. He respected the power of that focus. He wished he'd never had to see it directed at him.

For just a second, he considered popping off one of the irises that edged the garden. Handing it to her, as if that would make a difference.

"I wasn't allowed to say anything," he said instead, not moving. "It is a trip on behalf of the government."

She considered him, as if weighing the truth of his words. "Why tell me now?"

She still hadn't softened her stance. She looked instead like the goddess of judgment, her posture unbending, her aristocratic nose a bit in the air. And he hurt for her and wished he could just pull her into his arms. A worse idea than the iris, though, from her posture.

"Besides the fact that I just asked you to put your life into my hands?"

"Besides that."

"Because I found out your father already knew. And because for some reason I trust you more than the government."

A smile? No. He didn't dare risk it as stern as she still looked.

"The government?"

"The government asked me...well, *strongly suggested* I go."

"Why? I know you don't go to a battlefield. We have recently dispensed with those. What else demands such alacrity?"

He shrugged, feeling more and more uncomfortable. This had all been so clear to him when he realized how well the marriage would serve him.

Serve *him*.

But it meant so much more now. He wanted to hold her. To lay her head against his shoulder and promise that she would always have his support. She would never have to carry another burden alone.

But she would, of course. In a matter of little more than a week.

"Because I trust you," he said, not pausing when he heard the disbelieving huff, "I will share what I am not supposed to."

"And it will be the truth."

His instinctive reaction was to bristle. One look at the brittle expression on her face convinced him not to. "It will be the truth. From now on, it will always be the truth." He took a breath and a quick look out to the blooming flowers, peonies and primrose and lilacs. And useless damn iris. "When I was on the Continent, I was asked to perform a few...extra...commissions beyond my duties. I am fluent in French, German, and Spanish. It came in handy."

"I imagine it did. Was it during these extra commissions you kept running across my brother and cousins?"

Well, that took his breath. "How did you know?"

She shrugged. "I suspected. Things they said to each other when on leave." Finally, she afforded Grey a wry smile. "Men have a disconcerting habit of underestimating the comprehension of women. We kings figured it out long ago." She stopped for a moment, as if struck by a revelation. And not a happy one. "Oh, lord. You're part of Drake's Rakes, aren't you?"

Grey opened his mouth and yet couldn't seem to get anything out for the longest time. "Drake's...how do you know?"

She huffed in frustration. "I'm fairly certain every girl who attended Last Chance Academy knows about Drake's Rakes. Except I thought they were only the sons who weren't allowed to fight on the Continent who helped the government in...shall we say, other ways. How did you come into it?"

"Last Chance...?"

She waved him off, much like her father would have. "The nickname for our boarding school. You are a member of Drake's Rakes, then?"

He shrugged. "I'd call it more a cadet branch."

"And my brother and cousins as well."

He nodded, feeling more than a bit disconcerted. "I also served with them on the line. They are fine officers."

"If a bit reckless and impulsive."

He smiled. "If that."

"And now that Napoleon is on Elba?"

His first instinct was to lie. He truly wasn't used to breaking confidences, especially if they were state secrets. But if he could not trust her with this, he could not trust her with his children. And if he did not tell her the truth now, she would never be able to trust him again.

"Possibly an even worse problem. We have caught whispers of Napoleon having received aid from some highly placed British citizens, who, it seems, might well be working to help him escape. One of our men who has been working undercover has gone missing. I am to go to Paris to evaluate the situation under the guise of being a military liaison to Wellington as he settles in as ambassador."

She took a moment to let that sink. in. "When?"

"When? Well, they want me to go now. I told them I needed a week."

"And how long will you be gone?"

He drew in a breath. "I don't know."

"Days? Weeks? Months? Years?"

All he could do was shake his head.

After a tense moment, she nodded. "How convenient, then, that you found yourself compromised with a woman who had long experience in childcare so you could continue your adventures."

So, he wasn't about to be forgiven.

"What would you have me do, Georgianna? I have done my duty for this country for ten years. Do you expect me to walk away from it just because I find myself in my cousin's shoes?"

She huffed again. "If you expect me to help you this way, you could at least do me the courtesy of calling me by the name I requested. My name is Georgie. Georgianna is the Duchess of Devonshire, and I most certainly am not she."

"Good, because I don't want her. I want you."

She froze, eyes widened, breath frozen.

His own heart suddenly thundering with the chance he was taking, he leaned forward, elbows on thighs so he could impress her with the truth. And honestly, so he could catch that fresh flower scent in her hair he found so tantalizing. "Did you ever expect you would react to me like you did at the ball?"

She abruptly stiffened. "I never..."

He just lifted a single eyebrow. She didn't blush, but she looked damned uncomfortable.

"I wouldn't have asked if I hadn't reacted just as strongly," he assured her, reaching across to take her hands, whether she liked it or not. "I will be perfectly honest with you, Georgie. I have been attracted to you from the moment I saw you so deftly handling my scapegrace wards. I will not deny it. But when we stepped out onto that balcony, something completely different happened. I'm sorry, but I will not apologize for it, and I certainly won't deny it. Whatever else you believe about me, please believe that I am asking you to marry me because I like you, and...I want you."

Taking a breath, she closed her eyes. But she didn't pull away. And before her lids came down, he saw her pupils dilate. He saw her nostrils flare just that much and felt the heat pulse off her like a fire in winter.

His own body responded in the most primitive and understandable way. Which meant that it was probably better he was seated and leaning forward. He wasn't sure she was ready to see just how attracted he was—or that he was ready for her to see. She might have a pack of brothers and male cousins milling around her house, but he didn't want to take the chance that she might not have figured out the working parts of a randy male.

"You cannot deny you feel the attraction as well," he gently urged.

Her eyes opened, and he saw arousal, impatience, frustration. "I cannot," she admitted.

He was relieved that she was at least honest about it. And then she yanked the rug out from under him.

Pulling hard, she freed her hands and lurched to her feet. He followed, only to find her pacing down the garden walk as if responding to a bugle.

"Georgie?"

She shook her head and walked for a few more paces. "This changes everything, of course."

His stomach lurched just as abruptly. "What everything?"

Please God, don't say you won't marry me. He'd barely comprehended that surprise prayer before she whipped around and stopped, a martial light in her eyes that stopped him in his tracks.

"Get married. Go on your trip. But for the foreseeable future this marriage will be in name only."

If he hadn't stopped before, this would have done it. "What?!"

She took in a breath, hands clenched at her waist. "I have no intention of waiting here always pregnant and raising babies while you gallivant about the world," she announced baldly.

If she hadn't been clutching her hands together as if seeking purchase, he would have reacted quite a bit more strongly.

Well, he had told himself, he valued honesty. He wondered if it had to be quite so blunt.

"Why?"

She shot him an impatient look, as if trying to decide how to tell him he was an idiot. He probably was, at least about this.

Besides, his cock was beginning to make demands again he didn't want to ignore.

"Why?" he repeated.

"Because our marriage will be difficult enough as it is for a while. Especially if you keep taking these surprise trips. I will need to wade into your world and attempt to assume at least temporary command, comfort and support the little girls, and survive with a reputation as a wife who had been deserted at the altar."

"It's not—"

She gave him a little wave that reminded him again of her father. "You know it and I know it. But believe me when I tell you that society will be more than happy to jump to its own conclusions. Especially since they will also be assiduously counting the months until we have a blessed event. It is a far more choice bit of gossip that I forced you into marriage for my own benefit, than that you did me."

She was right, of course. He just didn't want her to be. He wanted her to feel as consumed by her attraction to him as he was becoming to her. He wanted...

"I know ways to prevent it." He hated the fact that he was sounding just a bit desperate.

That bit of brass earned him a glare that should have shaved two inches off his height. "Thank you, no. I don't trust you."

"You don't trust me, or you don't trust yourself?"

Her scowl just grew. "I am not the one who trapped another person into marriage."

It took him a second to answer. Not because she had no reason to make that statement. Because she did.

"Is there a way past?" he finally asked.

Again, she had the courage to look him directly in the eye, allowing him to see the emotions that roiled in hers. "I hope so. Just not now."

He nodded, wishing she would have given him a pat 'yes,' even if it wasn't true. "Then what do you mean to do?"

She sighed and looked over to where pale purple wisteria seemed to rain off the back wall of the house. "Play the comfortable newlyweds in public and shake hands at our bedroom door. At least for the foreseeable future. I'm still not certain I even want children."

"I must have an heir." He couldn't believe that came out of his mouth.

She gave him another shrug.

He tried again, already feeling ridiculous. "We must consummate the marriage, or it isn't legal. You know that."

That earned him more well-deserved disdain. "Don't be absurd. Consummation or non-consummation is not the issue. Inability is the issue in an annulment. And I have no intention— or need," she added, casting a quick glance at the evidence of his arousal, "—to call your...capability into question. I assume you wouldn't want to, either."

And damned if she wasn't exciting him by the very act of standing up for herself. Basely he wanted to prove he could convince her otherwise. He wanted to prove that he could overwhelm that reticence with just his mouth and hands. He wanted to know how she knew that bit of law, but knew this wasn't the time to ask.

Without realizing it, he had moved closer to her again, close enough that he caught that elusive hint of flowers that didn't exist in that all-too-fragrant garden.

She lifted her face and stood perfectly still.

"We could still kiss," he suggested, his voice already raspy with lust.

He saw her eyes go dark and her breathing hitch. But she didn't move as he lowered his face to her, as he touched her lips with his, once, twice, longer, until she leaned in, until he wrapped his arms around her, his hand in her hair, his heart thundering, his brain dissolving into mush.

She was lush in his arms, so warm, so open. Even untutored and new to it, she followed his kisses like a waltz on a dance floor, until her own arms finally came up and wrapped beneath his jacket to set fires along his ribcage and back. His cock was ready to burst, and his lungs had forgotten how to work. His body was too consumed with the naked, surging, primal need to mate. With this woman. With *his* woman.

It was the mewling sound he heard that brought him back from the edge. He was inches from cupping her luscious breast in his hand when he heard it coming from her, not a sound of participation, but distress. As if she found herself on the very edge of a very tall waterfall and couldn't think of a way to step back.

Which was when he knew that it was up to him to do it for her. If he ever wanted her to trust him, he needed to earn it now. He needed to stop.

His cock was raging and his primal brain roaring out protests, but as gently as he could, he pulled back. Even as she instinctively went up on her toes searching for more, he set her just enough away from him that she would know he was abiding by her wishes, not punishing her.

But oh, sweet suffering God, it was a struggle. Her eyes were closed, those long dark lashes fanned against her cheek. That perfect chignon was pulled just a little loose, and her mouth was as plump as berries with his kissing. And he thought he would never escape the scent of exotic flowers. Or want to.

"Georgie?" he said, leaning his forehead against hers, his breathing labored.

Hers was no easier. "You stopped."

"I'm not sure if you're offering praise or protest."

Her smile was soft and dreamy. "I'm not quite sure myself."

Opening her eyes, she pulled her head back so she could face him again. "You do that well."

"Starting or stopping?"

"Both. Thank you. You have set my feet on the road to trust." She screwed up her face. "Oh, bollocks. I sound like a Minerva Press novel."

And then she pulled herself out of his arms, her breathing still a bit labored, her hand to her chest. She shook her head, as if to clear it. "I am still not sure whether you are good for me or not, Grey, but I suspect there's nothing left but to formalize this thing."

"I agree."

"After I see my grandmama."

All the way home he was plagued by the fear that that would set things back all the way. Then he thought of that kiss and couldn't help smiling. Well. Maybe not *all* the way.

"GRANDMAMA, WHAT DO I DO?"

There she was seated on the little bench opposite her Grandmama's six beehives, bees contentedly swooping and humming about her and the mixed scent of the spring garden rich in the air. To add the perfect coda, she also faced an old woman bent over a lilac bush.

Anyone in society who had ever been tyrannized by the Dowager Countess of Clevedon would have walked right past the old woman in her comfortably faded round gown and cottage bonnet, deadheading the first of a dozen lilac bushes. But then most of them had never been invited to her lush, oversized garden.

"Do you love him?" came the imperious voice.

"Love him? I don't even *know* him!"

But then her grandmother straightened, turned, and fixed her with the kind of look that forbade dissembling. "But given the chance."

Which left Georgie with the uncomfortable need to squirm. Except no one squirmed in the presence of the Dowager Countess, cottager hat or not. So, she settled for a sigh and the truth. "Given the chance, might I could. But I *resent* him too much to find the room for it."

Those wise green eyes softened a bit. "Well, you had better find a way. Otherwise, you will find life tedious at best. Especially when you begin to bear him children."

Georgie ducked her head. "I told him I want a marriage of convenience." When she heard the gasp, she looked up. "For now. So I might have the chance to maybe find something of my own in my life, instead of spending the entire thing as nursemaid, nanny, and broodmare."

Her grandmama considered her a moment more before turning back to her lilacs.

"I'm afraid it is the way of women," the old woman said. "I had to wait for my old age to be given the chance to do what I loved."

"And if I don't live that long?"

Grandmama shrugged. "Your mother has carved out a way for herself."

"Are you so sure that is what *she* wanted for herself?" Georgie asked.

"Ask her."

"I am almost afraid to. What if I find that she is miserable with all of us? And how do I tell her that I refuse to have my life governed by pregnancy? I have spent my life in child-rearing. I am frankly tired of it."

Snip. Snip. "And those little girls?"

"What about them?"

"Do you intend to abandon them because you have had your fill of children?"

"Of course not. Those little ones need me far more than my own siblings ever have."

Oddly enough, that was what brought her grandmama upright, her expression fearsome. "Do not *ever* think such a thing again. Personally, I worry about how they will get on once you're married."

Georgie couldn't help a grin. "I don't suppose you'd like to move in."

That earned her a huff of disdain and a return to the flowers. "Not likely. I have earned my peace."

If peace included a prodigious correspondence and frequent forays into society with the purpose of stirring the pot. But Georgie admitted that overall, her grandmama had fashioned an exquisite retreat for herself out of a rather plain Queen Anne house near Richmond. The dowager often said that after the strain of keeping up with Clevedon Castle for forty years, she was quite delighted with only eight bedrooms, a full stable, and a garden that challenged Kew. And her bees. It did not do to neglect the bees. Whom Georgie still had to tell.

"Mama and Papa are interviewing for another tutor for the boys."

There was another impatient huff above the lilacs. "Your father should never be involved. For a man in politics, he is woeful at reading people."

"Which is why Mama is involved. And me." Georgie rubbed at her temple, which had begun to ache. "Can the little girls not be enough for now?"

"Only you can know that, child. But I wouldn't expect a man to be very patient with your restrictions."

"But why?! Why cannot I have something of my own? We women have nothing! Not our money, not our belongings. Even our bodies end up in service to the children we bear. Not to mention our home, which is not our own. We are only allowed to live in it until our son finds another woman to take charge. We are mere visitors in our own lives!"

At that, her grandmama not only straightened, she came over and sat next to Georgie. Cradling the clippers in one hand, she took Georgie's hand in the other, and Georgie saw how wrinkled and sinewy her grandmother's hand had grown, the joints knobby and angular. Worn, like the graying of her once blonde hair.

"How did he react when you made such a bold statement?"

Georgie sighed. "He was actually quite nice about it. I don't know if that *largesse* will last. But I at least have a bit of a window. He is taking a trip right after the marriage."

Grandmama nodded. "Might be best. With only one household to manage you might just find the time for that direction you claim to want. Do you know what you think you want, or is it just a supposition?"

"I might have some ideas."

"Do they have to do with that visit you make every Friday?"

This time Georgie shared a conspiratorial smile. "Oh, I think it might."

Her grandmama patted her hand. "Just remember. The decision is yours on how you go forward. If you respect this man and think you could love him, then fight for your place next to him. Begin as you mean to go on."

Georgie sighed. "That sentiment terrifies me even more than it reassures me."

"Well, here is another. There are ways to prevent becoming *enceinte*."

Georgie stared at her exceptionally proper grandmama, who was suddenly grinning back at her.

"That is what he said," Georgie retorted. "Truly? You know them?"

"Child," the old woman said with a squeeze of the hand, "We women have been taking care of each other for a long time now. It is simply your turn."

"Can you guarantee it?"

Her grandmama sighed. "No. But it certainly lessens the chance. We'll retire to the stillroom when we finish here."

Georgie blinked, feeling a bit stupid. "Er, you don't still need..."

Her grandmama had a way with a raised eyebrow herself. "Be sensible, child. I am not the only woman in my house, though, am I?" She shrugged. "Or my village, come to think of it. My still room is for everyone, as you know. That doesn't mean merely poultices and cough remedies."

Georgie shook her head. "I never guessed."

"I told you. We women must take care of each other." She spent a moment considering the old clippers in her hand before turning back to Georgie. Georgie was surprised to see color on her normally pale white cheeks. "Something else, which I suspect your young man knows quite well already. Something I suspect your mother will not think to share with you. You can share love in many ways that don't risk conception. Quite lovely ways, in fact. When you trust him, ask."

Even though Georgie never blushed, she was certain she was fire engine red. "Love? Who said anything about love? Grandmama, I have barely known him a week."

"But there is attraction."

"I wouldn't...."

Grandmama gave her quite a look, her one eyebrow raised in challenge. "Child, please do not try to convince me nothing happened out on that balcony."

Georgie ducked her head, her body remembering all too well what had happened on that balcony.

"For now," her grandmother gently informed her, "attraction will suffice. He is a good man. You are the best of my grandchildren—" Chuckling, she leaned closer. "Although try not to let any of them know."

Even Georgie smiled at that. At one time or another grandmama had named every one of her grandchildren as favorites.

"Trust me on this, Georgianna. This will set the tone for your marriage."

Georgie sighed. "I'm not quite sure I have the courage."

Grandmama patted her hand. "Of course, you do. Because you will want too much to know. I will tell you this much, my sweet girl. A good man will see to your pleasure with his hands and mouth and oh, especially his arms, which can hold you up when you feel you have nothing left in you."

Again, Georgie found herself stunned silent, clear images racing through her brain of Grey doing that very thing. "Grandmama," she finally said with a sigh and a shake of her head, "you are a never-ending font of wisdom."

Her grandmama just smiled and patted her hand. "It is what grandmamas are for. One final piece of wisdom. Do not allow him to leave you without assuring his own pleasure."

Georgie managed to open her mouth but found she could think of nothing to say.

Her grandmother flashed the grin of a much younger woman and tapped Georgie's cheek. "You may not know what is involved, but I assure you he does."

"And it doesn't involve...?"

"Not necessarily." Another tap, and her grandmother pulled a key from her pocket. "Now. You still have time to tend to your area of the garden before you go. But before that—" Standing, she walked to the hives. "You need to tell the bees your news. Come."

And Georgie followed her, walking slowly so as not to seem a threat to the hive. The buzzing was such a comforting sound, a hymn of contentment and industry. She loved the bees her Grandmama had introduced her to and cherished the privilege of being in their world.

As the owner of the property, Grandmama tapped the nearest hive with the house key, as she always did to announce herself. "We have news in our house, my friends," she said, her voice almost as melodious as the bees. "Come listen."

Georgie waited long enough to believe the bees might have paused in their endeavors to listen.

"I am to be married," she said just as quietly, the words suddenly portentous. "His name is Peter Greyville, Lord Coleford. But I call him Grey. When the ceremony is done, I will return with him and a piece of the cake. All right?"

With the music of the bees in her ears, her grandmother's hand holding hers, and the spring morning bursting with life around her, Georgie felt that this moment sealed her fate and future. She had told the bees. It must be real.

Now she just had to find a way not to lose herself to it.

10

———

Three days later she was standing back before the hives, this time holding Grey's hand and bearing a piece of wedding cake. For all the anxiety over it, the wedding had turned out to be a bit of an anticlimax. Grey had obtained a special license that allowed them to marry right away at St. Mary Magdalene's, her Grandmama's home parish in Richmond, where it had been assumed there would be less notoriety. Not to mention the fact that Grandmama demanded it, stating she hadn't the energy to deal with the fuss and bustle at the more fashionable St. George's in Mayfair. Georgie's mother had ruthlessly limited the invitations to only family, which was quite large enough to fill the homely brick church, even without Grey's family who hadn't the time to make it down from Tewkesbury.

Georgie had been relieved. She had never been one to long for a big wedding. Any wedding at all, truthfully. But under the circumstances a big celebration would have done no more than increase her feeling of panic. This way she hadn't had to stand before the altar for more than a few minutes. She hadn't even minded the few bystanders who had gathered on the street to see her enter and leave the church in her cream dotted muslin dress, green spencer, and green-lined bonnet.

Charlie and Eddie stood up as her dual maids of honor, while Amelia and Sophie acted as official bridesmaids. Georgie had to admit that it had been a real joy to see those little girls so excited and awed by the whole thing, especially wearing the brand-new dresses Grey had bought for them in pale pink merino with a bit of Honiton lace. As for Grey, his friend Rob Glenn did the duty of standing up for him, both resplendent in the sharp scarlet and gold of the First Royal Dragoons.

And now, standing in Grandmama's garden with the dowager in her regal purple, her lion-headed cane on one side, and the smartly uniformed Grey on the other, Georgie was faced with her next task. Her cousins stood behind her, as familiar and comfortable with the process as she, each holding the hand of a wide-eyed little girl, whom Georgie had instructed in the tradition while they sat beside her holding *her* hands, just that morning, weaving their way more tightly into the fabric of her life. Making her feel at once more joyful and more cornered. Which made her even more frustrated because she should have been able to freely adore them.

Once again, Grandmama tapped on the first hive with her house key. "We have news in our house, my friends. Come listen."

Tugging on Grey's hand, Georgie brought him a step closer as she reached over and laid the cake at the base of the hive.

"As I promised, my friends. Here is my new husband Peter Greyville, Lord Coleford, whom I call Grey. Please say he is welcome in the family."

For the bees' part, they circled overhead a few times and then returned to the hive.

"Good," Grandmama said with a solemn nod. "Then when it

is my time, your husband may accompany you to share the news."

Georgie opened her mouth to protest, but one look from her grandmother quelled her.

"Now let us go in," the old woman said with a thump of her cane. "I don't know about you, but I have been looking forward to my own piece of wedding cake."

Georgie took in a rather shuddery breath and prepared to face a swarm of Packhams. She could already see the younger members crowded by the back windows waiting for her.

"May we say hello, too?" she heard behind her.

She turned to see her grandmother considering the two little girls now holding hands with each other. Georgie knew how frightening her grandmother could be. Lord knows the old woman could ruthlessly crush the pretensions of the unworthy on a ballroom floor and sway the vote of an MP with a single raised eyebrow.

But young Sophie stood straight and tall before her, and never even flinched when Grandmama stepped her way, the thump of her cane a statement. Georgie ached with pride.

"Both of you?" the dowager asked, looking from Sophie to Amelia, who was looking to her big sister for direction.

"Yes, please," Sophie said in her best grown-up voice, even though Georgie could hear the faint tremor. Amelia just nodded, making the pink ribbons in her hair bounce.

Georgie also felt Grey instinctively move toward the girls. One squeeze of his hand held him still. She looked over at him and gave a surreptitious wink. She had grown up around the dowager, after all, and knew that little girls were never her targets.

After a moment's consideration, the old woman passed off her cane to Georgie and held out her hands. Amelia gave Sophie a glance and then both girls advanced to accept the invitation. Georgie realized she was beaming.

"My friends," Grandmama said to the hives, "I also have some new friends I would like you to know. And they wish to know you. This is Lady Sophie Greyville—make your curtsy, child." Sophie gave a very credible curtsy. "And this is Lady Amelia Greyville."

Amelia's curtsy was a bit more wobbly, but her smile was huge. "Hello, bees," she sang. "Will you be our friends?"

And as if they all expected an answer, everyone turned back to the hives. There seemed to be a pause, and then, quite wonderfully, a swarm of bees came to swirl over the girls' heads. And rather than be afraid, Sophie and Amelia giggled up at them in delight.

The dance was done, the bees returned to the hives, and Georgie felt Grey relax beside her.

"Amazing."

She grinned. "It is, isn't it? But now I think you need some champagne."

Letting go of her hand, Grey turned to the girls. "I believe a thank you is in order, young ladies. I suspect you have been given a great honor."

"Indeed, you have," Georgie assured them. "When my brother Michael tried to introduce himself, he was stung on the head. But he wasn't nearly as polite as you girls."

"He was a beast," Charlie assured them. "But no worse than my brother Gabe."

"Or Rafe," Eddie agreed.

"Thank you, bees," Sophie sang out as both girls offered another curtsy. "We are most honored."

"We like you," Amelia assured them, then turned to her uncle.

"You were very polite too, Uncle Grey," she assured him. "But you need to bow."

His grin was sudden and bright, doing strange things to Georgie's heart.

"You are correct, of course," he said.

Turning, he gave the hives his best court bow. Everyone else curtsied, and then it was time to celebrate.

"I must admit," he said as he watched the girls scamper after the dowager toward the house, "I have attended quite a few weddings. One in a gypsy camp and another under artillery fire. I still believe mine own is the most unique of them all."

Georgie meant to follow everyone in. Suddenly, though, she couldn't move. Her chest felt so tight, as if acid were being squeezed into her lungs. It was the bees, she realized. She had actually suspected that they would react badly to the news, refusing to fly or attacking her for being foolish and unwise and asking for sorrow with her commitment. But the bees buzzed happily on, courting the flowers like hesitant swains and filling the soft spring day with music. Which should have made Georgie feel better. Which did, in one way. She was taking the first step in creating a lasting marriage. She loved those little girls, and she liked and respected Grey. Which in any other marriage would have been the answer to a prayer.

But for her, it also meant that she had walked right into a closed room at the very moment she should have been escaping out the doors. She had worked so hard to earn her freedom, and she had just given it away. Now, she suspected, she would never know what she was truly made of. What she could have been. Who. She would end up being what she always was, the one who took care of everyone else. It made her feel as if she was struggling to breathe.

"Are you all right?" Grey asked quietly, slipping his hand into hers.

Her first reaction was to bat it away. She didn't, of course. "Fine," she assured him with a bland smile, afraid that he could see all too well that she wasn't *quite* fine.

Grey turned Georgie toward him at the edge of the patio as the rest of their group trooped into the house, chatting and laughing. "But not happy."

She looked up to see that there was a furrow between those intense seawater eyes of his. He wasn't just asking out of custom.

"I'm still getting used to the idea," she admitted, wishing she could just savor the harsh beauty of her husband, that she could run her fingers along that soft mouth that belied the strength of jaw and forehead. That she could kiss those ghostly eyes closed and simply breathe in the open-air scent of him. But panic was not a very romantic feeling. "It is a lot to manage all at once," she said instead. "Marriage, motherhood, decorating, marchioness-ing. And you going off in—"

He went very still, his frown suddenly apologetic.

She waited, but he didn't answer. Her heart plummeted. "What?"

He dipped his head, took a breath. Had the courage to face her again. "I'm sorry. I was hoping we would not have to deal with this at least until we enjoyed our wedding."

That robbed her of what breath she had left. "You're leaving."

It took him a second when she could almost hear the thud of his heart, sense the new weight on his shoulders. But finally, he gave her a rueful smile. "You suffer from an excess of intelligence, Wife. I suspect I'll never be able to hide anything from you."

"Something to remember," she retorted, even as she felt his news weigh on her as well. As her heart ached harder for her future. For *their* future, all four of them.

"There have been some developments in the case I am investigating, new very important questions," he said very quietly. "We need answers, and it is my job to find them as soon as possible." His smile grew sad. "My boat leaves in two days."

Her first instinct was to tell him not to worry. That she would take care of everything. That she could handle whatever needed to be done while he was gone so he could face his task with a clear head and heart. It was, after all, what she had always done. What had always been expected of her.

Not this time, she decided. She might do as she always did— she would, of course—but she could not think of one reason to sound happy about it. It would serve him right if she told him exactly what she thought. At the top of her voice. While dragging her fingernails across his face.

She never would, though. She was too well-trained.

But oh, for a seething hot minute, she was tempted.

"What?" he nudged, his expression just a bit whimsical.

She scowled, wishing she didn't already like him.

But what could she do, really? What could she ever have done?

"Husband, I believe it is past time to drink a surfeit of champagne."

He dropped a kiss on her forehead and one on her knuckles. "Wife, I believe I will join you."

GREY WAS ASSURED that the wedding breakfast was a classic Packham celebration. If that was true, he was shamefully grateful he was escaping in two days. He couldn't imagine how Georgie not only withstood the cacophony but seemed to relish it. She had children crawling all over her, at least two older women grilling her about something, and house staff dropping by to check with her about some preparation or another. Her gleaming mahogany hair, usually so sleek and tidy, was coming a bit undone, and she had what looked like a raspberry jam stain on her beautiful white dress. And she was laughing. He wasn't sure he had ever heard her laugh. And no more than an hour or so earlier he could have sworn she was near violence.

Even so, even with the laughter and gleam in her eyes, oddly enough, she sat there like the eye of a hurricane, the only calm in the room. The center around which all else spun. It was her special gift, he thought, a sense not so much of tranquility in the madness, but of a lodestone which drew everything to it. He wondered if she even realized it.

He was fascinated by it, by her. He wanted to be pulled into her orbit, to let her calm him as she did the little ones too enlivened by too much sugar and too many co-conspirators to settle. He wanted to see what that magic could work on a man who had seen and done too much and was about to head off to face more. He selfishly wanted her to focus all that magic on him.

Was he selfish enough to wish he could convince her that it might be fun to delve beneath that air of calm she wore like a protective cloak to find the furnace beneath? He knew it was there. He had tasted it on her lips, heard it in the rasp of her breath as they had kissed, traced it with his thumb across the furious pace of the pulse there at the base of her sleek throat. He could strip that cloak bare; he knew it. He could waken the sleeping sensuality that had scorched him the two times he had kissed her. Gods and little green fish, but he wanted to be inside of her. He wanted to hear her scream his name, wanted...

Grey dragged in a ragged breath and looked off before he gave himself away even to the children. Maybe he could talk her into leaving. Surely, they had spent enough time entertaining all the Packhams. Tossing back his latest glass of champagne, he headed her way.

He'd only made it three steps when a young man stepped into his path. Blast. Georgie's brother. It had to be. He had those same green, green eyes and that broad forehead. Thirteen, maybe fourteen years old, his limbs still out of proportion to his thin torso, ankles, and wrists visible beyond the hem of his suit, and shoes completely outsized for his age. He was frowning with intent.

Grey ruthlessly reined in his previous aim. He wasn't getting to his wife as soon as he thought.

"My lord..." The boy began, his voice balanced perilously close to breaking.

"Grey," Grey corrected him, trying not to notice that beyond the boy, Georgie had her head back laughing at one of her cousins, baring that delicious white throat. Taunting him without even knowing it.

The boy blinked, assessed, and gave a nod of concession. "Grey. I am Georgie's brother Harry."

Dragging his attention back to the task at hand, Grey held out his hand. "Not an archangel?"

The boy's face cracked into a quick grin as he took it and shook. "No, sir. By the time they got to me they were down to Zachariel, and my mother drew the line. But I am Georgie's oldest brother here. Our brother Michael is still on the Continent."

Grey nodded. He knew exactly where brother Michael was.

Harry cleared his throat, took a look at his overlarge shoes, and sucked in a breath. "As the oldest brother here, the duty falls to me to speak to you."

Grey badly wanted to smile. He knew better. There was nothing more devastating to a young man's pride than to be laughed at for what he considered to be a serious matter. Quashing his less elevated desires in order to focus on the matter at hand, Grey settled for a single nod.

The boy nodded back, dislodging a thick lock of hair the same color as Georgie's to fall across his forehead. He swept it back and took another breath. "I know the circumstances of this marriage," he finally said, voice squeaking only a little. "And I understand the need for expediency, to protect Georgie's good name."

Grey nodded again.

Finally, the boy gathered the courage to meet him eye-to-eye, and Grey was impressed with the determination he saw there. Suddenly Harry Packham looked older than thirteen.

"You haven't had time to realize how special my sister is," Harry said. "Or how her family feels about her. But since Michael isn't here, I am the one who will tell you that if you hurt my sister in any way, physically, emotionally, or mentally, I will probably not act the gentleman about it." He shrugged. "I'll probably kill you."

It was Grey's turn to blink in surprise. Not a thirteen-year-old at all. Not only for the excellent defense of his sister, but the suspicion that he really meant what he said about killing Grey. Grey had survived the last ten years by making lightning assessments of situations and characters. Without a doubt, he knew this minute that Georgie was so precious to this boy that he would act without any remorse at all. And probably do it with a fair bit of competence.

"Harry," he said, quite seriously. "You are quite right. I haven't had the time to learn what I want to know about your sister. But I do know that it will be my greatest honor and pleasure to spend my life correcting that lack. I am already awed at her devotion to you all, her good sense, her humor, her patience. If I do hurt her, I will deserve whatever punishment you mete out."

If he thought that would be the last of the threats, he was as wrong as assuming he could winkle his wife away for some time alone. One by one, various children waylaid him and promised dire retribution if he hurt their Georgie. Then the aunts, an uncle named Samson Packham, who evidently was married to Lady Charlie's mother, Lady Clevedon's intimidating twin, and who ran the estates—who also had a bad habit of slapping a fellow on the back and smiling while mentioning shooting accidents—the twin aunt herself who just glared, and finally both of the other kings.

"Don't bother," he told Georgie's cousin Charlie, his hand up. "I've already been threatened by everybody here but your mother's pug." He motioned to the bright hue of her hair. "If that is any indication, at least three of them belonged to your family."

She gave him a gimlet glare. "So long as you got the message."

If he hadn't by the time he'd gone through all hundred-twenty-seven Packhams crowded into these rooms, Georgie's mother came along to put a coda on the message by patting him on the cheek like one of her children.

"You'll do fine," she assured him with that serene smile of hers. "Fine."

He couldn't help it. "Because if I don't?"

Her smile grew wider and less serene. "We're not called the Mad Packhams for nothing."

He had already figured that out. There was nothing left to do but nod and smile.

He finally ran out of patience, lobster patties, and champagne and headed over to dig Georgie out from under the various Packham progeny. Evidently he had one more confrontation to make it through, though.

He had set his champagne flute down on a table by the back doors where he could envision escape, when a boy of about seven marched up to him as if on parade, holding the hand of a wide-eyed little girl in a spring-green dress.

"I'm Geoffrey, sir," he said with a very adult bow, which Grey found himself returning. "This is my sister Emily. You were with the First Royal Dragoons?"

It took Grey a second to follow the sudden shift of subject, even as the dark-haired little boy bounced a bit on his feet and young Emily watched with wide eyes as she sucked her thumb.

Grey accorded the young man every dignity. "I still am for a bit, yes."

"And you were at Torres Vedras and Ciudad Rodrigo and Badajoz?"

Grey wasn't sure whether he was impressed or worried. The boy even had the pronunciations down. "I was."

The boy's eyes lit like jack-o-lanterns. The little girl, standing quietly by, sucked that thumb and nodded, as if she knew of what he was speaking.

"Will you tell me of them?" Geoffrey asked, coming up again on his toes. "My brother Michael will not. He won't talk of any of it, which I consider ever so unfair. I must get all my information from Georgie."

Grey found he wasn't surprised by either fact. He didn't want to talk about it either. And he was quite certain Georgie did know everything young Geoffrey had been taught.

"Horse mad or army mad?" he asked with a small smile.

The boy grinned like a pirate. "I shall replace my brother Michael as the family military man when he has to come home and be earl."

That almost broke Grey's composure. He wondered if the current earl knew that his bloodthirsty progeny already had him planted. "I see."

"I was hoping to speak with someone who had gone up with the Forlorn Hope at Badajoz, but, well..."

"Sorry. Dragoons don't seem to have the necessary skills."

Thank a merciful God. He could still hear the screaming.

"What *did* you do there?"

Grey never would have called the Dowager Countess an angel, but she certainly saved him then.

"Not today, you barbarous little monster," she snapped, waving her cane at the boy, as if pushing him off. "The Marquess must go now. His bride awaits."

She gave him a look that said *whether he wants to or not*. Thank God and little fishes, he thought.

He gave her his best non-threatening smile. "Thank you for letting me know."

She was scowling, but her eyes twinkled. "Your girls will stay with us for tonight. Give you two a chance to get to know each other."

Which meant she already knew about his change of plans. He suspected it would be pointless to ask her how.

More importantly, she was encouraging his time alone with her granddaughter. His body reacted predictably to the offer. Alone with Georgie Packham, the focus of her prodigious attention. Maybe he could convince her of her mistake after all. Maybe she would enjoy a bit of seduction...

He got a swat from the cane across his shins to remind him of his manners.

"Thank you, my lady," he said with a very proper bow. "I'll be off then, shall I?"

"Excellent idea. On your way, you might ask Georgianna what she and I discussed the other day."

Grey was considering a follow-up question, but she was already turning to her young grandson. "Come along and harass your tutor. That's what we pay him for."

Reaching down, she took not only young Emily by the hand, but Geoffrey, Grey suspected so the boy wouldn't go running after him demanding stories.

But the boy surprised them.

"Sir? One more thing."

Grey stopped just short of sighing. "Yes, lad."

"Take good care of my sister."

Good God, did every Packham have murder on their minds? It said something that the dowager didn't even blink.

"Or you'll kill me?"

The boy's grin was complacent. "Oh, no sir. I'm too short. I'd never reach you."

Grey couldn't help laughing. "Finally, somebody who is thinking this through."

The boy shrugged. "I'd put fleas in your bed."

After that, all Grey could do was look over to his new wife, who was hugging Amelia. "Wife?" he called. "I fear we must leave before your family does me in."

Considering the fact that the Archangels hadn't even had a chance to throw in their threats, he wasn't quite sure he was joking. For the first time he wondered if it might be safer for him in France.

11

It was inevitable that the goodbyes were long and protracted. Georgie hugged everyone—some of the little ones twice—bore up under her aunt's reminder that she shouldn't let the Packham name down, and accepted assurances of support and defense if she needed it from several children. She and Grey assured Sophie and Amelia that they would be picked up the next day and were pleased to see them skip off with the girls from her home. She wiped off tears from some little cheeks and battled a few of her own. But finally, Grandmama's cane came down with an unmistakable crack, and everyone stepped back to allow Grey to hand her into an elegant barouche, emblazoned with the Coleford crest and pulled by beautifully paired bays. The man did know how to make an impression, Georgie decided, settling her skirts around her in the forward-facing seat.

Oh, blast, she thought, brushing at the rich red streak she discovered on her bodice. *Shelly shared her tart after all.*

"It's charming," Grey assured her with a wry smile as he settled in across from her. "You might start a fashion."

She scowled and wiped again to no avail. "I never can escape unscathed from that band of scapegraces."

Giving up on the stain, she offered one final wave to her family as the coach lurched to a start, laid her hands back in her lap, and took in a breath. She was suddenly so tired, the nervous energy that had been propelling her along dying a jagged death. She would have slumped if she hadn't caught something enticing in the breath she took. Cedar. Citrus. Leather. Wind.

By God, he smelled good. She was so incredibly relieved that her new husband didn't smell like a town beau. He smelled like strength and comfort and escape. He smelled like a man who had claimed his place in the world. She blinked and almost grinned to herself. Whatever the blazes that meant.

"You look tired," he said.

She looked up and forgot what she was going to say. For the first time in days, she finally had a moment to simply take in the rugged beauty of his features. The strength. The spare lines and crow's feet that bracketed his lovely eyes. The scar slashing his forehead that spoke of what he had survived. Lord save her, she could simply soak for hours in the sight of that hard, fine face like lifesaving water. Lap it up with her tongue.

Just not now, she thought, fighting another smile. *I might frighten the poor man.*

"I am quite well," she automatically answered. Then she did grin. "Well, all right. I admit I have been burning the candles at both ends getting today put together to Grandmama's exacting expectations."

"*You* did."

She nodded and surreptitiously took in another breath so she could enjoy the open-air scent of him. "Mama and Papa have been entertaining some of the foreign dignitaries who came in for the victory celebrations. Besides, as Grandmama so aptly put it, it was my wedding. If I let someone else take over, I would have no right to complain when it didn't turn out the way I wanted."

"Did it?" he asked, laying his arm across the seat behind him. "Turn out the way you wanted?"

She considered the question. "Well, considering the fact that I have never been the type to fantasize about what my wedding should be, I imagine it was. We were there, the bees were there, and my family was there. I'm sorry yours wasn't."

He shrugged. "My family is not nearly as close as yours. Besides, in all honesty I must admit that I had enough to withstand with just your family threatening my health if I did not make you supremely happy. I don't believe I could have tolerated my sister's badgering on top of it."

Her chest ached with the news. "All of them?"

His reluctant grin was a delight. "Even down to a moppet named Emily, who sucked her thumb and nodded as a ferocious tyke named Geoffrey threatened me with an infestation of fleas if I made you unhappy."

She couldn't help it. She laughed. "Yes, I'm afraid the Packhams are a bit bloodthirsty."

"That should not have surprised me. After all, I know the Archangels."

She grinned, pulling off her gloves finger by finger. "They hold nothing on the younger lot. Especially Geoffrey. He is preparing himself to be the best cavalry officer in the history of the British army."

That was when Georgie realized that they had turned off Sheen Road which would have taken them to the Putney Bridge over the Thames and back to London.

"Are you kidnapping me?" she asked, looking out to see that they were heading in a more southerly direction.

Grey took his own look as if verifying her claim. "Rob

insisted that we not spend our wedding night in the townhouse with its rather gloomy décor."

"Gloomy?" She laughed. "It is positively gothic. I wonder you haven't gone screaming into the street."

"The bedrooms are even worse than the public rooms you saw. I'm hoping that one of the passions you would like to indulge in is decorating."

Just the idea of a bedroom suddenly squeezed her breath. She had demanded a *marriage blanc*, but he hadn't promised. And he was so large. So...so...what? He seemed to pulse with energy, even sitting quietly, his arm lying across the back of his seat, his uniform stretched over those broad shoulders, the size of him across from her filling her vision. If he refused to honor her request, she had no legal recourse. She had no protection. Why didn't she feel more threatened?

Because, she realized with a whoosh of held breath, as little time as she'd known him, she trusted him. How amazing. She just wished she didn't suddenly wonder about what Grandmama had brought up. Could she really enjoy Grey's hands, his mouth, his embrace enough to chance it? She had certainly enjoyed the kisses they had already shared. Enjoyed? *Delighted* in. Her body had hummed for hours, and he hadn't even let her enjoy his hands.

It had been so much easier to ignore when she had other things to distract her. And wasn't inhaling the very enticing scent of her husband.

Her *husband.*

"Georgie?"

She found herself blinking. Good heavens, her body was humming again, stealing her concentration. And he sat so close, his legs long enough to rest alongside hers. How could legs be so warm? How could they make *her* so warm?

She coughed, struggling to pull her thoughts back into order.

If she couldn't keep her mind away from those pictures Grand-mama had painted, she would never even make it through the carriage ride.

"Then what is our destination?" she asked, her voice just a bit hoarse.

Grey didn't seem to notice. "Rob has a little cottage along Putney Heath he said we could use. He sent word to the housekeeper."

She frowned. "A cottage? Who usually lives there? Please tell me it is not his *cher amie*."

Grey's laughter was delighted. "Absolutely not. Believe it or not, our Rob is a bit of a birder. According to him, the Heath abounds in migratory fowl, not to mention butterflies and the like."

"I imagine it does. I'm simply trying to envision our Rob sitting still long enough not to startle flocks of pigeons. And giving silent thanks we're not invading a love nest of some sort. That would be just a bit uncomfortable."

"A very polite way of putting it," he retorted. "Vile places."

She couldn't help gigging him a bit. "So, you have never had a *pied-a-terre* of your own?"

She surprised a smile out of him. "Would have been a waste. I spent the last ten years trotting around the world after the Beau. Besides, I have suffered other men's ideas of cozy retreats. Spindly furniture no man over ten stone could keep from shattering, and the overwhelming stink of perfume that's been sprinkled over the place like holy water from a Papist. And I cannot believe I'm even discussing this with you."

"It is nigh impossible to avoid the less proper side of society with so many males in the family. But I have a more important question." She was almost afraid to ask. "You have a sensitive nose?"

His scowl was even more endearing than his smile. Blast

him, he was making her body hum *again*. "I'm afraid I do. Oddly enough for one in my profession. But there are some things I simply cannot tolerate. The use of perfume, for instance…"

"To cover up an unwashed body!"

He looked surprised, especially, Georgie suspected, by her enthusiasm. "Well, yes. The season is unbearable for me. All those closed-in spaces with too many people and not enough air."

She nodded enthusiastically. "Especially routs. Too many people crammed into small rooms that get far too hot, and not being able to so much as move. And if Prinny is there, you cannot even open a window. It is absolute torture!"

His eyes lit. "I personally thanked Brummell for bringing bathing into fashion."

She laughed, delighted. "I kissed his hand! You have no idea how difficult it is for a lady to withstand the assault on her sensibilities when dancing. And we are forced to do it! One refusal and we sit out the entire night. And I adore dancing! Do you know the convoluted tactics I have had to employ to avoid certain gentlemen?"

"Too popular," he mourned with a shake of his head. "Such a trial."

She was distracted again. His fingers were stroking the leather seatback behind him. His long, elegant, strong fingers.

If only Grandmama hadn't destroyed her peace of mind. The bloody thing was wandering places it had no business being. Especially when she was also battling an odd exhilaration just from knowing they shared such an odd prejudice.

"Oh, I am not that popular," she said. "More the duty dance type. Well, except for the young ones just out of university who consider me safe training ground."

That brought an eyebrow up.

She huffed. "In perfecting the social arts, you perverse man.

They love to flirt with someone they know won't take them seriously."

"Why not?"

She shrugged. "It might be the fact that I am well known for refusing the unmitigated delight of accompanying certain people of the male persuasion out onto a balcony. Or a library. Or anyplace more evocative than the dinner room." She grinned. "I am also known for my deadly aim with a fan and the heel of my shoe." She shrugged. "And if absolutely necessary, my knee."

He flinched a bit. "And you enjoy this?"

"Defending myself from encroaching men?" She let go another quick grin. "I'm afraid so. Especially their astonished looks."

"You terrify me, Wife."

"Something else to remember," she advised with a nod. "But the boys learning how to go on in public? Actually, I enjoy them quite a lot. I feel I am performing a service for my sisters, who will benefit from their dance partners gaining a little polish. It is something you will allow, of course, knowing how innocent the interactions are."

"It is?"

"Of course. Every married woman must have her *cicisbeos*."

"May I at least grumble a bit, glare at one or two, just so they know I'm paying attention?"

Blast him, his easy smile stirred a brew of delight in her chest. She could quite well come to love this kind of banter.

"Only three grumbles per ball," she insisted. "More if it is to help me discourage one of the encroaching. Or the reeking."

"Now that," he said with a grave nod of his head, "would be my pleasure. After all, if you dance with one of them, you might bring that olfactory insult home with you. And that I will not allow."

They were both grinning now. "Oh, good. I will enjoy having a co-conspirator. The other kings aren't nearly as understanding."

He gave her a bow. "It will be my honor."

"You smell quite lovely, by the way," she murmured, leaning a bit closer.

That incited another risen eyebrow. "I do my humble best. I also quite appreciate the sense of a summer garden you carry with you. Very...evocative."

"Why, thank you. My friend Anastasia helps me make up the scent especially for me." She sighed a bit. "She says it reflects who I wish to be rather than what I am."

"You wish to be gorse?"

"I wish to be free to wander the woods back home, or possibly the moors, the headlands."

"To walk?"

"Or ride. Just the time and freedom to lose myself in a spring day without dragging all the family challenges along with me."

"Alone?"

"Yes." She closed her eyes and sighed. "Alone."

Although suddenly she thought she might not mind the company of a certain ex-soldier. Holding her hand, laughing with her as they watched rabbits skip away and red squirrels chide them from the plane trees. She had never once felt the need for company, not even her cousins. It frightened her that her dreams might be changing without her permission.

"Well," he said, "You are in luck. From what I understand, at least three of my estates have quite a bit of land to tromp over. Two are on coasts. Coleford Abbey itself is near Gloucester. Painswick Park, I'm afraid, is more inland."

"Oh, blast," she retorted, sitting up straight as she remembered the ball from the other night. "I forgot. Do you really have an estate in Wales? Will we truly be forced to rusticate there and challenge the ghosts for sleeping space while you're away?"

"Llanthony Court," he said with a nod. "Sadly, though. No ghosts. At least, none who have importuned me. And no. We can save that pleasure for later. "

But that brought up another rather urgent question. "I haven't even thought," she admitted. "Where *do* you expect us to reside while you're away?"

He did her the kindness of considering that a moment. "Until we can face the estates together to determine what needs to be done—which I'm afraid is undoubtedly a lot—why don't you stay in London and concentrate on bringing some life into the townhouse? We'll make the grand tour when I get back."

She nodded. "We can at least rid the place of that horrid, musty, leaky roof smell that follows one from room to room."

He scowled. "Noticed that, did you? I tried to have Mrs. Chalmers bring in fresh and dried flowers, but that is again like—"

"Perfume on an unwashed body."

Wincing, he nodded. "It has put me completely off my feed." His sudden grin was rueful. "Except for cinnamon buns, I'm afraid. Many more of those and I won't fit my uniform."

"They are quite tasty."

For a long moment there was no sound but the unhurried clop of the horses, no movement but the slow stroke of Grey's thumb against the seat back. Georgie didn't feel that hum, now. It was worse. She felt a welling in her chest, as if emotion had volume and weight, filling her, unsettling her, threatening her balance.

How dare he be so kind? So thoughtful? How dare he understand her insecurities better than her entire family?

"Will you miss it?" she asked.

She had no idea where that came from. She was sure it was

the most insensitive thing she had ever asked. But suddenly it seemed important. He was not having to upend only her life, after all, with his inheritance. And she suspected his answer would tell her more about him than anything she'd seen or heard so far.

Besides, his revelations had exposed her far too much. She needed a diversion from the raw emotions that roiled in her chest.

Oddly he didn't seem to think she was too forward. "The military?" He nodded. "I will. I know it sounds odd, but there is so much in that life that is satisfying. The camaraderie, the action, the sense of accomplishment." He shrugged, as if he realized he might have said more than he'd intended. "The satisfaction of training a great horse."

"The horses your family breeds."

He nodded. "Prime hunters and chargers. As I said before, when my father died my sister and her husband took over. They're quite a pair for breeding them. All I must do is ride them."

She nodded and took a considered look at her hands. "Would you be willing to speak to Geoffrey about that life?"

He frowned. "I will not glamorize it."

She sighed in relief. "Exactly what I had hoped. Geoffrey is like most little boys. He only sees the adventure. He has no idea of the cost."

"Nor should he. He's a gruesome little beast, isn't he? Wanted me to tell him of the Forlorn Hope."

She scowled. "I told him you would not have participated. I'm correct, aren't I?"

"You are. Thank all the heavenly hosts. Cavalry charges were quite enough to disorder my nerves."

She was nodding in commiseration when a jaw-cracking

yawn caught her by surprise. "Oh. Excuse me. I usually behave better than this."

Instead of answering he simply changed seats and tucked himself in next to her. Too close. Georgie caught herself just shy of jumping up. Getting away. At least changing seats to escape the inevitable hum of attraction. The melting, seething energy that pulsed off him that was far too compelling.

But that energy was simply too delicious to escape. She wanted to snuggle up to it like a fire on a raw autumn afternoon.

His smile was oddly gentle as he laid his arm over her shoulder and drew her close. "Shhhh. I have no designs on your person other than to let you rest. Wouldn't you like to relax for just a few minutes? Surely your back is aching from keeping it so rigid."

She sputtered at him. "Don't be absurd. I told you. I'm fine."

But she couldn't quite move herself to throw his arm off or push away from his shoulder where he urged her to rest her head.

"Of course, you are," he said. "You're always fine. But for this little time when nobody can see you but me, why don't you allow yourself to be tired? Why don't you let someone else take care of you for once?"

If he thought that should soften her up, he was quite mistaken. All it did was stiffen her spine even further. "Don't be absurd."

He used his other hand to tuck her hair behind her ear. "You said that already. What is absurd about wanting to offer my wife a bit of comfort?"

"You'll expect me to get used to it. And then you'll leave."

For a moment he didn't answer. But he didn't let her go either, and his arm, lying so comfortably over her shoulder was soothing in a way she couldn't define. He was casually stroking her arm with those long, elegant fingers, and suddenly she could hear Grandmama's voice in her head. "...a good man will see to your pleasure with his hands and mouth and oh, especially his arms, which can hold you up when you feel you have nothing left in you."

It wasn't fair. She couldn't allow herself to fall prey to his casual comfort when it couldn't last. She was so very tired of being yanked back and forth for other people's convenience.

"You're right," he finally acknowledged, pulling her just a little closer. "I'm afraid I will leave. But I will always come back."

She turned her head to meet him eye-to-eye. "Is that a promise you can make?"

He didn't smile. "The war is over. The worst danger I shall be in at the embassy is from French chefs and the Beau's temper. But I've never known him to toss a subordinate off a balcony. Now, lay your head back and rest a bit."

She wasn't quite ready. And they had just turned in through iron gates. "We're going into Richmond Park. Isn't that the wrong way?"

This time he did smile and stroke a finger down her cheek. "I might have told John Coachman to take us around the park a few times."

"You did? Why?"

"Well, I thought you might like a few minutes to get used to the idea of being my bride before you are forced to assume the mantle of Marchioness of Coleford. The servants at Rob's place aren't ours, but they will be lined up to welcome a Marchioness, you may be sure of it."

She not only laid her head back, she groaned. "Oh. That's right. I don't suppose I could just ignore all that."

"Not a chance. And then you shall have to face the staff at Coleford House tomorrow. My people have been waiting a very long time to greet an ally in the fight to civilize me."

That got her eyes back open, even though she'd finally given up and laid her head against his shoulder. His broad, comfortable shoulder. Blast it. "I have no intention of wasting my time on such a pointless endeavor."

"You like me as the savage I am?"

"No. I despair of you ever having the sense to assume your dignity. It might have something to do with how you deal with those little girls."

"*Our* little girls."

That brought her head back up. "Is that to be how we go forward?"

"Should we not? They have been sorely deprived of an actual family their whole lives. I'm afraid my cousins weren't...weren't..."

"Kind? Loving? Christian?"

She knew he heard the anger that still seethed in her over the defensive flinches and miserable self-condemnation from two beautiful little girls.

"All of those," he admitted, his voice heavy. "I haven't even had the courage to ask them yet. I just keep hoping that with enough stability and affection, they'll overcome it."

"Affection and stability never hurt anyone. I'll be happy to lend my support. They are dear little girls."

He sighed, sounding heartsore. "They are. But let us face that difficulty later. For now, why don't we simply enjoy the park? It isn't a moor, but it does have herds of deer and woodlands that I believe still have bluebells, which I will remind you smell lovely."

She smiled and closed her eyes. "That they do."

Usually, she couldn't wait to smell them. She would stand on the bank of that sea of sweet blue tucked into the shadows of an oak forest and simply breathe, storing up the pure rich scent of spring to get her through the summer of whatever trials and tribulations her family tossed at her.

They couldn't this time, though. Could they? She had only Grey's trials and tribulations to contend with, although those would be enough to fill her days more than adequately. Still....

"Did anyone tell you that you have a wonderfully comfortable shoulder?" she murmured, her eyelids too heavy to lift.

"I usually don't allow my comrades to fall asleep on my shoulder."

"Then I feel privileged."

"No," he disagreed. "I am the one who is privileged. I suspect it takes quite a bit for you to trust someone enough to relax this much."

She thought about it and admitted with surprise, "My first time, actually."

Wrapping his arm around her, he pulled her closer. "I suspected as much."

There was a long silence filled with no more than the clop of horse hooves, the rattle of carriage wheels over gravel, the whisper-soft brush of Grey's breath in her hair, the boldening scent of bluebells. And then, as if it were inevitable, she could feel his fingers stroking her hair, releasing showers of sparks all down her back.

"Stop that," she said, although she couldn't quite dredge up the outrage to sound threatening.

"Why?"

Why? Why was his voice so soft, so close to her ear? Why did it seem to multiply those sparks that now skittered through her chest and into her belly?

"Because I'm not quite certain if you mean to wake me or put me to sleep. And we need to settle far too much in too little time to allow me that luxury."

"What do we need to settle?"

She took a breath and sighed, quite certain now that he

meant to wake her, or at least get her undivided attention. He had it, just not the way she thought he wanted.

"I don't remember."

His chuckle resonated through her in the most delicious way. "Can I ask a question?"

"I suppose."

"What have you and your grandmother been talking about?"

Georgie sat up so fast she almost fell right off the seat. "What?"

He shrugged. "She told me to ask you."

Well, she wasn't asleep anymore.

12

———————

It was to be dread then. Anticipation that stirred itself through her like butter into bread dough. Distress, she was certain. Fear, although somehow it felt like exhilaration. Whatever it was, she didn't have the courage to face Grey with it. She stared hard at the little window in the front of the carriage as if the back of the coachie's head fascinated her.

"Is it that frightening?" Grey asked, his voice soft.

Georgie could tell he was smiling. He would, she thought unreasonably. *He probably talks about this sort of thing all the time.*

"I don't know," she finally admitted, trying so hard to keep what distance she could from him. She wanted so badly to curl back up in his arms, close her eyes and pretend her grandmama would never have interfered in her marriage.

"I think you had better tell me," he suggested, taking gentle hold of her hand, "before you expire from nerves."

She instinctively shook her head, but that wouldn't do. She *wanted* to know. She wanted an answer before she did expire from nerves.

Only the question itself was enough on its own, really.

So, she gently pulled her hand free of his, as if that would protect her somehow. "We were...well, we were speaking of this marriage," she said, looking down to where his hand now lay on her thigh. Unable to ignore the elegant grace of those fingers, unwilling to forget the memory of them roaming her body. Hoping suddenly that her grandmother hadn't been wrong.

His voice was gentle. "What about it?"

She couldn't quite face him with her question. Closing her eyes, as if that would protect her from her own brazen behavior, she pulled in an unsteady breath and leapt into the fray.

"She said...she said that there were...em, other ways than...than...what I cannot allow, in which to express our...er, regard for each other."

She felt him go abruptly still and all but jumped out the carriage door, moving or not. Only the lure of that unknown promise, of the memory of those wicked hands held her in place. Only the determination not to be thought a coward by this man who had faced cavalry charges.

"She said you would know." Blast. Her voice sounded so small.

He dipped his head toward her. "I do know," he said quietly, as if afraid he would spook her. "I know several...options you might enjoy immensely. I would very much like to show them to you."

"Without...?" She looked back up at him, needing to see his eyes.

His smile was kinder than she'd expected. "Without."

She wanted to close her eyes again, the only way she could hide. She wanted to stop the carriage and walk away, as if added space would calm her racing heart or dry her palms. She realized she was wiping them on her lovely green pelisse like a deb sitting at her first ball. She hadn't realized how very much she wanted this until he'd asked.

"You can trust me," he murmured, leaning forward so that his mouth was just alongside her ear, his voice almost a purr.

She turned to face him eye-to-eye, needing more than pat assurances. "Can I?"

Rather than answer, he smiled, the kind of smile that made a woman hungry for the feel of it, for the comfort and promise and joy of it. Of him. Lord, if her heart ran off any faster, it would tumble completely out of her chest.

He still didn't answer. He bent towards her, ducking under her bonnet as if he'd been there before, his eyes so clear, so seemingly honest and sure. And he kissed her.

He did not touch her with his hands; didn't wrap both arms around her and hold her up as Grandmama had promised. He met no part of her body but her suddenly sensitive lips. And he courted her. Gently at first, a quick brush, a meeting, a nibble from lips that were impossibly soft and warm. Lips she suddenly wanted to explore herself. So, she leaned in, laying her hand against his chest to find that his heart was suddenly racing almost as fast as hers. Why would that be? He should be used to this kind of thing. She knew better than to think this was his first time sharing a prolonged kiss.

She couldn't help it. She backed away, leaving her hand right where it was against his heart. "Your heart is simply galloping. You cannot be frightened."

His smile was wistful. "Can't I?"

That brought on a scowl. "Don't be—" She shook her head. "I know. I already said that. I am very new to this," she said. "I had assumed you are not."

He finally lifted a hand to stroke her cheek. "Truly? You've never sneaked down a garden path at a ball to enjoy the embrace of some young blade?"

She felt as if all the air in her lungs was caught in her throat. "Not like this."

That just widened his smile. "Good. It's selfish, I know, but I was hoping to be the first to see those amazing green eyes go languorous.

She blinked those green eyes, feeling more and more confused, frustrated, uncertain. "But it's not new to you. Why is your heart beating so fast?"

"Because, my inquisitive wife, it is new with *you.*"

That did not calm any of the turmoil that battered at her. "But..."

"I can see that I didn't sufficiently make my point." Lifting her chin, he stroked the corner of her mouth with his thumb. "We may not...*without*...but I am very anxious to show you how lovely *with* can be."

Even now she couldn't quite escape her logical mind. "In a moving carriage?"

He grinned. "There is something enticing about the sway of a coach."

His eyes were like lights in the shadow, compelling, incandescent. She couldn't seem to look away, even as his thumb strayed, tracing its way down her jaw, her throat, to come to rest on the first button of her pelisse.

"If you allow," he murmured, "I'd dispatch with this. It seems to be in my way."

She opened her mouth to answer and somehow couldn't manage to make a sound. She was still caught in those ice-blue eyes whose pupils had dilated as he spoke. As he used his finger and thumb to ease the button out of its hole and open the material a bit at her throat. As he slid open the next and then the next.

She should have been at least chilled. There was a late afternoon breeze sweeping in through the windows. Thank heavens, was all she could think. It was the only thing keeping her from incinerating on the spot.

His thumb...his fingers stroked along her collarbone, back and forth, inciting showers of chills that tightened her nipples to buds that were suddenly unbearably sensitive against the silk of her dress. Her breasts seemed to grow heavy and taut, just from his touch along her perfectly innocent collarbone, and she realized that if he didn't move that hand soon, she would rip the bodice of her own dress to give him access. Sweet lord, what was he doing to her?

He was bending forward to drop a kiss where his thumb had rested, right at the hollow of her throat. And then...*oh*, was that his tongue? How could he...but he was, licking at her as if sipping up water from the cup of a leaf. And suddenly she lost the strength in her spine. Her body was arching quite without her permission so she could allow him better access. So he could explore beneath the fairly modest collar of her dress. So he could kiss her collarbone and then run his tongue along the slight ridge, and...sweet God, was that her moaning?

"Should I stop?" he asked, his breath skimming against her slightly damp skin and setting off more chills that glittered through her like fireworks.

She grabbed his hair and pulled him against her. "Don't you dare."

His chuckle resonated right through her. She was suddenly having trouble breathing, and her own heart had long since outpaced his.

Oh, his hair. She hadn't thought of how luxurious it would be. He kept it so neat, but it was like thick silk, curling just enough to cling to her fingers as she winnowed through it. She wanted nothing more than to explore him herself. His throat, his chest, that hard, flat belly that was so well served by his beautifully tailored uniform. She loved that uniform. But she wanted it off. She wanted everything off.

Again, she pulled back, gasping for air and good sense. "You promise me," she demanded. "Your oath."

His smile this time was the stuff of a mother's nightmares. So sultry and sinful that it curled her toes in her slippers, and she felt a sharp heat low in her own belly. Very low. Exactly where she didn't want him to be.

"On my oath as an officer and a gentleman," he purred, dropping a series of small kisses along her jaw. "I am quite talented enough to instruct you in every way your grandmother promised without you risking pregnancy. Of course, it would help if you did some participating of your own."

She sighed. "I was hoping you'd say that. It's just…"

He slid his forefinger around the shell of her ear.

"Stop that. I can't think when you do that."

He chuckled. "Which is the precise purpose of doing that."

She shook her head. "Please. Can't we…." Another sigh, this of frustration as she looked out that small window at the front of the coach again. Where the coachie sat and the groom, who only had to turn a bit to see right into the carriage. Where she sat, her body arching right into the busy hands of her new husband.

In the space between heartbeats, the heat died. Trying not to groan in frustration, she pulled away. "I'm sorry."

He froze, his breathing just as harsh as hers. "Something is the matter."

She gave a faint wave to the front of the coach. "I am not comfortable with an audience. I'm a very private person, if you must know."

He stopped and just looked at her, his expression much softer. "It means we'll have to wait. Servants. Dinner."

She nodded, briefly closed her eyes and dragged in another calming breath, sternly telling various parts of her body to desist from all those feelings skittering through them. "I know. It's just..."

He was still smiling. "You're rather a private person."

She scowled. "If you're going to be disrobing me and licking me like a Gunter's ice, then yes. I would much rather not do it in a public park in front of witnesses."

Letting loose a bark of laughter, he dropped a final kiss on the top of her head and straightened. He didn't remove his arm from around her, but with the other hand he tidied his hair and knocked on the roof. "Your wish and all that. Would you mind a bit of kissing on the way, though?"

She wouldn't.

GREY HAD to admit he was in awe of his new wife. He still felt as if his bones had melted and his cock had turned to stone long after Georgie had herself tidied and ready to meet Rob's staff. Her hair was a bit disarrayed, and her lovely lips were plump and pink from a surfeit of kissing, but as they pulled to a stop in front of the tidy little brick three-story thatched cottage at the edge of Putney Heath, she was as comfortably put together as if she had come from morning visits. He was still busy commanding his cock to settle down. He knew the staff wouldn't allow itself to notice his condition, but it didn't help him support the dignity of the office and all that.

Fortunately, they had to wait a few moments to disembark so that the staff could line up on the stairs in two rows, neat and prim in Rob's grey and maroon livery.

"Ready, wife?"

The groom opened the door and set down the steps. Grey waited for Georgie to take in one of her calming breaths before stepping out and holding his hand out to help her down. She exited with a quiet grace that made him proud. Although the idea that the daughter of one of the premiere political earls in the land would not know how to greet staff was absurd.

The line of uniformed servants dipped in unison and a comfortably round middle-aged man with a bright red tonsure stepped forward. "My lord, my lady. Welcome to Cuckoo Cottage. I am Wren."

Georgie almost tripped. Her eyes went a bit wider. The butler, whom Wren obviously was, smiled.

"Did he hire you for your name?" Georgie asked with a smile of her own.

"I sometimes wonder, my lady."

They were introduced to Mrs. Wren, who was a perfect match for her husband, although with black hair, and then led on into the house.

"Your maid is already here, my lady," Mrs. Wren said, bustling in ahead of them. "Would you care to freshen up? I can offer a tour of the house. His lordship particularly wanted me to point out the garden."

Georgie brightened noticeably, which put another strain on Grey's patience, since he knew it meant a further delay in what he really wanted to do.

"Thank you, yes," Georgie answered the woman.

Mrs. Wren beamed. "And in a bit cook has gone out of her way to provide a special dinner."

Which meant an even longer delay. Grey was beginning to feel positively grumpy.

"In that case," he said, following his wife up the stairs. "I will take a brandy in whichever room leads out to the garden. Since I suspect that is the only tour she'll need."

"And the kitchen garden," she offered with one saucy smile over her shoulder before continuing.

He thought he should thank Mrs. Wren for showing the way,

if only for the chance to enjoy the sway of his wife's sleek derriere as she climbed those steps like a dancer. Except focusing on that once again threatened his *amour propre*. He deliberately looked away so he didn't have to adjust his clothing.

It was going to be a long afternoon.

GEORGIE WAS FEELING MORE unsettled by the minute. It wasn't the house; it was lovely, a simple cottage decorated for comfort rather than ostentation. It wasn't Grey. He was going out of his way to ease her progress. It wasn't even Rob Glenn's instructions to his staff, who all seemed to be smiling like proud aunts and uncles.

The garden out back was indeed delightful, a riot of early color and scent with pinks and pasque flowers, verbena, and wisteria and two apple trees perfectly espaliered against a red brick wall. The kitchen garden was just as compelling, with enough herbs to stock a sizeable stillroom.

The garden had its own bees, along with a few early butterflies tumbling about the flowers like brightly colored acrobats. The day was warm and the sun gentle behind the fluffy white clouds. A dream of a day. A dream of a garden, especially when she discovered the overgrown arbor against the back wall. Much like the arbor at her home, it had facing benches tucked within the profusion of soft lilac wisteria that grew so lushly it all but hid the bench from view from the house.

Maybe the arbor was increasing her anxiety. Because the minute he saw it, Grey grinned like a pirate.

"I'll wait a bit on that brandy, Wren," he announced and held out his arm.

Georgie didn't know what to do but lay her hand atop it and allow him to guide her in to duck under the fragrant bower.

Grey sat her down on one bench but did not take the other one. He took up the rest of the bench she sat on, crowding her with his deliciously hard body, hips and shoulders and thighs. Oh, those thighs.

She cleared her throat.

"Mrs. Wren was right," Grey said, laying his arm across the bench behind her. "This is a *lovely* garden."

Georgie refused to simper or shy, even if her body had started up that disconcerting hum again, that buzz of anticipation. Now it had an idea of what Grey could make her feel, and that shortened its patience. Georgie had the most disconcerting urge to hum right along with her body.

Grey eased his arm around her shoulders and stroked his fingers along her arm. She shivered. He noticed and smiled more widely. And Georgie unfortunately remembered another bit of her grandmother's advice.

Begin as you mean to go on.

No more secrets. No more evasions merely to get along. She needed to know what to expect.

So, she cleared her throat again. "I assume you have more than flower appreciation on your mind," she said, not quite able to face him.

He leaned in to kiss her ear, which of course set off new shivers. "I do. Do you mind?"

"No....er, well, as long as we don't miss dinner. Mrs. Wren was quite excited by the menu. Roast lamb and haricot verts."

Another kiss, a bit farther down her neck. "That's nice."

"I would also not like to be discovered imitating a Gunter's ice, if you don't mind."

"I can leave every stitch of clothing on you," he promised. She could hear his smile.

She looked over, trying to work that out. "How?"

His eyes were molten and so dark she could tumble right into them. "Do you trust me?"

She tilted her head in consideration. She did. Mostly. But she kept hearing her grandmother. *Begin as you mean....*

"Can I ask some questions first?" she asked, clenching her hands in her lap. "We haven't had any time to...well, make certain we're on the same page."

That brought his head up. "I thought we had, for which I believe you should be very grateful. It isn't every husband who can ensure his wife's privacy as long as I believe you wish. Especially when the husband considers himself a slave to that wife's beauty."

Georgie's head came back. "Please stop," she said. "You don't need to do that."

He actually looked confused. "Do what? Call my wife beautiful?"

She sucked in a breath. "I would only ask you to be truthful. I am not beautiful. My mother allows the terms 'striking' or 'gracious.' But you know perfectly well I am not in the fashion."

"You are in *my* fashion, madame."

That stole her thoughts completely. Good heavens, he looked like he meant it. Eddie was the beauty in the family. There were several of Georgie's sisters and cousins who would slay hearts as they aged. But Georgie was...utilitarian. Useful. Competent. Not...*beautiful.* She truly didn't know what to make of Grey's assertion.

He considered her again. "You don't believe me," he said, sounding very surprised.

She managed a shrug. "It is a foreign concept. As I said, my contribution to society is to educate siblings and ease young men into etiquette. Not to provoke or succumb to a mad passion."

He shook his head. "Poor fools. They don't know what they

missed." With another kiss to her neck, he reached down with his free hand and unclenched hers. "Now, what were those questions you wanted to ask?"

She blinked, still caught by his assertions. Beautiful. What a thought. And then there was his hand, his fingers callused just that much to set off more shivers.

Questions, yes. *Begin as...*

"Do you have a mistress?"

Well, that certainly caught his attention. He froze as if she'd called his parentage into question. "I beg your pardon?"

She briefly closed her eyes against the outrage in his. "Something Grandmama said. That I should begin as I mean to go on in this marriage. Well, you should know that I am terrible at pretending blindness and deafness as most *ton* wives do. I would rather know right up front where I stand. Where *you* stand...or sit or...whatever."

He took a long moment to answer, his head tilted in consideration. "You wouldn't mind my having a mistress as long as I notified you beforehand?"

It took quite a bit of her remaining discipline to maintain her poise when what she wanted was to pummel him for even suggesting such a thing.

"I did not say that."

"But you would understand if I met my needs while you are forbidding me them."

"I did not say that either."

"Then what?"

She briefly closed her eyes again, mortified but committed. She had to know. "Am I to truly assume you cannot control yourself for a few weeks until you are back home and we are able to truly begin this marriage?"

Again, he tilted his head, as if considering the wisteria over his head. "Well, I don't know. I have never been asked to before."

She found herself staring. "You have never...*refrained* from carnal activity for a few weeks at a time?"

"Well," he mused with a suspicious twinkle in his eye. "There was the time I was in that French prison. And the siege of Badajoz. Precious little fun there."

She surprised herself with a huff of laughter. "Then you could manage it again if you tried."

"If I landed in another French prison, perhaps."

Now, a frown. "But you expect me to refrain without complaint for years. Isn't that a bit unfair?"

"Grossly unfair. You are going to prey on my sense of justice, aren't you?"

"Do you need to be threatened?"

For a moment, there was silence, punctuated only by the hum of distant bees, a bit of birdsong. The ruffle of a breeze. The thud of her pulse.

But then, still smiling, he leaned down and kissed her. Just that. A meeting, an acknowledgement. A promise. "If you can promise not to run off with the head gardener while I am away, I imagine I can withstand the lure of any female I encounter."

She all but held her breath. "Can I ask for a vow to that?"

He leaned close, brushed her lips with his. Reached up to stroke her cheek with that deliciously callused finger. "I imagine you can. As long as you promise you will honestly consider the moratorium only to be for this trip."

"I will..." she reached up this time and kissed him. "Consider."

"In that case," he said, his voice unbearably soft, low enough to set up a resonance in her chest, in her belly, "would you like to meet back here after dinner, or is it too public for what I intend to do?"

She was beginning to find it hard to breathe. "What exactly is that?"

His finger strayed south along her throat, back towards her very sensitive collarbone. Just above where her dress skimmed the beginning swell of her breasts.

"Well," he murmured, leaning closer, his eyes all but pitch black, his smile again a thing of sin and temptation, "I thought I would begin by kissing my way along your pulse." His lips brushed the throbbing at the base of her throat. "Here, for instance, and here—" to the inside of her elbow, her wrist. Up to where she could feel her heart pound against her ribs. Just a touch, a feather against her breast that set it to puckering again, filling, all but reaching out to be touched. "I would very much like to divest you of all this clothing, dress, stays, stockings—I can promise you that rolling them down is quite a lovely pastime...."

She couldn't catch her breath at all now. He had run his hand down over her hip, along her thigh, to just behind her knee. Even through her dress, oh, who knew that spot could be so sensitive, so evocative? Who could imagine that faint touch could set off fireworks deep inside? Who could think that just those touches would make it impossible to look away from the kind of eyes that made more thorough promises than any words ever could?

"And then," he murmured, his hand moving again, back up her thigh, towards those fireworks, "I would introduce you to the delights that await you when you put yourself in my hands. I would be honored to show you exactly what your grandmother meant."

And just a brush against the place where her thighs met, where she swore she was melting and weeping all at once. Where she wanted more than anything to find out exactly what he meant. She opened her mouth to tell him. She reached up to cup his face. But before she could say a word, the dinner bell rang.

Again, abrupt silence. Except for the pounding of her pulse. The accompaniment of birdsong. The rasp of his breath against her cheek.

"Dinner," he said, his expression wry.

She would have thought him unaffected, but she realized his hands were trembling just a bit. "Dinner," she answered.

He leaned forward one more time and brushed his lips against hers. "I cannot wait for dessert."

13

———

*G*eorgie sat at the pretty dressing table in her room staring into the mirror, not at all seeing the work Minta was doing on her hair. She didn't even notice that with her sudden promotion to lady's maid, Minta looked more worried than elated.

For the moment though, she fought hard not to give way to a silly grin. It had been quite a day. Marriage, a surprising congeniality, and then...well, whatever it was Grey had in mind.

She had to admit that if it was anything like what he had already done, she might not make it through dinner. Just the thought of his tongue dipping into that little hollow at the base of her throat took Georgie's breath all over again.

"There you go, miss," Minta proclaimed, stepping back.

Georgie blinked. "Minta," she said, squinting at the sophisticated-looking woman in the mirror who was dressed in a gold silk gown with low squared neckline that betrayed the tops of her breasts. Her breasts that puckered all over again at the memory of Grey's fingers.

But it was her hair that reflected the biggest change. She

usually wore it in a utilitarian fashion, braids wrapped about her head so her hair would be out of the way. But now…

"My heavens, Minta," she breathed, trying to understand how a simple hairstyle could make her look so different. So non-utilitarian. "Where did you learn to do hair? This is lovely."

It had been gathered at the top of her head, held up with jeweled pins, only wispy curls framing her face. And if Georgie wasn't mistaken, constructed so that the removal of a couple of pins would send the whole thing tumbling down her back.

Behind her, Minta blushed and smiled. "Thank you, my lady. I been learning."

Georgie got to her feet. "You certainly have. I almost don't recognize that quite sophisticated lady in the mirror."

"Oh, she's you, ma'am. You just never let her loose before."

Georgie chuckled. "I'm not sure I should now."

Minta giggled. "If this isn't the time, ma'am, I don't know when is."

Georgie turned for the door, feeling surprisingly shy. Everything was suddenly different. Not just the house, the room with its comfortable chintz upholstery that reminded her of her own sitting room. Not just the new her. Her new life. She was stepping over a threshold, and she had no idea if she was ready for it.

He had given her security. He had given her possibility, even if it was given right along with more responsibility.

She came very close to succumbing to the urge to gift him in return. What could it hurt, one night? What danger would she face?

But she knew what danger. Her mother had made sure she knew. She simply could not change her decision, no matter what she owed Grey. No matter how she was feeling.

Begin as you mean to go on. And she had to establish her boundaries now, or she never would. And if she didn't, her marriage would be no better than her childhood, finding herself the person everyone relied on without ever knowing how to ask for something of her own.

Taking in a deep breath, she opened the door and stepped out into her future.

And immediately faced the most dangerous threat to her autonomy.

He was standing at the head of the stairs waiting for her, his uniform changed for a suit of midnight superfine and snowy linen, his neckcloth tied in a simple knot, his hair gleaming in the hall lamps. He was smiling and shaking his head.

"You do clean up well, Lady Coleford," he said, winging out an elbow for her to join him.

She laid her hand on his arm and lifted her hem for the stairs. "You don't do so badly yourself, sir."

"How soon do you think we can make it through dinner?" he whispered, so close to her ear she fought brand new shivers. "I would hate to commit unspeakable acts over the haricot verts."

Those familiar chills chased down her body. She smacked his hand anyway. "Behave yourself, sir. This might not be your staff, but they shouldn't have to witness bad behavior."

"Oh, I don't think it's bad. I think it's perfectly acceptable. After all. Your grandmother approves."

She couldn't help but grin. "You assume my grandmother is acceptable."

Heavens, how she delighted in this sparring. No one except the other kings had ever thought to do it with her before, as if she didn't deserve a bit of fun. Or maybe that she wouldn't want it.

That thought brought her up sharp. Could that have been her fault? Could she have had so much on her plate that she couldn't imagine any relief?

He laid his hand over hers. "Well, then, what do you suggest?"

For a moment she just stared at it, still caught in her unhappy question. But this was not the time for it. This was the time for serious discussion, whether she wanted it or not.

She accepted his offer and turned for dinner. "I suggest we get the discussions we must have out of the way."

"And those would be?"

But she made him wait for Mrs. Wren to guide them to what looked like the morning room where a small table had been set for two, including china, crystal, silver and flowers. Grey settled her into her place and then took his across from her. She couldn't help noticing that the candlelight was particularly kind to him, softening the harsher lines he had earned on the Peninsula and gleaming in his hair.

They were both well-behaved enough to wait until Mr. Wren had served the soup before picking up the conversation. It was better than admitting that they weren't tasting everything for the tension they both suffered.

"Have we been polite enough?" Grey asked with a sly twinkle. "What do we need to discuss?"

"Well," she said, setting down her spoon, "everything."

He cocked his head. "We can't put it off until after our wedding night?"

"Not if you still intend to decamp day after tomorrow. If you do not wish to come back to a completely alien household, you need to apprise me now."

He took a moment to consider. "Do you think I will not like your taste in decor? I've had no problems with your fashion sense. In fact, I find it elegant, clean and colorful with just a hint of whimsy."

She found herself battling a smile. "Do you like chintz?"

"I wouldn't know chintz if it came up and introduced itself."

"What about the Oriental Salon in the family home?"

She could see him looking back. "Yes, as a matter of fact. I do. Did you decorate that?"

She nodded, unaccountably relieved. "Each of the oldest girls got a salon to decorate for practice. Charlie and I fought over the scarlet wallpaper."

"Then I believe I may trust you."

Her soup was getting cold. She didn't notice. "And you are happy with your staff as is?"

"Exceptionally. Aren't you?"

"I don't know. I have only met them in snatches. But if, say for argument's sake, one of them hurts one of the girls. Deliberately, I mean. Or through neglect."

He never so much as took a breath. "Then they go. You also have my permission and blessing to hire more staff if you believe we need them."

She nodded and waited until the soup was exchanged for sole. "You do know that the girls need a governess."

That brought him up short, fork halfway to his mouth. "Oh, no. Not so soon."

She nodded again, this time with purpose. "So soon. They are having enough upheaval in their lives. They need some stability. A nursery maid just isn't enough."

"What about you?"

"I'm not enough either."

"Can't you wait till I get back?"

"I'm afraid not." Especially since she didn't know when that would be. She forebore telling him, though. She figured he knew.

For a long few moments, he focused on his meal, and she focused on watching him do so, wishing with all her heart they could have a normal marriage. A *more* normal marriage. One in which she could rely on him to be available when she needed him.

She almost laughed out loud. Not that husbands she had known had been particularly observant of that behavior. Even her father, one of the smartest, most decisive politicians in London, could prove himself particularly absent when needed at home, as if all his skills were reserved for other people. But then, truth to tell, Georgie knew that her mother cherished her unique position in diplomatic circles.

Well. She thought she did. Did she have the courage to ask?

"What else, madame wife?"

His voice snapped her to attention. What else...?

She focused on her fish for a moment as she tried to prioritize. "Do you intend the girls should ride?"

He paused, considered. "Don't you think they'd enjoy it?" He seemed particularly interested.

She smiled. "You obviously haven't noticed the condition of the nursery rocking horse. Besides, Sophie needs something to spend her energy on besides climbing."

His grin was a thing of beauty that did unspeakable things to Georgie's equanimity. She caught herself rubbing her free hand against her dress, as if that would cure damp palms.

"Well," he said. "I can ask my sister if we could borrow Wilson from home to work with them. He put me on my first pony."

She nodded. "He can be trusted to pick the ponies?"

"Oh, good Lord, yes."

She nodded, trying hard to think of the arrangements they had to think of, but too distracted by the hum that wouldn't fade in her body. That anticipation that built inexorably.

"What about you?" he asked.

She looked up, startled. "What about me what?"

His smile was conspiratorial. "Do you ride?"

She blinked, struggled to focus on the matter at hand. "Oh. Yes. Yes, I do."

He took a sip of wine, and she was distracted by the sheen on his lips. "Do you have a horse you'd like to bring over?"

Finally, she was able to look away for a moment. Somehow a lovely piece of lamb had shown up on her plate, along with the haricot verts, which only made her think of unspeakable things.

Horse. Yes. He wanted to know about her horse.

"Lucy," she said with a nod. "Yes, it would be lovely to have her here."

He was smiling now. "Lucy?"

She finally was able to grin. "My little sister named her. Said she looked like a Lucy, although I'm not quite sure how a bay Arabian mare translates to Lucy."

"Probably an easier name for her to remember. Anything else of great import?"

She couldn't be anything but honest. "Not that I can think of right now. Will you be able to trust me to make the best decisions while you're gone?"

This time his smile was gentle. "I would not have married you and trusted you with our girls if I didn't, Georgianne."

"Georgie," she instinctively retorted. "The only time I've been called Georgianne is when I'm in trouble."

He nodded. "I've already sent the notice to my banker so he knows you are to draw on my account. All bills are to be sent to him. I'll give you all the pertinent information when we go back home tomorrow. Both the lawyer and estate agent will stop by as well so you may meet them. Will that suffice?"

For a moment she was swamped with a feeling of panic. Was she really ready for this? Certainly she took on much of the responsibility of running her own house, but this was different. There she had the support of well-loved staff, who watched out for her and filled in when she couldn't manage everything.

Could she truly walk into an established household that was going through its own upheaval and not fall flat on her face?

She didn't have a choice, did she?

Doors were closing in again, even as they opened, and she fought that feeling of suffocation.

But then he reached across the table and took her hand. Just that. And he smiled, that wonderful warm smile that lit his eyes and offered his complete support.

"We have time, Georgie. Whatever doesn't happen now, we can manage when I get back. And that is when we can focus on you. All right?"

She battled the sting of tears. He was such a good man. He was trying.

She nodded and squeezed his hand back. And knowing that they had a meal to finish, turned back to what Georgie was certain was a delicious dinner.

GEORGIE DECIDED she was very proud of herself. She made it all the way through dinner without decorating her dress in the food she might have dropped from distraction. She even managed to thank the staff for a lovely dinner, leaving them smiling. Leaving her blushing, as she strongly suspected that they considered themselves responsible for the coming evening. She even let Grey lead her away from the table, her hand on his arm and his other hand covering it.

"Why do I suspect that if we do not go immediately upstairs, we will severely disappoint the Wrens?" Grey whispered as he led her from the room.

Georgie was able to smile. "It is difficult enough to be responsible for my own success. I am not so comfortable being responsible for theirs."

He leaned closer so that she could catch the wind-and-sea scent of him. "What about mine?"

She almost tripped. "I imagine you'll let me know."

That made him laugh. "I believe we will do very well, Georgie." That statement would not have been so evocative if he hadn't been stroking her hand as he said it, if he hadn't matched his pace to hers as they neared the stairs.

Georgie couldn't help herself. She grinned up at him. "I'll let you know."

She was coming to count on that soft rumble of laughter in his chest. She found herself wanting to lay her hand against it, just to feel the vibrations, to lay her head against it to better hear it. To hear it and his heart, which she realized was accelerating again.

"I believe, lady wife," he murmured, guiding her up the stairs, "that we might save the arbor for another day. I have an overwhelming hankering for acting like I'm at Gunter's. The staff might not understand."

She wasn't sure she did. It didn't matter. His words set off a firestorm inside. The growl of his voice settled low in her belly where those new sensations had been plaguing her. She was so tempted to ask him what they were. He already knew she was inexperienced. Surely he would understand her trepidation.

In the end, she couldn't. She simply nodded and climbed the stairs toward the small bedrooms they had been allotted.

"You might want to send your maid to dinner herself," he said. "Braxton will surely keep her company."

Well, there went her breath again. Too clearly she could see what that would mean. "You sent him away?"

"I have long since learned to disrobe all alone. Besides—" He leaned closer again, spilling chills down her neck. "I suspect we can manage quite well without them."

And all Georgie could do was nod again. More than her

palms were suddenly damp. Her breathing had gone a bit short. And Grey kept stroking her hand, back and forth, back and forth, sending shivers racing up her arm and beyond, even making her breasts pucker.

She came so close to asking if they couldn't postpone the next few moments. So close. But then they reached the door to Grey's room, and he turned to her.

And he smiled. And that smile took the rest of the stuffings out of her knees.

"Don't tell me you are nervous," he said, that smile melting more than her knees.

It seemed pointless to lie. "Dreadfully."

He lifted her hand and kissed it. "Then we'll have to do something about that. Since you'll be letting your woman go for dinner, don't you think we can help each other from now on?"

What exactly was she supposed to say? "Can I help you first?"

That widened his grin nicely and deepened the anticipation in her chest that felt like dread.

"I thought you'd never ask."

She was amazed at how quickly he set up the next act of this little play. Stepping into Georgie's room, he smiled at Minta and suggested she look for Braxton in the servants' hall. Then, after Minta had received Georgie's permission by way of a mute nod and retreated toward the servants' stairs, he guided Georgie into his room. Well, Rob Glenn's room, which was decorated in an aggressively masculine theme of oak paneling and dark blue walls filled with paintings of birds. Oddly enough, it seemed that the birds were watching them and weren't happy about the intrusion. Georgie looked around and shook her head. This was going to be stressful enough.

"Why don't we move on to my room instead?" she asked.

Grey gave one last distracted look around and reclaimed her hand. "Unless it's all pink ruffles, it has to be better than this."

It was better. In fact, it was very nicely decorated in soft spring greens, blues, and rose. It soothed rather than challenged. Georgie led Grey inside and let him close the door.

"Much better," he pronounced with a decisive nod. "Now I can focus on more important things than whether that heron back there will poke me in the back with his beak."

Georgie's giggle was a bit breathy. She still had hold of Grey's hand and suddenly didn't know what to do with it. With him. With herself. Her grandmother had assured her she would know what to do. Her grandmother had been wrong.

It was up to Grey to set the tone. He wasted no time doing so. "Would you like the room light or dark?" he asked, lifting his free hand to cup her face.

She swallowed. "I don't know."

He leaned down and gently met her lips with his own. "Personally, I would love to enjoy the sight of your loveliness. But as you have said, I'm not brand new to this."

Another swallow. An instinctive stretching of her neck to welcome his gentle touch. "It feels a perilous decision to make. Can we just move forward and see how we do?"

He dropped another kiss, this longer, more thorough, his hand cupping the back of her head to him as he explored her mouth. "I knew I could count on you for common sense. Do you think we're wearing too much clothing?"

"I think you could certainly dispense with that tight jacket... maybe your neckcloth?"

Another kiss, this one nudging her lips open a bit to feel his tongue stroking the seam. She was truly having trouble breathing now. And oh, how her breasts ached. Could she ask him to touch them? To hold them so they didn't feel so suddenly heavy?

"And you won't mind my loosening the ties at the back of your dress?"

She shook her head. He smiled and she wanted to lick his lips in return. Instead, she watched him shed that sleek blue jacket and toss it onto a chair before the fireplace. He held out the edge of his neckcloth that trailed out of his arrangement. "Would you like the honor?"

She caught her breath. She had undressed her little brothers. She had never come so close to a grown man. Certainly not one who looked intent on swallowing her whole. Even though her hand trembled, she reached up and took the end from him, and then took the other end, and began to unravel the knot. As she did that, he reached around her to find her ties. Too easily, she thought in distraction. Too cleverly. He had indeed done this before.

And then she couldn't think at all, because she pulled off the line of linen from around his neck to open a V in his shirt. And there she came across his throat, that same little dip he had sipped from on her. And below it, curls of dark hair, and oh, she wanted to touch them, winnow her fingers through them to learn their texture. She wanted to yank that shirt over his head and find out what the rest of his chest looked like. Was it as muscular as it seemed? Was his belly flat in a way that invited her to explore?

"You can, you know," he said with that same smile of invitation.

She startled and looked up at eyes that suddenly seemed black and languorous, hot. Mesmerizing.

"Can what?"

"Pull off my shirt. It will have to happen sooner or later. After all, I have your dress and your stays unfastened."

Could he look any more devilish in that moment when she realized that her dress, her lovely cream silk dress, was sagging at her shoulders? Cool air snaked in around her waist and set up fresh chills. She wanted to wrap her arms around herself. She wanted to close her eyes and pretend she was somewhere else. Back in her room. Back at the castle, where this kind of thing was no more than fantasy.

But oh, her body would never forgive her.

He was still smiling. And she had never considered herself a coward.

"All right," she said and reached for his shirt. And yanked it up right over his head to find that every one of her wishes had come true. His chest was magnificent—sleek, broad, decorated in that lovely curling hair that narrowed at his torso and arrowed right down like an invitation to explore. To explore...oh, dear. She had brothers. She had a mother who had made sure her daughters would never be ignorant enough to put themselves in danger. So she knew that the rather impressive bulge in Grey's trousers meant that he was excited as well. Anticipating. Readying.

She quickly looked up to see his expression gentling. "Yes, my dear," he said, once again running a soft finger along her throat. "That is what you do to me."

"You won't...."

His smile broadened. "I won't."

"But won't that...hurt?"

He shrugged. "We'll figure a way around it."

"In fact," she retorted with a sudden grin, "I insist on it."

His answering grin matched hers exactly.

She couldn't help it. She motioned to his chest, his broad, strong chest. "May I?"

"I wish you would."

She did. Finally, she reached for him, tentatively laying her hands against those muscles, winnowing her fingers through those curls of hair, sating herself on the texture and strength and heat of him. Tracing with reverence the two scars she uncovered, one up by his collarbone, another along the side of his torso, long scars that still looked angry.

"What about these?" she asked, compelled to lean forward and lay her lips against them.

He shuddered with her touch. "Mementos of a long fight with a tyrant."

"I'm sorry."

He kissed her forehead. "Thank you."

She leaned back a bit and looked up. "I'm having all the fun. Shouldn't we do something about that?"

And then before she could change her mind, she shrugged her gown off her shoulders. She saw him draw in a breath and suddenly felt stronger. Surer. She actually had power over this magnificent man, and it changed her forever.

For the briefest moment, he closed his eyes. And then he lifted his hands. "May I?"

"I think it only fair." She was still winnowing her fingers through that silky hair and smiling.

"Maybe we'd better find a more comfortable place to do this," he suggested, and before she could even answer, had her lifted in his arms and was on the way over to the bed, leaving her dress on the floor behind them.

He didn't even bother to pull the covers down. He just laid her out on the bed like an offering and followed, settling right alongside her so that he could reach her as easily as she could reach him. So he could run his callused finger along her collarbone, down the very center of her chest, then around her breast that ached for him, her nipple a hard nub.

She was having a hard time keeping her eyes open. They wanted to drift closed so she could better focus on the delicious sensations he was unleashing. But if she did, she wouldn't see the lambent light in his sea-blue eyes. She wouldn't see him dip his head so that he could follow his finger with his lips, kissing, nibbling, oh Lord, licking with slow, exquisitely delicious strokes of his tongue closer and closer to her breasts, her aching, hungry breasts. Did that mean it was up to her to dispense with her chemise? She was just about to ask when he simply closed his lips around her breast and kept licking.

She heard herself gasp as her body arched completely without her permission. As she caught his head in her own hands and held him to her, urged him to continue, to increase the torture he was inflicting. He pulled away from her breast and smiled down into her eyes, his expression the stuff of maidenly dreams. And then he kissed her again, nibbling at her lips now, using his tongue in unexpected ways.

"Open for me, Georgie," he murmured.

She had no idea what he meant, but when she opened her lips to answer him, he slipped his tongue right past them. He caressed her breasts with his fingers and her mouth with his tongue until she caught on and met him, tongue-to-tongue, dipping in and out of his mouth until she couldn't seem to separate the almost frightening new sensations from her mouth and her breasts. Until she opened her legs because she couldn't bear them closed anymore, and she heard him growl low in his throat. She felt his hand slide right down her belly to raise her chemise until the night air chilled her, there between her legs, chilled her where that low hum had first alerted her to his power over her.

He never broke the kiss, even as his fingers reached the curls at the juncture of her thighs. Even as Georgie flinched at the foreign sensation. Even as she instinctively tried to close her legs together.

"You'll like this," he murmured with a kiss to her ear. "I promise."

She couldn't help it. She opened again, flushing with the

sensation that she had become wanton. Because she was afraid. But she was more afraid he would stop.

And oh, his fingers set off a firestorm there, flicking and stroking, dipping inside her where she was weeping with the want of him. She came so close then to forfeiting her commitment, to yanking his breeches open and demanding he fill her to her core. She couldn't catch her breath. She couldn't calm her body. Somehow, though, she held onto her control enough to keep her mouth shut. At least figuratively.

"Do you trust me?" he asked, his eyes glowing.

She nodded.

His smile was the stuff of fantasies. "Then believe that you'll love this."

And without another word, he slid his whole body down, laid his hands along the inside of her thighs and opened them even more.

Georgie lurched up. "What....?"

He smiled again and she was lost. And then, dipping his head right there where his fingers had been, he treated her like a Gunter's ice.

Except nothing was cold. She was so hot, her body was clenching, a wild keening feeling coursing through her. His tongue, oh, his tongue, sliding up and down and then darting inside, just like his fingers had, only sweeter, slicker, even more thrilling until she was keening right along with her body, her hands clenched in his hair, her head thrown back, her body caught in a storm.

And then, he brought his finger up. He found a spot that shot lightning through her, and he stroked it with finger and tongue, and she swore she could feel the vibrations of him humming in this throat until he dipped in one more time, and her body seized and she cried out, the sensations too much to hold, the exquisite pleasure sweeping through her like a thundering surf. She wasn't sure if she pulled him up or he came on his own, but suddenly Grey was holding her, her head tucked against his shoulder and his hands stroking her back.

She was still shuddering when he stopped stroking and lifted her chin. "Are you crying?"

For a long moment she could do no more than nod. Finally with a rather watery smile, she stretched up and kissed him back. "Thank you. I would never have imagined...."

Again, she shook her head. This time he kissed her, and she tasted herself on him, which oddly excited her all over again. Which, even still replete with surprise chills still chasing through her, made her remember more of her grandmother's advice.

She lifted her head back from his shoulder and faced him. "It seems to me we have not completed the evening's festivities."

His grin was brash. "You want another round?"

She shook her head with what she hoped was a salacious smile of her own. "No. I want *you* to have a round."

He seemed to freeze a bit. "You don't have to...."

"My grandmother said that I did. And since I am a proponent of fair play, I agree with her."

He shook his head with a rueful grin. "I have to spend more time with your grandmother."

Georgie chuckled. "She'd like that. She likes handsome men. And the bees welcomed you. There's just one thing." Now she battled a fresh blush. "I am not...er, conversant with...er, technique? I mean, I know the basic equipment, but I'm not exactly sure how to make the most of it. Will you guide me?"

For the longest moment Grey couldn't seem to make a sound. Georgie looked up to see that his eyes were all but black, his nostrils flared. His scent had grown darker, somehow, and it called to her. She knew she should have been petrified, awash in shame for being so forward. But her grandmother was right.

Now that she was able to focus on something besides her own cataclysmic bodily responses, she realized he was stiff, holding himself exquisitely still. She wasn't even sure he was breathing.

He couldn't be afraid.

Georgie figured she had better make the first move. Running her hand down his chest, his torso, which was damp with sweat, she laid her hand over the placket of his trousers. "If you can untie my dress, doesn't that mean I should unbutton you?"

He briefly closed his eyes. "I only have so much restraint, Georgie."

She shouldn't allow his admission to delight her, but it did. She had never been irresistible before. She decided it would be a waste of time to be polite. She opened a button and then another, intrigued by the fact that as she slipped her fingers inside the placket, the muscles of his abdomen rippled. She wanted to lick them. Next time, she decided, when they both knew the rhythms of the dance.

Another button.

Another.

His breathing was growing harsh, and her fingers had reached a nest of curling hair. And...oh, my. Oh, she hadn't expected that. Well, she had noticed how big the bulge had been, but she suspected it hadn't been completely...involved.

She couldn't stand it anymore. She bent and laid a kiss on his belly and was rewarded by another low growl and a ripple of muscle, even as she gained enough access to curl her fingers around his...what was it the boys called it? Shaft? Man spear? Cock? Somehow that didn't seem to...er, encompass the physical presence of it.

"You know what..." she murmured, pulling the placket fully away. "If you could dine on me, why couldn't I..."

That got a real groan out of him. "Please," he begged. "Not now."

She looked up to see actual pain on his face. "Am I hurting you?"

He managed a rather grim smile. "Only in the best of ways. Help me get these things off so we can enjoy this interlude a bit better."

Her own smile was delighted. She helped him shuck the rest of his clothing and spent a moment taking in the sight of his... man spear? That was much larger and rounder than she'd imagined, all cushioned in that nest of curly hair, a shade darker than that on his head.

This time she didn't ask permission. The idea of 'supping' on his shaft intrigued her, but she thought this probably wasn't the time, if he was this uncomfortable. So she satisfied herself by using her fingers, her hands, and one kiss right on the tip where a pearl of liquid had formed. She delighted herself testing the texture of him, like silk stretched over steel. She cupped his sacs and inhaled the earthy male scent of him. She heard him groan again and decided this wasn't the time to waste on education.

"Tell me if I'm doing this wrong," she said, wrapping her hand around him and sliding it up and down, delighted when he seemed to jump in her hand. "Grandmama was not explicit."

"You're doing just fine. Only one thing..." And before she could object, he pulled her back up to him and met her mouth to mouth, so that she lay along his body, relishing the hard strength of him, delighting in the heat, relieved that she could still reach his shaft so she could focus on it along with the kiss, and his hands roving her body, his groans, his smiles.

"Are you sure I can't..."

He kissed her again. "I'm sure." His voice was so strained, that she gentled her hold on him. But he protested, wrapped his own hand around hers to show her what he liked. She kissed him this time as she began to stroke, feeling him growing even larger in her hand, throbbing, stiffening, until it seemed it would burst. It excited her so much, this mastery over him. He was setting her body alight again, but she was all but shattering his control.

And then, with a cry, he pulsed in her hand and spent on his belly, and she met his mouth again, lips and tongue and teeth, furious to meet him, to succumb to him, to triumph over him. He hadn't even finished when he reached down and began to stroke her just as he'd done before, faster, lighter, tormenting her with the silk of his touch, his fingers just callused enough to rasp against her most sensitive flesh, bringing it back to shuddering, seething life. Bringing her back to her own ecstasy as she moaned into the kiss, as she writhed, as she wept with the perfect moment they shared.

14

───────────

She should have felt wonderful. Well, she did; her body feeling weightless and...she thought for a moment and wanted to smile. Glowing. It glowed. Or it should have. She had spent the night exchanging pleasure with her new husband, safe from pregnancy, and now lay in his arms, her ear resting against his chest where she could hear his heart and smell the scent that was curiously his.

His skin was so warm, his body so solid, as if she could rely on its protection always. As if she could lean on him, when she hadn't been able to lean on anyone in her entire life.

But she knew better. And that was why, when she should have been safely asleep and sated, she lay in his arms, dreading the day to come. The week, the month. She should have been able to enjoy this interlude without qualm. But the fact was she would lose it, lose the chance of it, for how long? She would be weighed down with the responsibilities of his family, his estates, his title, while he gallivanted off to the Continent. And heaven only knew what she would still have to settle in her own family.

"You're thinking too hard," she heard and felt the rumble of that delicious voice all through her.

"It is unavoidable," she countered, not moving. "We have already overslept, and we have two girls to rescue from the madness of my house."

"Two girls I suspect are having the time of their lives."

She couldn't help but smile. "Oh, I hope so. At least if they have imaginations to feed. They can choose from a pirate ship or a magic wood with fairy houses or a circus."

That ended his relaxation. "A circus?!"

She smiled. "Several small dogs who love doing tricks and being dressed up in funny outfits. Oh, and an elephant."

That froze him. "You're joking."

She chuckled. "Perhaps. The problem is that we must finally climb from this comfortable bed if you want to find out."

He began playing with her hair. "I'd rather leave the world outside."

She closed her eyes against the delicious chills he was setting off. Chills she knew perfectly well she shouldn't become used to. "As would I. But someone in this room managed to schedule a boat trip two days after his wedding. And he hasn't even introduced his new wife to his staff yet."

"They saw you."

"A completely different matter, and you know it. If I stand a chance with them, I must establish my presence before you go. Not to mention with your solicitor and estate agent."

For a moment there was just silence, the distant ticking of a clock somewhere. Then Georgie realized she could hear furtive rustling in the next room, more of it farther away. She had just run out of time.

Before he could challenge her, she lifted her head, dropped a kiss on his chest and rolled out of bed. "If I stay here any longer I will waste away from hunger," she said. "And my poor maid will die of mortification from waiting for me in your room. Make certain you have at least some semblances of clothing on before going through that door."

She took a chance to look at him and almost faltered completely. He was impressive enough dressed and groomed and upright. It was nothing compared to him lounging in bed, his arm behind his head, his hair tousled and the sheet only covering his most pertinent equipment. She fought an intense desire to jump back in with him.

Instead, she shook her head. "Lord, I am tired of always being the responsible one. Get dressed, your lordship. We have places to be, and the staff is waiting to see us on our way."

"You're sure about that."

She scowled and tied the dressing gown Minty had left for her. And then, she waited. And he smiled. Which did nothing to improve her mood.

"Please," she said, feeling worse by the minute.

She wanted like mad to stay. To crawl back in and fill herself with the weight and size and smile of her husband. She wanted to pretend that everything else would simply disappear.

But she knew better.

Finally, his grin positively piratical, he climbed out of bed and stretched like a giant cat, knowing perfectly well that she couldn't keep her eyes off his battle-hardened body, that tantalizing line of curls right down his abdomen, the taut leanness of his hips, his horseman's thighs. Everything else. And then he just swooped her up and kissed her as if he'd just returned from a year away. And she realized her grandmama had been correct. His arms could hold her up when she felt that nothing else would. But before she could enjoy it, before she could even really take it in, he kissed the tip of her nose and strode perfectly naked through the door into his room.

Georgie certainly hoped poor Minta wasn't in there.

THE WRENS WERE SO dear in parting that Georgie fought a surprising sting of tears. Oh, she wished they were her new staff instead of Grey's, whom she still had to win over. She wished she could stay at the cozy breakfast table sating herself on toast and eggs and Mrs. Wren's comforting smile. But they had little girls to see to, little girls who were going to lose a bit more stability by the next morning.

She had, as ever, responsibilities.

And so, with a final wave, she let Grey help her into the carriage.

The ride back into the city was more comfortable than she'd expected. Grey sat next to her, holding her hand, and he filled her in on everyone in his London staff, from Chalmers the butler, who had let her in that first day, to Midget the scullery maid, who had been brought in like several of her compatriots from a foundling home.

He admitted he didn't know all of them well, since he hadn't spent much time at the London house until very recently, but he couldn't think of one she would have problems with. She sincerely hoped he was right.

The good news was that she had quite a bit of experience with staff, from hiring to firing. The difference with his staff was that their loyalty would never be first to her.

By the time they reached her house she felt more settled. After all, managing staff was her forte. She'd been doing it since she was fourteen. And if the reaction of her staff at seeing her was any indication, she hadn't been awful at it. Clarence, the first footman, welcomed them in with a deep bow and handed them off to Weems with a broad smile. Weems looked like a proud father, and Mrs. Barnes, rustling and jangling up, did everything but genuflect.

"Well now, Lady Coleford, welcome back. I assume you've come to collect those scamps who've become our latest circus performers."

Next to Georgie, Grey stiffened. "I thought you were joking."

Georgie grinned. "Heavens, no. Dogs, tumbling, or elephant, Mrs. Barnes?"

Mrs. Barnes chuckled. "Oh, all of it. Especially Lady Sophie. She and Master Geoffrey have been learning somersaults."

"And Lady Amelia?"

"Holding the cat."

She nodded. "Come, my lord, and see the Packham circus."

It wasn't quite as out of control as she'd led him to believe. The circus, just like all other activities for the children, was contained in the nursery, which took up the third floor of the combined townhouses. Besides the dogs, which were indeed attired in brightly colored jackets and frilly collars, there resided a large mobile wooden elephant, two somnolent tabby cats dressed as tigers, and a swing that hung from the ceiling, upon which Amelia was kicking her legs back and forth to try to gain some height. Grey almost objected until Georgie surreptitiously held him back with a hand and a minute shake of the head.

"Are you having fun, Amelia?" she asked quietly.

Her new niece gave a beatific smile. "May we have a swing in our nursery, Uncle Grey?"

"We'll see," Georgie answered for him. "Miss O'Toole, has it been a good day?"

A tall, almost skeletal-thin woman of indeterminate age unfolded herself from a seat in the corner, a mass of knitting in her hands. She had the smile of a mystic monk.

"Ah, they've been grand, milady," she said with a very precise dip.

And then she made a noise between a throat-clearing and a hum, and the half-dozen of Georgie's young kin came charging forward to give Georgie and Grey their own version of bows or curtsies, most giggling. Georgie giggled back. Which was when she noticed that Sophie and Amelia did not join in. In fact, the two of them froze, as if caught in a crime. Amelia slid off the swing and Sophie, who had been riding the elephant behind Geoffrey, stumbled forward to stand just next to her sister. Clutching hands, the two of them, produced stiff little curtsies, their heads and eyes lowered.

"We are sorry, my lord," they chorused.

Georgie felt a chill slither down her back. She gave Grey a quick glance. The color had leeched from his face.

"Have you been having fun?" he asked with a step forward.

Both girls edged back. "Yes, Uncle Grey." In chorus. "It is good to see you."

Grey froze in place, obviously confused. So Georgie took over. Stepping past her crew, who were looking at the girls as if they were foreign objects, she crouched down to her knees right in front of the girls.

"Your manners are excellent," she said, just for them. She got both sets of eyes up to her, although both girls looked far too afraid. She truly hoped they couldn't see how blazingly angry she was. The last thing any of them needed was for the girls to think she was angry at them. "But as you can tell from these monkeys," she continued, "we are not used to being formal here. It makes me nervous, isn't that true, Geoffrey?"

Geoffrey switched his attention from the girls to Georgie and back. He saw her slow wink and nodded. "My sister isn't very formal, you know."

"In fact," Georgie continued, fighting hard to keep from just grabbing those little girls to her. "I don't prefer it at all. Certainly not here in the nursery. After all, Miss O'Toole wouldn't have it when I was a girl. I don't think she would now. Would you, Miss O'Toole?"

"Formal manners are a lovely thing in the drawin' room," she said, her voice soft and sure. "But as I told you yesterday, I far prefer to see my children have fun up here."

Both girls looked back and forth as if trying to interpret a foreign language.

"When you were a girl, Aunt Georgie?" Amelia asked.

"Oh my, yes," Georgie said with a bright grin for her old nanny. "Miss O'Toole taught me my manners, you can be sure of it. And if she says fun should be had in the nursery, it should. What if we try it in our nursery as well?"

Sophie risked a look up at her. "What?"

Georgie shrugged. "A hug? I love hugs."

"She does!" the other children chorused.

It didn't quite thaw the girls, but they looked at each other and shrugged. "We could try," Sophie said. "It is just that we are wild savages, and we should be very careful to present a good face."

Georgie thought she would be delighted to share her opinion of that teaching with whoever had inflicted it, except she thought it might be long too late. "You present an excellent face," she assured them, holding her arms open. "Isn't that right, Uncle Grey?"

She heard the growl of emotion in his voice. "A most excellent face."

Finally, the girls ran into Georgie's arms and let her hug them both until she had them giggling as well. Then she handed them off to their Uncle Grey who knelt just next to her, his eyes suspiciously bright.

"I have an idea," he whispered to them, kissing both their heads. "You may present an excellent face to everyone else. But your Aunt Georgie and I would be far happier if you were just yourselves at home. Just like her family is. Because now we are family. All right?"

Both girls backed up and checked both Georgie and him. "Truly?" Sophie asked.

"If it would suit you," he said. "Because I become very sad if my girls feel uncomfortable around me."

"As do I," Georgie agreed.

"Would the bees?" Amelia asked, her little face puckered in concern.

Georgie almost choked. "Did the bees mind when you introduced yourselves?"

Both girls shook heads. "They sang to us!" Amelia declared.

Georgie nodded, her hand on Grey's shoulder as he held on to his little girls. "Well," she said. "No one knows better than the bees. "

Finally, *finally* the girls surrendered themselves to Grey and Georgie. It was only then that Georgie saw O'Toole surreptitiously wiping her eyes.

"There was concern?" she asked the family nanny as Grey was collecting the girls' clothing.

O'Toole shrugged. "They seem much concerned that they behave correctly."

Georgie sighed. "I'm afraid Grey's was the first kind smile they have seen."

"I was afraid so." The nanny patted Georgie on the shoulder. "Well, they have landed in good pasture now."

Georgie smiled. "You're sure. When I was twelve, you claimed I would be the death of etiquette and culture."

O'Toole smiled back. "Sometimes etiquette and culture are overrated. You will be the perfect person for those girls." Then her smile grew. "As long as you bring them over here frequently for a bit of mayhem."

"That," she said, giving her old nanny a brisk hug, the only kind the nanny would accept, "I believe I can guarantee. I would also consider it a huge favor if you would help me screen nannies for the girls."

Miss O'Toole cast another surreptitious glance at the girls, who were in the process of chattering at their Uncle Grey about their adventures with the Packhams. "Shall I send out feelers?"

"I would be grateful."

And as briskly as that, Georgie knew O'Toole would find the perfect nanny for the girls.

"Time to go, I'm afraid," Grey said, regaining his feet. "Say goodbye to your new friends."

"May we come back?" Sophie asked.

"Absolutely," he assured them with a nod from Georgie and Miss O'Toole both.

Georgie formally introduced her husband to her old nanny and then took hold of Amelia's hand as Sophie accepted Grey's. The general farewells were cacophonous and repeated when they returned downstairs to be met by the kings and Georgie's mother. Georgie was ruthless, however, in getting them back out of the house. She had very limited time left with her husband, and part of it had to be taken up with explaining to the girls why their brand-new substitute father would be deserting them so soon.

IT WENT JUST AS BADLY as Georgie had feared it would. Not that there were tears or tantrums. Worse. There was silence and an odd retreat, as if they had shrunk away even as they sat there.

"Where will we go?" Sophie asked from where she had moved to sit right next to her sister, Amelia's hand firmly clasped in hers.

"Where?" Grey repeated, obviously bewildered. "Why, nowhere."

The girls went stone still.

"He means that you will stay right here with me," Georgie assured them gently, her heart in shreds for the distress so obvious in the rigid posture and small voices. How many shocks did these two have to survive in their young lives?

Grey blinked a couple of times. "Well, of course. You didn't think I would send you away, did you?"

That was exactly what they had thought. This time, Georgie saw the pain reflect in Grey's eyes and wanted to hold his hand.

Abruptly he got to his feet and walked over to insert himself ruthlessly between the two girls on the settee, one of their hands in each of his.

"My two little gooses," he chastised them with a frown. "We are a family now. And I do not know what you believe a family is, but in my house, a family stands by each other. They work together and play together and if one of them must ever leave— as so often happens—the others wait for him—or her—to come back. Maybe they could even bake cinnamon buns to lure him home. I just got my family. I am not giving it up for anything!"

"But you're leaving," Sophie protested.

"And will be coming back," he assured her. "As soon as my work is done. And in the meantime, your Aunt Georgie will be here with you. And she will help you finish settling in. I suspect she would even help decorate the nursery and your rooms."

"With a swing?" Amelia asked, her voice still far too hesitant.

Grey smiled down at her. "As long as it is safe."

"I was hoping you two would help me redecorate here," Georgie offered, wanting so desperately to hold the girls as well. Knowing how important it was that Grey be the one to lay the foundation for them. "Maybe we can make it a little..." she looked around and scowled. "Brighter?"

"But what if Uncle Grey doesn't recognize it and can't find us?" Amelia protested.

Lord, would her heart ever stop hurting.

It was Grey who settled that question. "You could paint this house purple and wrap it in fur, and I would still find you. You will never ever be lost again, Sophie. I promise that. Because even if I am not here, your Aunt Georgie will be. And Chalmers, and Mrs. Chalmers, and Bill the gardener, and Midget, and especially Bark. Isn't that right, Chalmers?"

The butler, the image of stiff propriety could be heard clearing his throat. "Indeed, my lord. You are our little girls as well, my ladies."

Georgie swung a quick, surprised smile at the very proper butler, whose eyes shone just a bit too brightly.

"And just to be certain," Grey continued, his voice sounding a bit rough as well, "you also have all the Packhams. You might not have realized it yet, but when Aunt Georgie made you her daughters, she made you official Packhams. Even if Aunt Georgie and I aren't handy, the Packhams always will be."

"And they're always easy to find," Georgie assured them.

She knew they weren't convinced. Their history was too harsh to trust quite yet. And neither Georgie nor Grey had had enough time with them to convince them differently.

And then, worst of all, Amelia's little voice coming from a bowed head. "Is it because we were bad?"

The silence was devastating. Sophie was watching Amelia with terrified eyes, and Grey was watching them both with tears in his. Even Bark, lying on the floor at their feet, had his head up and cocked.

"Sophie," Grey said quietly. "Would it be all right if I talked to Amelia about this? Will you listen?"

Sophie didn't face him, but she nodded, as if she knew it was a question too far. At least it would have been with her family.

With a kiss to the top of Sophie's head, he reached over and plopped Amelia onto his lap and wrapped her in his arms. Amelia sat like a stone.

"Is that why you think I am leaving tomorrow? Because you did something bad?"

For a long, fraught moment she held still. Then, without looking at him, she gave a jerky nod of her head. "It's why my father was gone so much."

It was all Georgie could do to sit still. She had filled her life with responsibilities to children. But she had never been faced with a child so broken she had to begin by rebuilding.

Holding on more tightly to Amelia, Grey gathered Sophie into his arms as well. "Thank you for telling me. It will help me understand some things better. Do you know who the King is, girls?"

Both gave shy nods.

"Well, he has personally asked me to make this trip to help the country. And girls, as impatient as I am to begin our new family, do you think I can disobey my King?"

Wide eyes and shaken heads met the question.

"The King?" Sophie asked. "The *real* King?"

He nodded. "King George himself. I hope you understand that it is the only way anyone could make me leave you right now. Do you believe me?"

They both looked up at him. "Yes," they whispered.

He nodded. "And the only person I trust enough to care for you while I'm gone is your Aunt Georgie."

"And Mr. and Mrs. Chalmers," Amelia piped up.

Sophie pointed at Georgie. "And the Packhams!"

He grinned. "And the Packhams. Are we all right now?"

"Will we see you tomorrow?"

"See me? You shall take me to the docks to wave off my ship. And if I know Aunt Georgie, she will tell you all about pirates while we're there, and take you for ices on the way home."

"It has been a very long day," Grey said with a prodigious yawn as he pulled off his cravat.

It had been. After getting the girls settled, Grey had made the formal introductions to his staff, from Chalmers and his wife, who acted as housekeeper, all the way down to the scullery maid Midget, a tiny redhead with an amazing amount of freckles and a gap-toothed smile. The only two people she would have to wait for were the estate agent and Grey's solicitor, who would stop by before Grey left in the morning. Georgie began to memorize names and responsibilities and enjoyed the relief of knowing that most of her new staff were at least glad for her presence, especially with the little girls to care for.

Things were looking up. The girls were tucked into bed with Bark stretched out by the bedroom door, and Georgie could concentrate on her new husband, whom she suspected she was falling in love with.

Looking up from where she was dispensing with her slippers, she bestowed a suggestive smile on him. "Oh, dear. And here I was thinking of continuing my education tonight."

Even as she'd made it a point to join Grey in tucking the suddenly chatty girls into bed, it had been all she could think of. A bit of comfort, some closeness to help ease that pervasive feeling of helpless rage for those two little girls who were still far too tentative and uncertain. Even more, some time selfishly dedicated just to each other before the rest of the world intruded once more.

Stopping at the sound of her voice, Grey gave her a sweet smile. "I was hoping you'd say that. You're not too tired?"

Georgie met his gaze with every ounce of heat that had suddenly ignited in those new places she had discovered the night before. She almost told him the truth. *Hold me for just a little while. Let me rely on your strength and savor your taste and the exhilaration of your excitement.* Instead, she shook her head. "Not for another test of Grandmama's theory."

Just the thought sent chills racing through her. She was going to have to work harder on maintaining an emotional distance from her husband. It would be a lot easier if he weren't so dratted precious with those two little girls. If he didn't have eyes that melted her with one look. If he didn't smile at her as if she were a syllabub and he had a spoon.

She could enjoy a bit of carnal sport and mutual comfort without becoming too attached, couldn't she?

Couldn't she?

His cravat dispatched, he went to unbuttoning his shirt. Slowly. All the while watching her with that maddening little half-smile of his. Blasted man. He was making her knees weak with that smile. And he knew it.

So she fought back. Lifting her leg onto an ottoman, she slowly pulled her skirts up to bare her knee and reached for her garter. Slowly rolling it down, she followed with her stocking. Slowly, her fingers sliding along her leg as if inviting a look. A touch.

She could hear the most curious growl, and looked up to see Grey frozen, his hands on his buttons, not moving. His eyes on her own hands.

"Woman," he said, his voice raspy as he slowly shook his head, "You are going to kill me."

"Don't be silly," she said with her own sly grin. "You have far more experience in these matters than I do. Surely you have built up a...tolerance."

He glared, taking a step forward. "Familiarity does not necessarily equate to tolerance. You are trying me, Wife."

"Well, I hope so," she retorted, changing legs and repeating the motions, "or I'm wasting all the suggestions Charlie had for me."

That stopped him in his tracks. "Charlie? What did she tell you? And how does she know?"

"She reads. Incessantly. And undoubtedly not the sermons most mothers would want her to read. She is particularly interested in researching the married life. So she is prepared if she ever gets around to it."

"Remind me to warn the men of London."

She chuckled until he stepped around the bed and gently pushed her hands away from where she was rolling down her stocking. Without taking his gaze from hers, he took over the task, his fingers just callused enough to incite another cascade of chills.

Maybe she could just enjoy herself, she thought briefly. Make tonight special so she could remember when she was lying in that lonely bed next week. Maybe it would be enough to cast caution to the wind, just for tonight. Just for the joy of seeing his eyes grow dark and his nostrils flare. Just for the chance to tempt him to the edge of his control.

So she pulled her skirt up even higher. Slowly. Leaning just a bit forward so he couldn't miss the swell of her breasts or the scent of her soap. So he could almost see what lay just under the hem of her dress as she held it against her thigh.

"Are you sure you want to waste your time with that stocking?" she asked, smiling with that flush of power she was becoming so attached to.

He stepped right up to her to brush her hands aside. Then, reaching his one arm around her back to hold her against him, he reached beneath her hiked hem and sought out the very spot that had begun to ache. She arched against him, opening to his fingers, welcoming his touch. Savoring those calluses that betrayed a life of purpose and risk.

And, there. His eyes grew almost black, and his nostrils flared. His hand trembled just a bit, and his breathing grew harsh. She did that to him.

She leaned a little more into him so she could catch the spice of his scent. So she could begin to tremble herself. And when she saw his smile, an acknowledgement of how close to madness she was driving him, just by opening herself to his touch, she knew the power of being a woman. She savored it like the scent of his skin, like the rasp of those fingers that were tormenting her beyond bearing. She heard herself groan and decided to stifle such a needy sound by reaching up and opening her mouth to his. She met his tongue with her own, fencing with him, tasting the wine that lingered on his breath. She leaned in just a little more and reached over to stroke the bulge that betrayed his impatience.

She was humming now, relishing the symphony of arousal, hungry for his bare skin. He must have heard that in her, because with a rakish grin, he simply swept her into his arms and carried her over to bed. And within moments they were skin-to-skin, the feel of him delicious from the soft curl of his hair to the abrupt ridge of the scars he had carried home. And before he had the chance to satisfy her, she took hold of him and took control. She delighted in running her hands up and down his shaft, measuring, tracing, swirling her fingers over the head so that he jerked in her hand, so that his breathing became gasps. So his body arched to give her better access, and she took it. Took him in her mouth and feasted, not only on his shaft, but the coarse groans, the quick tremors that built, the sweat that salted his skin. She brought him to release and smiled as he cried out and seized in her arms, his seed again anointing her belly.

"Now," he growled, changing places. "It's my turn."

And it was.

They didn't sleep for hours, until exhausted, wrapped around each other, they pulled up the covers and finally rested, sated and sweaty and smiling. And for that moment, life was perfect, and Georgie couldn't have asked for more.

15

She should have known better. She had actually believed things were looking up. The next morning proved that she had just walked from one circus into another.

It didn't get worse right away. She sat down at a lovely early breakfast with the girls, Grey, and Bark, who parked himself right in between the little girls, where the most food landed when falling off plates. Mrs. Peters, the unusually thin blonde cook, had a way with bakery items, as Georgie knew all too well, and Grey was happy to serve both tea and coffee, which Georgie had grown to like on her brief forays to the Continent. The conversation was desultory and comfortable, and Grey only checked his watch twice to make sure they would have time for the estate agent and solicitor.

"He is bringing the papers that will give you supervisory power along with him while I'm gone," Grey said, stirring his tea.

Georgie nodded over the list she was making of her most immediate tasks. "That sounds perfect."

And then she met the estate agent.

"How long has he been in his position?" she quietly asked

Chalmers, as Grey met Mr. Hartman, the estate agent, and Mr. Deevers, the solicitor. "Mr. Hartman, I mean." The estate agent, who wasn't even looking at her.

Chalmers did look over at her, evidently surprised by her question. "About six months, my lady."

She nodded. "I see."

Mr. Deevers was no surprise. He looked much like most solicitors she had interacted with. Businesslike, tidy, greying, with a smile that conveyed caution. Georgie immediately liked him. He reminded her of her Uncle Samson. Mr. Hartman, though....

Georgie trusted her instincts. They had seen her through some difficult times, fractious relatives, and powerful acquaintances. And right now, they were lifting the hair off the back of her neck.

She couldn't quite put a name to it. Maybe it was the fact that when Grey introduced them, Mr. Hartman offered a smile that was pure condescension. Maybe it was the fact that he just looked too slick, his attire just a bit too finely crafted for an estate agent, or that his boots were definitely Hoby. Suddenly she had an overpowering urge to see the estate books.

"You just leave everything to me, my lady," he said with that too-smooth smile. "We'll get along fine."

No, she knew suddenly. They wouldn't. So she sat in on the meeting with the three men, surprising both of their guests, even though she offered nothing more than the occasional nod and a few signatures alongside her husband's on authorization papers after she read the terms quite closely.

"You really want to read all that legal mumbo-jumbo?" Hartman asked, still smiling.

She smiled right back. "I don't like to be surprised."

The terms were there. She and the solicitor had control over the estate until Grey returned from the Continent. She needed to make sure, though.

"If you gentlemen won't mind," she all but purred. "I need to check with my husband about a personal matter. I'm sure Chalmers would be happy to serve tea in the parlor."

The two gentlemen bowed and let Chalmers lead them out.

"There's a problem?" Grey immediately asked, his voice pitched low.

Georgie kept looking after the estate agent. "Your cousin hired Mr. Hartman?"

Now Grey looked that way, as if he could still see the man through the closed door. "He did. Why?"

She shrugged. "I don't know. I just have a…"

"Feeling? Why?" He was smiling. "It couldn't be because he just tried to patronize you."

She couldn't help but grin. "Well, that too. But there is something that just doesn't fit. I need to see the estate books."

"Because his clothing is too well-made and he acts like a politician?"

She looked up to see that knowing smile in his eyes. "You noticed, too?"

"I am new to this," he said, looking back toward the parlor, "but I admit to some suspicion. I just haven't had the chance to dive into the situation yet."

"The estate hasn't been bringing in the income you thought it would, though, has it? What was his reason?"

"A need for maintenance that my cousin fell behind on."

"Why do I have a feeling the rents have been raised without your knowledge?"

He looked back at her, betraying a surprise that should have annoyed her, but didn't. He really was new to all of this. "Are you asking me if you can take care of this little problem while I'm gone?"

"I am."

He cupped her face in his hands and kissed her. "You have my full faith, my girl. Just be careful. He won't be happy if you show him the door."

"He'll be more ready to go if I show him the magistrate. Who is he, by the way?"

Now Grey was frowning. "Well, at Coleford Abbey it is Squire Handy. I wish I could be here. I hate dumping all of this on your plate."

Georgie was proud of herself. She didn't smile and say she would be happy to handle it. Instead, she kissed her husband back. "I wish you could, too. I wish I could wait for you to come back to handle this. But..."

His smile was rueful. "You have a feeling."

GREY THOUGHT he would get out of the house without more problems. His luggage was piled on the carriage, and he was just about to help the girls don their coats when Chalmers showed up at the salon door looking frantic.

"My lord, I...."

Before he could finish, a whirlwind shoved right by him and stomped into the salon, feathers quivering from her puce hat and the floors vibrating beneath her hard heels.

"*There* you are, you lecher. Do you not stay home to care for these poor defenseless girls anymore? Or are you too busy in your debauches? Or is that luggage out there not yours?"

Grey felt the girls freeze all over again and fought the urge to jump in front of them and battle this fury. It was vital, he knew, to assure the girls that they were safe or they would be right back to where they had been a week ago. When he heard Bark growl out beyond the green baize door, he knew he had to act.

It took exactly half a minute to realize that he didn't have to jump to anyone's defense. His wife kissed the top of Amelia's head and passed her little hand to Grey before stalking toward the interloper, a Valkyrie on the march.

"Might I have an introduction, Grey?" she asked, never looking away from the bristling hedgehog of a woman with suspiciously yellow hair and a voice like a foghorn.

"I apologize, Georgianna," he said, still holding onto his girls, who were poised for flight. "Please meet Mrs. Philomena Keyse, the girls' grandmother. Mrs. Keyse, my wife. Lady Georgianna Packham Greyville, Marchioness of Coleford."

One of them should have curtsied. They stood as still as mountain goats readying to butt heads.

"Lady my arse," Mrs. Keyse snorted, looking Georgie up and down as if she were a chorus girl in a sacristy. "She's one of your trollops. That's what she is. If not, I would have been invited to the wedding. And I won't have it!" This with a foot stomp, as if she were six herself. "These girls need a better foundation than your wild escapades! Tell him, Sophie! Tell him, Amelia! Don't let him force you to stay here!"

Grey felt the girls trembling and squeezed tighter. He moved just in front of them. His instinct was to get them out of the room, but Georgie made a minute signal with her hand that kept him in place.

Georgie tilted her head at their grandmother as if she were trying to solve a puzzle. "If you cannot speak in a civil manner, ma'am, I cannot see even letting them stay here now, much less go with you."

Mrs. Keynes shot Grey a scowl. "Aren't you going to do anything?"

If the girls hadn't been literally trembling, he would have happily laughed at Philomena's cherry-red face. "I did do something, ma'am. I gave my daughters security."

"Your daughters?" the woman all but screeched. "*Your* daughters? They are no more your daughters than I am."

He held even more tightly to the girls. "I beg to differ. According to the terms of Francis's will, they are indeed now my daughters. And I suspect the Chancery court will agree."

It actually sounded like she growled. "We'll see about that. Those girls don't belong with a thief and his doxy. They belong with their grandmother, and you know it. "

"With you, Mrs. Keyse?" Georgie countered in a terrible, quiet voice. "A woman who spouts such obscenities in front of her own grandchildren? I sincerely doubt that, madame."

"How dare you?!" the girls' grandmother sputtered. "You have no right to keep my granddaughters from me!"

"But I am not. I will be happy to work out a schedule so you and the girls can spend time together if they choose. Here, if it is agreeable to the girls. But I will tell you now, ma'am, that I will not allow anyone to act in a crude or threatening manner around them in their home. I am not certain where you came from, Mrs. Keynes, but in my family, we do not frighten children."

"Your family," the old woman spit. "*Your* family? Who are your family, if anybody, who would raise such a termagant?"

Grey took a step forward. Georgie motioned him back and took her own step.

"I would be delighted to introduce you to my own grandmother, the Dowager Countess of Clevedon, and let her deal with you if you prefer."

It seemed that the Dowager was just as fearsome as Grey had suspected. His cousin's mother-in-law blanched as if Georgie had threatened her with the guillotine.

Without moving, Georgie seemed to be taking up quite a bit more space. "Now, I am certain the girls would be delighted if you visited, if you only give me some notice. But right now, we are about to accompany their uncle to his ship. If you have any questions, you might ask Mr. Deevers, the Marquess's solicitor. But please let us settle in first."

"Settle in?!" Mrs. Keyse snarled. "Take over. Usurp my daughter's precious memory. Shoving her out of her daughters' life!"

"Which cannot happen if you regularly visit. If you share your most lovely memories of your daughter. I would consider it a great favor if you would send around a note when you are next free. Maybe in a few days? Girls, please give your grandmama your best curtsies."

Grey gave the girls a gentle push and kept his hands on their shoulders for support as they dropped rigid little curtsies.

And before Grey could say a word, Georgie guided the woman out the parlor door and into Chalmers' waiting hands. The woman was out the door before she could protest, as if she were a person begging for a donation.

Grey couldn't help but stand there staring. No one in his memory had ever dealt so efficiently with that woman.

"I'm sorry," he said. "I should have warned you."

Georgie flashed a brilliant smile at him and the girls. "Oh, you did. It's the lovely thing about growing up at the foot of my grandmama. You learn such useful lessons. Like how to dispatch with annoyances. I must thank her when I see her again." Then, without turning, she addressed Chalmers who had reappeared, looking just a bit chuffed. "Chalmers, do you think Cook has some biscuits the girls could take along on the ride?"

Chalmers bowed as if he were addressing the queen. "He does, my lady. I shall be happy to see to the matter personally."

"Excellent. Thank you. Now," she said, kneeling before the girls. "I am very sorry you had to see your grandmama upset, but she was not in a very agreeable mood, was she?"

She got a pair of wide-eyed shaken heads. She nodded back.

"I would have let you hop off with Chalmers when your Grand-mama came, but your Uncle Grey and I wanted you to see that we are always on your side. We are family, now, aren't we? And nothing is more important than family. It will be your decision about whether to visit with anyone. And if you decide to visit with your grandmama, it will always be here where you are safe and everyone in the house—" As if on cue, Bark gave a rousing howl out in the kitchen. Georgie grinned. "Especially Bark—is here with you. Maybe even the Packhams. Is that all right?"

The girls looked at each other and then to Grey before offering tentative nods.

It was Grey's turn to kneel. "I think sometimes you haven't felt safe," he said, holding their hands. "But from now on, Aunt Georgie and I and Chalmers and Mrs. Chalmers and all the staff —and the Packhams—will be here to help Bark keep you safe."

The nods were still tentative, but Grey knew it was still too soon for certainty. So, he hugged them both and stood up.

"Now," he said. "Are we ready to go, Aunt Georgie?"

She smiled and held out coats. "We are, Uncle Grey."

And for the first time since Grey discovered two frightened little girls in his front parlor, he felt positive about leaving his household to do the government's work. Somehow, he had been gifted with the perfect wife to handle things at home while he was gone. Even if it was the last thing she wanted to do.

It was as they were seated with the girls in the carriage wending their way toward the docks that Grey realized that his wife was just a bit too bright, her posture a bit too perfect, as if she were bracing herself. As if she were protecting him and the girls from the real impact of the morning's meetings on her.

Suddenly he realized he really didn't want to go right then. He wanted to call out to Braxton to tell Drake to stuff his mission. Grey had more important things to do.

Except, in the greater scheme of things, he didn't. It was

absolutely vital he find Gracechurch and learn what intelligence he had unearthed. And he had to do it as quickly as possible.

"I'm sorry," he said very quietly, glad the girls were focused on their ginger biscuits.

Georgie turned, betraying surprise. "What for?"

His smile was rueful. "Dumping this all on you. I'm not sure who will be the biggest nightmare, Hartman or Philomena."

He'd been hoping for a real smile. What he got was a carefully drawn in breath. "Oh, if worse comes to worse, I shall call for Grandmama to back me up. I have yet to meet anyone with the brass to challenge her. And then, when you return home, I will have toted up the cost of your absence, which will be paid with support for my projects."

Smiling, he took her hand. "Gladly," he assured her. "You never told me what they are."

Her own smile was private. "I know."

"I don't get a hint?"

"When you are ready to stay home. I'll have the tally by then."

He had the dreadful suspicion that cost was going to be high.

"Well, at least I gave you a safe place to escape to, if necessary," he offered. "If worse comes to worse, you and the girls can always run away to Painswick Park."

"One of your properties?"

He stared a bit. "No. In fact, one of yours."

Georgie blinked. She blinked again. "Pardon?"

Grey sighed. "You didn't read the settlements? I was sure you would."

She shook her head, suddenly looking truly shaken. "I was so busy. Father assured me you had settled sufficient funds."

Grey scowled. "But he forgot to mention you have your own estate."

She was still profoundly silent.

Gray nodded. "You can read my copy when you get back to the townhouse, if you'd like. It is in the wall safe. You are in control of one third of your dowry and have control of Painswick Park, allegedly a nice little piece of land and manor house in the Cotswolds. Also near Coleford Abbey and Gloucester, come to think of it."

Georgie began to shake her head. "I don't understand."

He smiled and picked up her hand. "Georgie. Because of you, I will be allowed to recover the heritage my cousins squandered. The least I can do is share some of it with you." Lifting her hand, he kissed her knuckles. "Although if I end up being as profligate as my cousins, I may have to ask you for a loan."

"An estate," she said, as if the word were foreign. "It cannot be in my name. I'm a woman."

"It is held in trust. Deevers can explain it all. He has the paperwork and is the trustee, and I am told there is an excellent steward on site. You can control it all yourself, leave it all to them, or have me handle it. Although I admit I am a neophyte at this estate business. I was rather hoping I could get advice from you."

He'd thought she knew. He'd thought she hadn't been that impressed. Looking at her now, he realized he had just given her the shock of her life.

"Georgie," he murmured, lifting a hand to her cheek. "The estate is to provide you stability, no matter what. It is not meant to be another burden."

Georgie shook her head, as if the weight of his gesture threw her off-balance. "So, if I wanted, I could turn the estate into a home for fallen women or climbing boys?"

"As long as they bathe."

"A military camp?"

"Same rule."

She kept her gaze on Gray's, her eyes wide and glistening. "You mean it."

He met her gaze without flinching. "I do. I know what a burden I am putting on your shoulders. I wanted to lighten it even if just a little. No matter what happens in the future, you will never have to rely on anyone else for your safety."

"And the girls?"

He shook his head again, this time feeling a bit disappointed. "Your father really didn't let you see the settlements. The girls are taken care of as well, thanks to the generosity of your dowry. You and Deevers are their guardians. And I do thank you for that. Their well-being means a lot to me."

Georgie nodded. "Me as well."

This time he didn't kiss her hand, he kissed her lips. A small kiss of companionship, a grace bestowed, a thanks. "This old soldier thanks you, Lady Coleford. You have relieved him of his greatest worry. The rest can be managed. Especially since I don't have to worry about charging an enemy on horseback any longer. Whatever the cost, I will happily comply.And then I hope we can really begin to become a family."

It was two hours later as they stood on the dock, each holding one of the girls' hands, that he knew exactly what the cost would be.

"Have a safe trip," his brand-new wife said to him, then gave a very slow wink. "Because when you get home, you and I have unfinished business."

He almost didn't get on the ship at all.

There were times he wondered if he was really as devoted to the Crown as he thought.

16

———

It didn't turn out to be as bad as Georgie had feared. It turned out to be worse. And the problems didn't even wait until she and the girls made it home. The carriage was working its way through traffic back up towards Mayfair when Amelia began to whimper.

Georgie looked over to see that her little face was pale. "What is it, sweetheart?"

She didn't look up. "Do I need to call you Mama?"

Georgie had to admit that that was not the question she expected. She reached over to smooth back the little girl's hair to realize it was a bit damp. "Not if you do not want to, my dear. I would never ever want to take your mama's place. Would Aunt Georgie do for now?"

She nodded, still looking miserable. Even Sophie was looking over now.

"Aunt Georgie?" Amelia asked, still not looking up. "I think... I..."

"Oh, no," Sophie suddenly piped up, jumping off the seat. "She's going to puke!"

Georgie was about to chastise Sophie when Amelia looked

up, and Georgie knew that not only was Sophie correct, but they had run out of time. Pounding on the roof of the carriage, Georgie bent to throw open the door. John Coachman pulled over at the same moment Georgie unlatched the door and grabbed the little girl under the arms.

It was close, but she managed to get Amelia's head safely over the side of the carriage before she lost the cinnamon buns she had gorged on that morning, not to mention the biscuits Georgie had added.

"Milady?" Barney, one of the grooms asked, hopping down.

"We're fine, Barney," she said, making sure her voice stayed calm as she pulled a handkerchief from her reticule. "Amelia? Is that better?"

"Usually she only does it once," Sophie assured her with an older sister kind of nod.

"Amelia?" Georgie asked.

She shook her head. "I want to go home."

Georgie wiped the little girl's face and looked up to motion to Barney. Waiting until Georgie was certain it was safe to close the door, he obliged and climbed back up.

"We're on our way right now, sweets," Georgie said. "Does this happen often?"

"Only when she eats too much and we're in a carriage," Sophie told her with another of those nods.

Georgie gathered Amelia into her lap as the carriage lurched to a start and rested the little one's head against her shoulder. "Well, the good news is that we're not far from home. We shall be there in a minute."

"Not *that* home," Amelia whined. "*Our* home. I want to go *h-o-o-o-o-o-m-e!*"

Georgie looked up at Sophie, who shook her head. "It isn't our home anymore, Amelia. Papa sold it to that man, remember? This is the only one we have now. I *told* you."

Georgie hugged her new daughter just a bit more tightly. "Well," she corrected, "not the only one. But I don't believe this would be a good time to go searching out the others."

The others. Including the one Grey had given to her. That quickly Georgie was swamped with longing, loss, regret that she had not trusted Grey more. She owed him so much, suddenly. She wished she had properly thanked him, because he had given her unheard-of independence. He had given her autonomy, if she wanted. Sanctuary. She just had to convince the solicitor she could manage it.

Painswick Park. She might have to change the name. Maybe Thoughtful Husband House. Marvelous Marquess Manor.

Oddly enough, that was what made her smile.

Considering the fact that even though Amelia had recovered from her vomiting, she developed a heretofore unheard whine, the pitch and volume of which would have sent a saint's teeth to grinding, Georgie was afraid it was going to be a very long night. After all, she was no saint herself. And even as familiar as she was with her own siblings' unerring knack for that unbearable pitch, it still set her teeth vibrating.

The good news was that Barney helped carry the little girl inside, and Minta met them at the girls' bedroom.

"Ah, the poor wee thing," she said. "Let me have her, milady. I know how this goes. Got sisters of my own, don't I?"

The bad news was that when Georgie helped Minta get Amelia out of her dress, she realized the little girl was hot. Which meant it was not just a surfeit of sweets this time. So, she got to visit with her family physician Dr. Banks, a gruff old graying veteran of wars and diplomatic families, who promptly answered her call to reassure her that this child's fever was no different than the others she had survived for years with her own family. Which also meant she spent the rest of the night dealing with a stubborn fever.

The next morning, when Minta and Sophie—and Bark—took over the whimpering Amelia's care, Georgie skipped much-needed sleep to first gather the entire staff in the large foyer. She didn't know many of them yet, but she needed to deliver a message.

"As you all know," she said, "the Marquess had to leave on diplomatic business yesterday. Which means we are left behind to not only maintain his home but brighten it—" Scowling, she took a look around. "—considerably."

For that she got smiles. She nodded. "If you have any concerns, please feel free to bring them to Mrs. Chalmers, and she will bring them to me. I am quite open to suggestion. You see, if any of you didn't know already, I was rather in charge of my father's home these last five years or so. So, I know how households work."

Seeing the smiles on most of the faces, she paused. Time to send the real message "I also know by the surprising appearance of Mrs. Keyse yesterday, even before the wedding announcement was in the papers, that someone on this staff alerted her to events here. I will not demand a confession. I will say that I suspect others on staff knew about this, and that it ends here and now. I do not tolerate disloyalty, not to the Marquess, not to me, and especially not to the little girls, who deserve your kindness most of all. If I find that anyone is sharing information about this house without either myself or Mrs. Chalmers knowing—they will be summarily discharged without reference. And make no mistake. If that sharing involves anything illegal or harmful to our girls, I will not hesitate to bring down the law. Do we understand each other?"

She got a forest of head bobs and curtsies. She nodded back. "I would also appreciate an appraisal of any extra staff we might need. I am already looking for a governess and nursery maid. And a groom for the girls' ponies, which should arrive soon."

Accepting another round of nods, she nodded back and smiled. "My primary aim right now is to make this the most comfortable home I can, not even primarily for me or the Marquess, no matter how much I like him. It is for the girls. I would appreciate any help. Thank you. And thank you for welcoming me into what was your home first."

Having sent that message, her next task was to sit down with Mr. Deevers, so she could get a decent overview of Grey's holdings and responsibilities. It told her a lot about Deevers' relationship with Hartman that he didn't even question her getting her information from him rather than the estate agent.

The good news was that except for the horse farm in Ireland, the estates were all within a reasonable distance. The bad news was that somehow Hartman had taken control of all of them except Painswick Park. Which meant that she would also have to think about hiring men at each estate to supervise their running. Once she broke the news to Mr. Hartman, anyway.

With that information in hand, she sent grooms for the estate books and a note to Mrs. O'Toole to begin the search for not just a governess, but a nursery maid. And then Georgie took a bit of time with not only Mr. and Mrs. Chalmers, but the three footmen who staffed the house, to see which she could trust to protect all of them when out and about.

"Any of them can, milady," Mrs. Chalmers said, posture betraying her sense of insult that Georgie couldn't trust her or the mister's hiring. "They're all good lads."

"I know they are," Georgie answered from behind the small desk tucked into the corner of the library. "In a normal circumstance, that would be enough. But if my suspicions are correct, Mr. Hartman is about to find himself in need of new employment, and some things I've heard make me distrust his good will."

At that, the stolid middle-aged housekeeper straightened

like a Grenadier and offered quite a frown. "Well, we can't have that, now, can we?" She seemed to think a moment and then broke out in a quick grin. "You might also find a way to get hold of one of his handkerchiefs or some such so Bark knows his scent. Can I also suggest that our new tiger, Mick Tuesday, might be helpful there? Mick has rather a history with acquiring other people's handkerchiefs."

Georgie looked up in surprise and ended up grinning right back. "I knew I could count on your knack for efficient planning, Mrs. Chalmers. We shall see it done."

She wasn't truly surprised that Hartman refused her request for the books. She had actually put a contingency plan into action for that possibility. Her uncle had an assistant at the Castle, the son of a tenant, who was quite promising but constrained by the fact that Uncle Packham would never loosen his own hold over the Packham properties. Maybe young Winslow would enjoy a chance at the Greyville holdings. Besides, it would give him and Minta a chance at the life they wanted. Even better, he was a strapping young man, even larger than the footmen. She could send him after the books, and even let him study them without worry.

She didn't tell Minta until she had contacted Uncle Packham, who answered her plea for help promptly and with enthusiasm.

This is just the chance he needs, the answering note read. *He always has a place here if it doesn't work out.*

And so, with a beaming Minta to greet him, young Peter Winslow gladly accepted the promotion and his instructions as to first inspecting the properties for Georgie to assess their various needs and then after, conferring with her to address the various problems. After, of course, dispensing with the problem of Mr. Hartman.

Which, of course, brought Hartman racing to Mayfair to confront the uppity woman who didn't know her place.

"But I do know my place, Mr. Hartman," she said to the red-faced man who paced her library. "It is to protect the Marquess's holdings until he returns."

"You'll pardon my saying so, ma'am," he retorted, hands on her desk as he leaned in. "But that is *my* job, which I've been doing since long before you showed up."

Georgie was sure he thought he was threatening. He hadn't grown up with the Packham boys. She just hoped Winslow had taken advantage of Hartman's absence from the estates to get all the estate books collected. She also hoped he'd been able to check Hartman's cottage for an extra set of books or ill-gotten gains.

"What would a woman know of the needs of an estate this size?" the about-to-be-fired estate agent demanded, with an unwise amount of disdain. "This isn't planning dinner and counting linen."

"Mr. Hartman," she said with absolute calm, "you were there when my husband informed you and Mr. Deevers that I was to be apprised of all the estate's business. You nodded, as I recall. You cannot suddenly claim surprise. I would think you would be glad to have the Marquess and me involved in the running of the Greyville properties."

His scowl was ferocious, but Georgie was working on very little sleep and the distraction of a sick daughter, and didn't have the patience for his theatrics.

"I assumed he meant normal ladies' duties," he countered.

She smiled. "Those, too."

She almost threatened him with her grandmother as well. But then she saw the calculating look come into his eyes and knew quite clearly that his days with the Greyvilles were numbered.

"I have contacted my uncle who runs the Packham estates," she said before he could set off on another attempt at control, "and asked for his advice, along with the aid of one of our land agent's assistants to help you and me with this transition, Mr. Hartman. I know you will accord him every courtesy. He is a bright young man, and anxious to be of any help he can."

That straightened Harman like a shot. "I don't need any help. We've been doing fine here."

They hadn't, but she nodded anyway. "But there is always a transition when a new master takes over. Which will be complicated by the Marquess's obligations to the Crown. I know you agree that we need to do all we can to help ease his responsibilities as we care for his properties."

She knew he was grinding his teeth, but there was really nothing else for him to say. With a sharp nod of his head, he spun around and stalked out. Without her permission, she noted. Just as well. She needed to get up to check on Amelia and make sure Sophie was all right. And then she had to go over staff needs with the Chalmers. And somewhere in there she had to fit in some sleep.

After that, her days were completely taken up with the burden of dispensing with the responsibilities she had left behind at home and learning about the different Greyville estates on the one hand and her new children on the other. Her family helped with the second, thank heaven, especially after Amelia slept off her fever and needed distraction. Mrs. O'Toole helped find the extra nursery staff needed, but Georgie had to interview governess candidates. She didn't even manage to get away for her regular Friday forays, which made her all the more surly, even though the only people who were questionably privileged enough to witness it were the kings, who dropped by when they could to help. The girls loved them, Bark showed them his belly, and Georgie swore they carried sanity on their shoulders. She also began to systematically load them back down with the duties she was trading for those at the Greyville properties. Charlie, she handed the farming tasks, and Eddie, the household tasks.

There was no one she could hand Mrs. Keyse off to, so she suffered through three visits, not leaving the girls for a second while the slyly poisonous woman was in reach. Nor did she let Bark leave them, his eyes unerringly on the source of the tension in the room. Georgie had to admit that she was secretly delighted that he threw Mrs. Keyse off balance. It also helped her equilibrium that she surreptitiously let Bark get a good sniff at the older woman's clothing.

The good news was that she and Grey wrote back and forth. Georgie relayed edited news about Mrs. Keyse's visits and Winslow's trial employment. She mentioned Winslow's investigation into the estate books, but might have left out her own findings, since there was nothing Grey could do about them till he returned.

Her instincts had run true after all. When she reviewed the books with Winslow, it was to find them showing a higher cost of supplies than the purveyors remembered, and that rents had indeed been raised regularly without mention in the ledgers. Grey would find out about that and her remedies when he returned.Instead she filled her letters with news of the girls and their greetings in the form of sketches of Bark and the barn cats. The bad news was that Grey only corresponded once a week, sending not only what would have been considered harmless news from the embassy, but little gimcrack gifts to the girls and sketches he'd drawn of the people and places he saw on the street, like an organ grinder and monkey, a magician, and, of course, the street vendors.

Every night, much too late for real rest, Georgie fell into bed. And every night, she fought the shearing sense of loss at missing

Grey. Not just his wit and sense and sly humor. The simple warm comfort of his body lying alongside hers. The open-air scent of him and the rumble of his laugh. She had slept with him one night. One. And she missed him all out of proportion. Wouldn't it just be an irony if she went ahead and fell in love with the man once he was out of reach?

Had she really had to demand a white marriage? Would it truly protect her in any way, when she already suffered not having him here? Couldn't she have had that one night when there could have been no boundaries between the two of them? Couldn't she just once have felt the fulfillment of the marital act?

In her saner moments she knew better. Her burden was heavy enough as it was, especially knowing the confrontation that was coming with Hartman. The last thing she needed on top of that was a pregnancy.

So, she went to bed alone, although on occasion she would wake to see little faces standing by the side of her bed and invite them in for the rest of the night. She woke alone except for the newest maid Mary, who sneaked in to lay the fires.

At least she did not eat alone. The last thing the girls needed when trying to settle into a new—and evidently completely unknown—structure of family life, was to be banished to the top floor while their new mother—well, their Aunt Georgie— ate in lonely splendor in the dining room. So they all ate together in the breakfast room, sometimes alone and sometimes with their new governess, Mrs. O'Toole's niece Kathleen, a bright, calm redhead, who loved little girls only a little more than she loved big dogs.

And then again, alone to bed with only the comfort of weekly letters and the memory of one night to comfort her.

~

THE CONFRONTATION with Hartman inevitably came. Georgie was wise enough not to face him alone. In fact, her Uncle Samson was gracious enough to sit alongside her, along with Winslow, footmen in the hallway just in case of problems, and Bark seated right next to Hartman's chair, the dog's attention razor sharp, his lips every once in a while curled back to show very sharp teeth.

"I doubt we need to show you the books," she said, Uncle Samson perched silently beside her behind the desk, his silver hair gleaming in the morning light. "In fact, I am not at all certain why you're still here. If I tried to present this imaginative accounting to my employer, I would have long since caught a ship for anywhere else."

Hartman gave Georgie one scathing look and kept his silence.

"In fact," she said, tapping the ledgers with her finger. "We have discussed it, and we have decided that if you want to avoid prosecution, you should definitely be on a ship by end of the day. This way you may pick the location of your choice instead of being shackled on a vessel on its way to Van Dieman's Land. I will be happy to offer you transportation to first take you to recover your personal effects and then safely transport you to the docks. I have a list of ships about to sail, if it is necessary. Oh, and that little stash of money hidden behind the loose brick in your bedroom won't be going with you. I'm sure you have enough in the bank."

Hartman was on his feet so fast Georgie had to focus not to flinch. "You'll regret this," he snarled.

Uncle Samson gave him a dry smile. "I was afraid you would say that."

Which was how Hartman was bodily escorted to his house for his things, down to the docks, and onto a ship for the

Western Hemisphere, three footmen watching from the dock until he was a distance down the river.

At last able to relax a bit, Georgie dove into the family finances, the redecorating of the London townhouse, and the curriculum and schedule for the girls. She was even able to get hold of Grey's old stablemaster, who promised to be there within the week with two ponies who would be perfect for little novice riders. After little more than a month—that seemed like six—things were beginning to settle. Which made it an even worse shock to see who showed up at her door.

She was on her way out of the small library she had taken as her office, her arms full of estate books, when someone made use of the door knocker. She knew she undoubtedly should have waited for one of the staff to answer it, but Chalmers was in the wine cellar arranging the shipment of claret she had just secured, and the footmen were most likely helping carry out debris from the renovations that were in progress. She had just finished changing over what she fondly referred to as the Mud Parlor. She and the girls had decided that it should be a sunny yellow with royal blue settees and a Tintoretto of Venice over the fireplace. Now that they had repaired the roof, it even smelled better. She couldn't wait for Grey to see it all. It was why she was driving everyone so hard. She wanted it done when he came home, all the once-peeling, moldy, grimly dark rooms rehabilitated and welcoming.

In the meantime, though, the visitor made another foray with the knocker. Georgie stopped in the middle of the hall and looked around, but there was no help. She should be able to answer her own door, really. She was a marchioness. Couldn't a marchioness open her own door if she wanted? What could go wrong?

She knew the minute she swung the door wide. She heard the echoing thud of the books dropping onto the marble floor. She thought she heard a moan and wondered where it had come from.

"What are you doing here?" she demanded.

For there on her stoop stood three uniformed officers. One dark and fierce, one golden blond, one with hair the color of fall leaves. Three Archangels in the flesh.

Just standing there, as if waiting for a command to stand down.

Georgie wasn't sure if it was the door or the thudding books he heard, but suddenly Chalmers was standing behind her. She could hear him catch his breath.

"What are you doing here?" she asked again of the three on her doorstep.

Even before they answered, she felt a great hole tear open in her chest. She couldn't breathe. She couldn't think. She couldn't bear for them to answer.

But they did.

"We need to talk to you," Michael the Warrior said, his grey eyes grave, his posture in his Guardsman red rigid.

They even looked like their namesakes, she thought absurdly. Michael the Warrior, dark and fierce. Gabriel the Messenger, golden blond. And Rafael the healer, with hair the color of blood. Her family.

Still, she couldn't seem to move. "Chalmers?" she asked, fighting to keep her voice level so she didn't begin shrieking like a madwoman.

Grey. Oh, Grey.

"Where are the little girls?" she asked without turning.

"In the park, my lady," the gentle voice answered behind her. "With Miss Breck."

She nodded. "Please send someone to advise her to keep the girls there for a bit. Until I call for them. I imagine I will also need to assemble the staff in about an hour."

"Yes, milady."

"And Chalmers."

"Yes, ma'am."

"Send for Madame Marie. I believe we will be needing black."

Without a word she turned to led the way up the stairs, not so much as motioning her brother and cousins to follow. She knew they would. They had news to deliver. It was the only reason they could be here. In England together. At her new house. The house of the Marchioness of Coleford. She knew there was something else the Marchioness was supposed to do at a time like this, but her brain suddenly felt as frozen as her heart. As useless.

Grey.

Incongruously she led them into the Yellow Salon, as if bad news could be eased by bright walls. She motioned for them to sit. She took the newly upholstered royal blue settee to one side of the Adams fireplace. The Archangels shared the settee opposite, easing down in perfect unison, two Guardsmen in sharp red against that blue, and Rafael, who had never felt the desire for the flashy garb of the Guards, in his flat olive Rifleman green. Hands on knees, backs barracks-straight.

"Tell me."

She was trembling. She couldn't tremble. She had no place to fall apart. She had no right. Evidently, she didn't have enough force of will to win. But she could keep the Archangels from seeing it. Hearing it in her voice. Recognizing it in her eyes, where she thought the devastation should have been painfully obvious. Tears clogged her throat, but she had enough will to force them down. Tears would do no good. Tears could wait, just like always.

"I'm sorry, Georgie," her brother Michael said, his severe face even harsher. "Our superior dispatched all three of us to be with you."

She nodded. She did nod, didn't she? She wasn't quite sure. Everything suddenly felt encased in ice. Even her trembling heart.

"How? The battles are over."

"He was freeing one of our people from a prison. There was...an...explosion."

That hit like a punch to the chest. She was suddenly terrified that every time she closed her eyes, she would see Grey disintegrate before her. She would hear his screams, whether he'd screamed or not. She couldn't ask.

"Did he save the other man? The one he went to find?"

"He did."

She nodded. "Can they..." She swallowed, cleared her throat. "Can they bring him home for burial?"

Michael didn't even shake his head. She could see the devastation in his eyes as well. And Rafe's. And Gabe's.

"I should be comforting you," she said, reverting to what she knew best. "You knew him far better than I."

"You were married to him," Gabe protested.

She managed a smile, although she suspected it looked like a rictus. "For all of two days." Then she laughed, as if the irony of the situation really did amuse her. "In fact, we've been married so short a time I don't even know which estate has the family plot. At least we can put up a stone. Have a service." She realized she was rubbing at her temple and pulled her hand away. She didn't have time. She had no time. She had so much to do, and she hadn't even told the girls.

Oh, sweet God, the girls.

"His man of business should know," Michael said. "About the plot."

She managed another grim smile. "I am his man of business. It was an added bonus to the marriage. Along with my money came my expertise. It is just that the expertise never extended to where to bury my husband."

She could tell she was appalling Rafe. Rafe the healer. Rafe should have known though, how she would react. It was the only way she had ever been allowed to react to anything.

"Should we call for Mother?" Michael asked.

She shook her head. "She and Father will be at the military review in Hyde Park. And later a spectacle. All the heads of state are here."

She sounded so matter of fact, as if she didn't feel as if she were the one disintegrating, collapsing into that terrible void that had opened up inside where there was room for nothing but pain and tears.

Tears she didn't have time for.

She must have been silent for too long. The boys were looking uncomfortable. But then, what did one do after delivering the kind of news that tore a person apart?

"Will you..." She had to swallow again. "Will you tell the family for me? Tell them to not come stampeding over, please. The girls won't need all that fuss."

"Is there anything else we can do?" Rafe asked, Rafe the Healer.

She blinked. Tried to think. Couldn't come up with anything. She couldn't even comprehend the idea of asking them for help. That was her job. It was always her job.

Just like now.

"Not right now," she finally managed. "I need to tell the girls. And the staff. And I imagine Grey's solicitor. There is an heir who needs to be found."

They stood up. She stood up. Michael came up to her and wrapped his arms around her. She returned the gesture. After all, Grey had been Michael's friend.

Had been.

Had been.

She hoped they left soon. Suddenly she was afraid she would vomit all down the front of one of those uniforms.

"Thank you," she said into the soft wool of Michael's scarlet jacket. "For coming yourselves."

He pulled back, still holding her by the arms and looking down at her as if assessing the risk of his leaving.

So, she smiled. "I am all right, Michael. Truly. Like I said. I only knew him a bit more than a week."

A week that had opened her world in ways she would never reclaim. A week of his gentle smiles, wry humor, and clever hands. A week of planning and sharing and anticipation.

All gone. Disappeared to leave a world even smaller than the one she'd been trying to escape. A world suddenly painted in pain and loss. And little girls who had to be told.

The men were turning to leave when she did remember something. "Braxton," she said suddenly. "Where is he? Was he involved?"

Michael turned back to her. "He suffered some burns, a few broken bones."

She nodded. "Where is he?"

Michael's eyebrows went up. "At his sister's in Stepney."

Georgie swallowed. "Can you have someone check up on him, please, and make sure he has everything he needs?"

She knew Michael thought she was mad. She truly didn't

care. "It's the least we can do. Please tell him I will visit when I can."

And with that, she sent the Archangels on their way. She gave her cousins their own hugs and then led them down the stairs and out. And for the longest time, she just stood there in the foyer with the sun streaming in through the window over the door and stared at nothing. It was where Chalmers found her.

"Go get the girls," she said and turned away.

SHE SHOULD HAVE KNOWN her family wouldn't stay away. She was curled up on the overstuffed royal blue settee in the yellow parlor, an arm around each little girl as they huddled against her like puppies caught out in a storm, Bark curled up at their feet. It had been hard. It had been harder than anything she had ever done, and it would get harder. They were suffering the first shock now, but when that wore off, the girls would have to once again face an unsafe world. And all Georgie could do was hold them. Because suddenly she understood that.

She had known him for a week. A single week, and he had upended her life. And then gone. He had begun to change the shape of her future, change the focus of her life. Change completely her relationship with her own body, which ached now as if she had been physically attacked. Sharp pain seemed to live in each breath she took, which like a tide, kept rising until it choked her. Until it deafened her and stole her voice. Until it left her too useless to do anything but hold two little girls who hurt even more than she did.

He was gone, and he had taken something with him. Something vital and dear, something she knew she would never find again.

He was gone and she was left alone again to do what she always did. Tidy up, correct, reclaim.

"Will we have to leave again?" a tiny voice suddenly piped up from her lap.

Would they?

"I don't know, my love," she said, squeezing a little tighter. "We must see what the new Marquess has to say. But never fear. If we cannot stay here, we can live at the Packham house with the other children. But whatever we decide, we stay together. Because what did Uncle Grey call us?"

Sophie sighed. "Family."

"That's right. Wherever we go, families go together."

Or they could go to Painswick Park. She couldn't even think that far yet.

She had talked to Mr. Deevers. No one had any idea who the heir was. They had never had to look. So, she and the girls were once again suspended over a chasm without a familiar way forward.

At least they knew where to put up the headstone. But she would think about that later.

"Milady," Chalmers murmured from the door.

But before he could finish, there was a whoosh and suddenly her mother was standing before her. Georgie wasn't exactly sure what to do. Her mother was a lovely, serene person, but not much of a hugger. Bark struggled to his feet as her mother gently nudged him out of the way. It said everything about her mother that Bark let her near his girls.

"What do you mean *don't bother my mother*?" she asked without preamble, which told Georgie all she needed to know about how upset her mother was. Amelia and Sophie sat up and scrubbed damp faces with the backs of their hands.

Georgie's mama promptly crouched down and threw open her arms, and the girls tumbled straight into them. Georgie admitted that she stared. Who was this person? She wondered vaguely. She couldn't remember her mother ever being so demonstrative, never mind wrinkling her dress so egregiously. Slowly, feeling as if she had suddenly developed arthritis, she unwound herself from her place on the couch.

"I asked your cousins to wait a bit so I could see you first," her mama said as she stroked little girls' hair. "Your grandmama would not be put off, however. She is on her way."

Of course she was. And here Georgie had thought she couldn't feel more exhausted.

"Chalmers," she said, her voice perfectly placid. "Did I hear Miss Breck was bringing a tea up to the girls to fortify them? With cinnamon buns?"

"You did, milady," he allowed with a small bow.

She nodded. "Girls, may I speak to my mama alone for a bit? Miss Breck is waiting to give you treats."

Both girls straightened. Sophie met Georgie's eyes head-on. "You will not leave?"

She met her eye-to-eye. "I will not leave. When you have gorged your fill, you may come back to find me right here in our new yellow salon."

"Is that all right, Grandmama Packham?" Sophie asked, so suddenly small and uncertain.

Her mama dropped a kiss on each forehead. "I will watch over Aunt Georgie while you are enjoying those cinnamon buns," she promised.

"Good," Amelia said. "We are sad today. Uncle Grey died, you know. You're not going to die, are you?"

God bless her mama. She gave the girls another good squeeze. "Everyone dies sometime," she said. "But today I will be waiting for you right here."

The girls both nodded and dropped unsteady curtsies, and then Sophie took hold of her sister's hand and led her and Bark out of the room, Chalmers closing the door behind them. Sitting down without a word next to Georgie, her mother did something she never did. She wrapped her arms around Georgie. And Georgie did what she had never in her life done before. She burst into tears.

18

———

Georgie had no idea how long she cried. She knew she cried to exhaustion. She knew she lost every barrier and bit of training that had seen her through her first twenty years, the same discipline that had allowed her to take control of every kind of situation her family had faced. She knew she had never once so much as dampened her mother's clothing. Well, she did now.

At one point she thought she heard the door open and quickly click close. She wasted no attention on it. She knew that her mother, the most quietly controlled woman she'd ever known, watered Georgie as well. She knew that sooner or later she would have to get back on her feet and take control again. It was her duty. Her responsibility. Her privilege. At least her Aunt Berenice would put it that way when she saw her again.

But for now, she was a lost child who needed her mother.

"You fell in love with him," her mother said very matter-of-factly, pulling back to hold Georgie's face in her hands.

Georgie fought fresh tears. "Silly, isn't it? I barely knew him a week. I was married for two days—a day-and-a-half, really. Is that a record?"

Her mother briefly rested her forehead against Georgie's, still holding her face. "Not silly at all. I fell in love with your father the first time I saw him laugh. You have been falling in love with Greyville ever since you began reading his name in the dispatches to Geoffrey. During that week you spent with him you were just lucky enough to realize he was the man you'd hoped he'd be."

Georgie sucked in a ragged breath. "I was lucky, wasn't I?"

Her mama just nodded. Georgie squeezed her eyes shut against the pain.

"Your grandmama is here," her mother finally said when both their eyes were once again fairly dry. "Will you see her?"

Georgie wanted to say no. She wanted to send everyone away and crawl up to her bed and curl into a small ball and sleep. She wanted to close her eyes and keep everyone and everything out. She knew better, though. Nothing, in the end, was changed. She still had to create order out of disaster. And she had to begin to do it now.

"Of course," she said, sitting up to find her mother holding out a sturdy man's handkerchief to her.

"Your father won't miss it. I figured a woman's handkerchief simply didn't have the volume needed to handle this situation."

Georgie accepted it with a smile. She noticed her mother had another for herself that she applied briskly. Then Georgie climbed to her feet and walked over to the bell pull.

"Please have the Dowager join us," she told Chalmers when he immediately responded.

Georgie caught her breath. Chalmers already wore a black armband for mourning. He saw her attention and touched it, as if that would make it real. "We have a store of these still from the last marquess. I hope you don't mind."

"Of course not," Georgie assured him, her chest feeling too

tight to take a good breath. "Thank you for your prompt attention."

For just a moment, Chalmers betrayed his own grief. He opened his mouth to say something, but after a moment, simply closed it again. Shaking his head, he turned for the door to bring in the Dowager.

Georgie and her mother immediately stood. And for the second time in her life, she was the recipient of unheard-of comfort. Her grandmother also wrapped her in her arms and simply held on. It almost broke Georgie all over again.

"I saw the girls," Grandmama said, her own voice sounding a bit shaky. "They have suffered too much. Too much."

Georgie gave her grandmama one final hug and separated herself. "I wish I could make it better."

"Move home," Grandmama said. "Let them run about with our brood for a bit."

Georgie sighed. "I'll think about it."

For a long moment, Grandmama just looked at her in silence. "You must tell the bees," she finally said.

Georgie reared back as if she had been slapped. "No," she said, stepping away. Lifting her hand, she waved at her grandmother as if shooing her away. "No."

Grandmama frowned. "You know they must be told."

Georgie turned around. "Not yet. Not...yet. The girls are not ready."

I am not ready, she thought wildly as she rubbed at the fresh pain in her chest. She didn't bother to consider that in fact she would never be ready.

"Georgie..."

She shook her head. "Let them pretend for a while that everything is still all right. Don't rile them until we need to."

She knew that her grandmama was looking at her mother, as if for support. She had no idea what her mother did. Her own eyes were closed, and she was digging the heels of her hands into them to stop further tears. She had to calm down before the girls returned. She had to be their rock now. No more tears. No wailing as if the banshee hovered in the room.

Two days.

Two. Days.

Georgie almost couldn't believe it, but her grandmama finally nodded and backed off. They sat like civilized people and discussed arrangements for the memorial stone and service. Eventually the girls returned, giving Grandmama a stiff little curtsy, and Grandmama held her arms out as well.

At least the girls would get all the support they needed. Perhaps it had been a good thing after all that Georgie had been forced down the aisle, even for two days, so that the girls, who had so often been deserted and discarded, had the cushion of their new family to comfort them.

IT WAS inevitable that the kings came. They took over the redecorating and cared for the girls when Georgie was pulled away to plan a funeral without a body.

She hadn't thought to have anything elaborate. Family, of course, which meant that notice had to be sent to Grey's sister near Tewksbury. Room had to be found for her, her husband, and their daughter. Braxton, of course. The Packhams. Those who could take the time to go to Gloucester to attend service at the cathedral and reveal the memorial in the family crypt. But then, evidently word got out to those who had served under and with Grey. Those families who mourned his lost men. Wellington himself, which along with her parents meant the diplomatic corps, and amazingly, the Prince Regent. It turned into a spectacle.

Mama helped with the diplomatic side of things, Michael with the military. Georgie took advantage of Eddie's list-making skills and Charlie's contacts. Georgie was the most organized, competent person she knew. But this was beyond even her.

And then she learned from Winslow that Coleford Abbey was in no condition for guests. It was in no condition for even family. So instead of leading a procession into Gloucestershire for the obsequies, the funeral itself was moved to St. George's in Mayfair, with the crypt ceremony limited to family sometime later.

Actually, Georgie was relieved. The girls could stay where they were comfortable and where she could easily get to them if needed, and she could be where it was at least familiar, and close to her family.

At least it all kept her so busy that when she fell into bed at night, she slept. It demanded her attention and her skills and her time so she didn't have to think far past the funeral. She could get herself and the girls fitted out in black, and confer with everyone involved, and make the best decisions she could. The good and the bad news was that she was truly in her element. It meant that the funeral proceeded with swift competence and ended up, she hoped, being worthy of Grey's life.

She met Grey's sister and was relieved to find that she truly liked her, this horse-mad woman who had taken over their father's work. She visited Braxton at his sister's home. She even greeted the new ponies Grey's sister had brought in for the girls and her own Lucy. And she saw her friend Anastasia Dunn, who had just returned from Vienna, and who promised her they would pick up the project she and Anastasia had been working on for so long. And to be honest, it all felt unreal, as if she were watching someone else's life pass her by. She was numb.

Standing at the door to St. George's, she greeted the Prince, who had known her since childhood. She greeted his brother, the Duke of Clarence, in his resplendent Naval uniform. She greeted the various foreign dignitaries who were in for the celebrations and came for her parents. She stood with her parents, who knew most of the players, and handed the girls over to the Kings and Archangels who kept them safe. She even met the Archbishop of Canterbury, a distant cousin, who came to sit regally in the sacristy in support of the service.

She did not, however, meet Wellington, who had evidently come to the service but avoided her. She briefly wondered why, but was too busy with the portentous service and later the gathering, which was held at her parents' home, since hers was still hip deep in scaffolding and paint buckets. She nodded and smiled and held out her hand to be saluted and hid behind the mourning veil and murmured pleasantries, especially to Grey's true friends, like Rob Glenn and Declan Bowdern, who was supposed to have been their sacrificial rake, and would have, she realized, played the part well. She even sat in on the reading of Grey's will, which he had somehow managed to draw up between his proposal and death, to find no surprises. She was cared for, the girls were cared for, and the longtime servants were cared for.

And she got through it all to finally find herself back in her now empty, echoing home, with none but the girls and the staff. And for the next while, everyone left them all alone. The weather was unnaturally cold, necessitating fires in most of the rooms and two extra blankets on her bed, which she dove under even in the afternoons.

"Recovering" her mother called it. Hiding, she knew. But now that the funeral was over, she had nothing to look forward to but the task of maintaining a lifestyle defined by her widowhood and the uncertain position she held in relation to the marquessate and its holdings.

All work. All drudge. Both leavened and burdened further

by two lost little girls who couldn't tolerate much more loss. Little girls who slept curled next to her like lost puppies, and who spent their days waiting for her to disappear as well. She knew she needed to get them out and about. They needed fresh air and company. She needed to answer the summonses from various Packhams to join them for any manner of expeditions. For now, though, she couldn't. For now, she and her daughters licked their wounds with none but the also-grieving staff and an oddly quiet Bark to shelter them. They would hide for a few more days, she decided.

Just a few.

IT WAS inevitable that the world came calling. Not just the Packhams, but neighbors from the girls' old house. Grey's friends, who wanted to check in on them. The Kings and the Archangels, who harried them out of the house when the weather was good enough, with Bark's exercise as an excuse. Mrs. Keyse, who kept threatening to petition Chancery Court to be made guardian of the girls. And Anastasia Dunn, who had evidently decided it was time to get back to work on their project.

"What do you mean your husband didn't know?" her friend demanded over tea and tea cakes.

Georgie shrugged. "There wasn't time. I promised him he would find out when he got home." She swallowed. "It was supposed to be an encouragement to not stay away too long."

Anastasia knew her too well to do something vaguely patronizing like patting her hand. "Well, I need some new scents. I believe I have Papa talked into the real perfumery. I even found some single ladies to help cultivate some of the gardens. But I need my nose."

Georgie scowled. "I'm not certain how fond I am of that designation."

"But you are," her friend objected with a bright grin, which just made her look like an elf with her bright red hair and green eyes. "You are the secret weapon that will make us a success. No one has a more delicate nose than you for mixing scents."

Maybe one person, Georgie thought wistfully, but he was no longer available.

"Please," Stasia begged. "We're so close."

And so, along with her other duties, Georgie began to mix scents for Stasia's perfumery. Which meant she got even less sleep. What with everything else going on, she had not a spare minute for herself, which at least kept the blue devils constrained. A bit.

Until the day she was once again walking out of the library, her arms full with fabric samples and pattern books this time, when the knocker sounded on the door. She didn't even hesitate. She knew that the staff was helping the girls decorate their bedroom. So before she could think of it, she yanked the door open.

At least this time she didn't drop her burden on the floor.

"I really must stop answering the door," she said to the three soldiers who stood on her stoop. In uniform. "Go away."

It was all she could do to keep the panic from her voice. Who was it this time? Which member of her family?

"I think you'll want to see us," Michael said.

"Oh, I don't think I will."

She grabbed the door handle, ready to tell him how unfunny their appearance was when, without a word, Michael and Rafe stepped apart.

And there on the front stoop was, in her best attempt at a description, a motley collection of splints, slings, and scars.

For the longest time, all she could do was stare. Her brain

simply wouldn't compile this ragged bundle of disaster into something—or someone—familiar.

And then the something smiled. "I hope you haven't told the bees."

For the longest moment the five of them stood there like a frozen tableau, the other four smiling at her, and her trying to make sense of the untidy pile of humanity leaning on a cane on her stoop. Finally, she opened her mouth.

"You bastard!" she all but shrieked. "Where have you been?! Do you realize we threw you a funeral only two flower arrangements shy of Nelson's?"

Michael, the clodpole, nodded at the apparition with a grin. "Definitely happy to see you."

She glared, as if her heart weren't slamming against her ribs and her chest unbearably tight at the sight of Grey's injuries. "Shut up. Get in here."

He was grinning, too. How could that collection of disasters be smiling? "If you let me into my house, I'll be happy to tell you."

Still, she stood there, frozen. Desperate to hold him tight, terrified she would break something fragile. Even more desperate to hit him. Just ball up her fist and wallop him right in the chest, across which his left arm was strapped. For causing her such pain by dying. By not dying but making her think he had. And his face. Oh, his beautiful face, now transected by a scar from his forehead to his chin. And burns. His eyebrows were gone.

Stepping back to let them all in, she glared at her brother and cousins. "Did you know about this? Did you enjoy destroying my world?"

All three threw up hands of protest. "We had no idea," Michael protested. "Not until this morning when we got a message to meet a boat."

She didn't know what to say. She couldn't even manage to form words. So she turned around without a word and marched up the stairs and into the yellow parlor, where it seemed all their little dramas now took place, assuming the Archangels would get Grey up the stairs behind her. It wasn't until she had made it inside and turned around that she realized the cousins were all but holding Grey upright, and he was looking around the room with pure delight.

"I knew I could trust you," he said. "Did the girls help you?"

She dropped her burden on a table and clenched her hands together to control their trembling. She pulled in a calming breath. She tried so hard to yell at him again for what he'd put them through, all of them, especially those little girls, especially really, her, even though she knew it wasn't his fault. And then, much to not only her surprise but everyone else's in the room, she did something for only the second time in her entire life. She burst into tears.

19

———

*A*nd Grey thought he couldn't feel worse. He'd made her cry. And he couldn't even really hold her to him to soothe her. Couldn't bury his face in her beautiful hair or wrap his arms around her waist and reassure her that he was not only still alive, but that he loved her, which he had inconveniently realized while lying in a hospital bed in a foreign country. Lying in bed while, evidently, the royal family showed up to wave him off this mortal coil.

And now instead of being able to carry her off to bed—or at least the settee—he was doing all he could to just stand up himself. Oh Lord, he hurt. But the pain in her eyes was hurting him worse. She stood there in the middle of the room alone sobbing, her hands over her face as if she were ashamed of her tears.

Desperate, he looked over at her brother and cousins. "Do something!"

But all three of them stood there staring at her as if her hair was on fire.

"Packham!" he snapped. "Haven't you ever seen a woman cry?"

Michael kept staring. "Not her," he finally said.

Both cousins shook their heads. Rafe even pointed. "Ever."

Grey swore. Then he did the only thing he could think to do. He limped up to Georgie and wrapped his good arm around her. And bless her, she nestled into his sore shoulder like a child.

"I'm sorry," he said. What for, he wasn't sure. For surviving? For taking so long to get back to her? For marrying her in the first place?

No. Not that. Never that. It sounded so trite, but one of the few things that had kept him alive was the idea of getting back to her. And now that he caught her fresh flower scent, he knew he was rewarded.

"I hope you don't mind," he said gently to the top of her head, "But you'll have to share the bed again."

She just nodded. He was beginning to think that he needed to sit down when suddenly she pulled back and straightened.

"Wellington!" she snapped, glaring at them all like a hanging judge. "He knew, didn't he? That was why he avoided talking to me."

Grey nodded. "I'm sorry."

"Why, though? Why not tell me?" She must have seen him waver, because even with the tears still wet on her cheeks, she *tsked* at him like an annoyed governess. "Oh, for heaven's sake, sit down."

He looked over at the settee and wondered if he could make it that far. She saw that, too.

"Michael!" was all she snapped, and with a rueful grin her brother stepped in and helped Grey to the settee, where he eased down onto the cushions with no more than a small groan. Georgie strode over to get an ottoman from the corner and very gently lifted his left leg onto it.

Even though it pulled his stitches, Grey smiled up at her. She *harrumphed.* She actually harrumphed.

"Why?" she asked again. "I need to be filled in before the girls hear us and come charging in here."

"Simple answer?" Grey answered. "Because we weren't at all sure I would be coming home. I didn't want to raise your hopes just to have them dashed again. Well..." He tried another smile out on her to not much success. "At least the girls." Raising his arm, he shrugged. "As you can see, though, I seem to be very hard to kill."

Giving the bell rope a good tug, she settled down alongside him and waved the Archangels onto other furniture.

"These miscreants truly didn't know?"

It was Michael's turn to smile. It was Grey who shook his head. He was just about to continue his explanation when they were interrupted by a loud gasp from the doorway. Chalmers had obviously responded to her summons.

Grey tried to smile for him as well. Considering what Chalmers looked like, he thought the old man might need smelling salts.

Swiping at her eyes with her sleeves, Georgie gave Chalmers her own smile. "No, Chalmers, you are not dreaming. Lord Coleford truly is home. Evidently, we were the last to know that he survived."

"Thank heavens no one brings gifts to a funeral," her unflappable butler said. "It'd be a treat getting 'em all back."

Grey couldn't help it. He laughed. Then he grabbed the side with his cracked ribs. "I knew I could count on you to act sensibly, Chalmers."

Georgie gave her eyes another swipe and turned to the butler. "First, Chalmers, make certain the girls remain up in the nursery until I can call for them." She gave a little sob that might have been a laugh. "Again. Then, I believe that for at least a month or so, we will need to turn one of the other salons into a sick room. His Lordship is in no condition to manage those stairs. And no random visitors. Can you see that done?"

Chalmers straightened like an outraged matron. "But of course."

Grey almost laughed. Georgie stared him down. "And some tea, please, Chalmers." She waited long enough to see everyone's reaction before allowing a sly smile. "And a bit of brandy, I think."

Even Chalmers almost smiled.

As Chalmers strode off in his best majordomo fashion, Grey leaned back against the cushions of a surprisingly comfortable settee and sighed in relief. He'd made it. He'd been thinking of this moment for the last four weeks. Now that he was here, all he wanted to do was look at Georgie. So his next order of business was to see the Archangels out the door.

Again, he had to quell the urge to laugh. Georgie was leveling a very telling look on them even before he could open his mouth. They were obviously well-acquainted with her silent communications. Michael Packham suddenly jumped to his feet.

"Let me alert Chalmers that the tea is only for two. We have...um, other places to be."

And so it took only five more minutes before he was finally alone with his wife. He wondered how long he would have with her before being descended on by the girls. Oh well. He might as well make the most of what time he had.

"Georgie," he said, reaching over with his right hand to take hers.

She swung around to him, her eyes still glistening with the remainder of her tears. Then she looked down at his hand to see the bandage peeking out from beneath his uniform, the only attire he'd been able to hold onto.

"Oh," she said softly, frowning and gently laying her own hand atop his. "Poor hand."

He almost rebroke his left shoulder to grab her. Instead, he feasted on the sight and feel of her. "I need to tell you something."

She stiffened. He realized a second too late that he'd sounded like he was prepping her for bad news. "Would you mind," he said, rubbing his thumb over the back of her hand, wishing so hard he could wrap his arms around her and hug her hard. Even one arm. Feeling absurdly shy, he smiled. "Would you mind if I told you I loved you?"

He imagined it took a lot to surprise his Georgie. This was evidently one of those things.

"You what?" Her voice sounded a bit strangled. Her eyes were huge.

His smile grew. "Please don't tell me you have fallen in love while I've been gone. All I've thought about for six long weeks is how much I wanted to get back to you to tell you that I was a fool to leave you without letting you know that I'd begun to develop feelings for you. Feelings that solidified while I was lying on that cot hundreds of miles away. I love you, Georgie. I really want for us to have a true marriage." Shrugging, he let his smile turn wry. "Although it won't be soon, I'm afraid. I'm still a bit..."

"Tacked and tied together?" she asked.

He chuckled. "Well put."

He had hoped she would smile. She didn't. She looked down at their joined hands. "But I have fallen in love," she admitted.

He thought his heart would stop beating. But then she looked up and he saw the truth in her eyes.

"I fell in love with *you*, you clodpole," she said. "I have spent the last two months torturing myself because I was idiotic enough to have waited to realize I was in love with you until you were hundreds of miles away." She allowed another small sob. "And then spent the last month certain I would never be able to tell you."

There were tears again, this time silent and steady. And not just from Georgie. Grey couldn't help it. Without another word, he let go of her hand and gathered her to him with his right arm, resting his head over hers. And for the very longest time the two of them shared silent thanks that they hadn't been stupid after all. That they would have all the time they wanted to nurture that love.

Very gently, Georgie wrapped her arm around him as well. He could feel her tears wetting his shirt and didn't care.

"There is one thing I should tell you," she said. "I did promise, after all."

He straightened and looked down at her suddenly impish smile. "What?"

She shrugged. "I have a job."

That was probably the last thing he expected from her. "A job."

"Yes, indeed. Well, shall we say an investment. My friend Anastasia Dunn is beginning a perfumery, and I am helping create her scents, for which I'm awarded a fourth of the company." Her smile widened. "She calls me The Nose. I thought you would appreciate that."

He couldn't help it. He laughed, even though it hurt. "The Friday trips?"

She nodded. "Just so you know. I might love you, but I am not giving this up."

"Don't be silly. Just tell me how to invest in it. And let me know if you need help. As you know, I have a rather prodigious nose myself."

The two of them were laughing together when the salon door flew open.

Grey was prepared for almost any kind of reaction. Not the one he got, though. Two little girls stood like statues in the doorway holding hands and frowning. He thought his heart would burst. They were thinner, far more solemn. He knew, seeing them then, that he had spent his last moment disappearing on behalf of the Crown. He had more important things to do right here.

"It's all right," Georgie said, her hand out to the girls, "he's a bit banged up, but it is your Uncle Grey."

Still, they didn't move. And then Bark nudged them out of the way to gallop across the room. Everyone yelled a warning, but the massive dog skidded to a halt right at Grey's feet. And he sat, his head to the side as if he, too, were evaluating the pile of splints and bandages on his couch.

Finally, finally at seeing the dog's quizzical look, Amelia let go of her sister's hand and stepped forward. She tilted her own head.

"Uncle Grey," she said, sounding suspiciously like a displeased governess. "Why aren't you dead?"

Grey didn't know whether he was closer to laughing or simply melting at her feet. "Because I had to get back to my three favorite girls, that's why."

The answering silence was a long one, born, Grey knew, of harsh experience.

"And I have decided something," he said. "I will never leave you again. If I must go somewhere, everyone goes along. Or I do not go."

Again, that silent consideration.

"Not ever?" Sophie demanded finally.

Very carefully, he shook his head. "Not ever."

Still, he suffered their careful consideration. He found himself clutching Georgie's hand like a lifeline, his breath held for the judgment of two little girls. Until finally, they looked at each other and smiled.

"Well, that's all right then," Sophie declared, and Grey knew she had declared them a family.

He couldn't wait to find out what that meant. He knew, though, when his girls very carefully wrapped him and Georgie in a laughing embrace, that they finally believed it. He could do no less. Nor could he want to.

EPILOGUE

"You're sure about this."

Grey tightened his hold on his wife and dipped his head to inhale the delicious scent of her neck. "Who is sure about anything?" he teased, beginning to let his hands wander over the softly curved body he had been dreaming of for the three months it had taken his various bones and bruises to heal. He'd never have his face back to its former glory, but Georgie didn't seem to mind. At least she didn't seem to shy away from his kisses. And oh Lord, had he been enjoying his kisses. Now, he was about *finally* to enjoy more.

"The girls are at your parents'?" he asked from somewhere near her collarbone.

She stretched her neck to give him more access. "For two nights." He could actually feel her grin. "At least."

"Mrs. Keynes?"

He got a sly smile. "Relocated to her other daughter's home in York. The stipend you settled on her helped. The girls don't say anything, but I think they're relieved."

"No more relieved than I. And the staff?"

"Have been given the night off. Except Braxton, of course, who lives in fear you will call out for help and he not be tucked in his room. I am free to make whatever lascivious noises I wish."

It was his turn to grin. "A challenge I cannot refuse. Where shall I deflower you?" he asked. "The desk? The floor? The bed?"

"What about all three? Starting with the bed, I think. I do admit that I have grown fond of the luxury of it."

He began on the buttons down the back of her gown.

She shivered. "One-handed. You seem awfully practiced at this, sir."

He refused to be distracted from his task. "Not since setting eyes on you, madame."

God, her skin was soft, tantalizing, all the way down the sweep of her back. All along the column of her throat, where he could lay his lips against her quickening pulse. Beneath her jaw, where he ran his tongue, just to get the taste of her.

He fought for patience so that he could give her the delight she deserved for loving his unworthy self. For her calm and compassion and patience with his quirks and crotchets as he'd healed. For just being his Georgie.

Ah, there went the dress, sliding down her arms, her waist, her delicious hips. He reached down to pick her up. She stepped right out of his hold.

"Don't you dare," she warned, her eyes sparkling. "The very last thing I need right now is for you to pull an almost healed injury and forbid me the reward I have been so patiently and graciously awaiting."

Giving him one last suggestive smile, she reached down and did away with her undergarments, and Grey damn near dropped to the floor right there.

He was so proud of himself. He actually took the time to

disrobe and follow her up onto the cocoon of her bed where they could hide amid peach-colored curtains and cloud-soft down. He held himself back from ravaging her as he finally kissed her to his heart's content, testing and tasting and tempting with lips and tongue and teeth, all the while savoring the sweet silk of her body with his own. He even let her hands explore his own body, from the curling hair on his chest to his flat abdomen and lower, oh Lord, lower, until she tested him past endurance.

And yet, he still took the time to christen her breasts, to taste and tease and suck until she bowed right off the bed, whimpering his name, a sound he knew he would never tire of. And then, when she was trembling and sweating, he slid his hand up her thigh to test the tight curls at their apex, to slip his fingers inside, to savor the slick, hot core of her, delighting in the fact that she was more than ready for him, that she was so responsive that her whimpers quickly grew to cries, to demands, to pleas. To the surprised gasps of a climax he could feel pulsing about his fingers.

Only then did he ease her legs wide and position himself over her. Only then did he ease his way in, pausing for her stiffening.

"I'm all right," she all but growled when he stopped. She yanked hard at his hair. "Don't...*stop*..."

So he didn't. He pushed through and then began to rock. She wrapped her legs around him, pulling him in, enclosing him in her heat until he was mindless with urgency, until he could no longer hold back, and with his own cry of surprise poured himself into her, so deep he knew he would never recover. Would never want to recover.

And finally, when she followed him, this time crying out, head thrown back, hands clutching his sides, body convulsing around his cock, when they both collapsed in each other's arms, he knew he'd taken his final step in coming home to his own family. Truly home. And that, just as he'd promised the girls, he would never leave again.

ALSO BY EILEEN DREYER

Last Chance Academy

Just One Kiss

Drake's Damsels

Twice Tempted

Ill Met By Moonlight

Dueling with the Duke

Three Times a Lady

Miss Felicity's Dilemma

Daughters of Myth

Dangerous Tempation

Dark Seduction

Deadly Redemption

The Kendall Clan

Jake's Way

Simple Gifts

Some Men's Dreams

The Cowboy and the Fairy Godmother

Drake's Rakes

Barely a Lady

Never a Gentleman

Always a Temptress

Once a Rake

Deadly Medicine

A Man to Die For

Brain Dead

Nothing Personal

With a Vengeance

City of the Dead

If Looks Could Kill

A Molly Burke Suspense

Bad Medicines

Head Games

Love on the Edge

A Rose for Maggie

A Soldier's Heart

A Walk on the Wild Side

Perchance to Dream

Timeless

Lighter Side of Love

A Fine Madness

Isn't It Romantic?

The Ice Cream Man

Playing the Game

The Cambell Cousins

Don't Fence Me In

Sail Away

ABOUT EILEEN DREYER

New York Times bestselling author and RWA Hall of Fame member Eileen Dreyer and her evil twin Kathleen Korbel have published over forty novels and novellas, and ten short stories in genres ranging from medical suspense to paranormal to multiple sub-genres in romance. She is thrilled to bring her work, including the continuation of her Drake's Rakes series, which she considers historical romantic adventure, to Oliver-Heber Books.

A native of St. Louis, where she still lives with her husband Rick and family, Dreyer is an RN, BS with two decades experience, including sixteen in trauma medicine before retiring to write full time. She is also trained in in forensic nursing, death investigation and Tactical EMS (as in being a medic on a SWAT team) (yeah, it was that cool).

A seasoned conference speaker, Dreyer travels to research, and uses research as an excuse to travel, including an unforgettable participation in the 200th anniversary Duchess of Richmond Ball and Battle of Waterloo. She has animals but refuses to subject them to the limelight. And yes. She was on Jeopardy. The way she puts the results is that she won the silver medal.

Visit Eileen's website:
Www.eileendreyer.com

A small press bound by the belief that every voice matters.

Sign up for our newsletter to learn about new releases and more.
https://oliver-heberbooks.com/subscribe/

Follow us on social media:

facebook.com/oliverheberbooks

instagram.com/oliverheberbooks

amazon.com/oliverheberbooks

youtube.com/@OliverHeberBooksPublisher

* 9 7 9 8 9 0 0 4 3 0 9 5 9 *